LIVE BY THE SWORD, DIE BY THE SWORD

KAREN WOODS

ACKNOWLEDGEMENTS

Thank you to all my readers, my family and friends for all their support. This is my thirteenth novel and I'm still pinching myself. I took a chance and it paid off.

Thanks to my children Ashley, Blake, Declan, and Darcy for all their support. Also a big thanks to my mother Margaret and my father Alan. Thanks to James for all his support.

"If you do what you have always done, you'll get what you have always got."

Follow me on Twitter @karenwoods69 - www.karenwoods.net

I'm working hard on my next novel now and hopefully my readers won't have long to wait. I'm a real person writing real stories. My last thanks as always goes to my son in heaven. "Goodnight God Bless Dale."

Love

Karen Woods

CHAPTER ONE

"THIS HAS TO BE the last time Larry, I'm getting married tomorrow. Are you listening to me or what? I'm being serious, this has to stop!" Dawn groaned as Larry's firm masculine hands ravished every inch of her body with her needy flesh pressed firmly against his. Her mouth was wide open; she was gagging for it as he suckled his ripe red lips against her neck. Who was she trying to kid, she wanted him as much as he wanted her, she was besotted with him. It was there for everyone to see. He was the forbidden fruit, her heart's desire, her guilty pleasure. But Larry Watson was the younger brother of the man she was about to marry. What the hell was she thinking? She was playing a dangerous game!

"Shut up yapping and get those knickers down. I've not got long; Linda will be looking for me soon. Come on; get them off while I slip it in. I'm going to burst in a minute." Larry shot his eyes behind him scanning the area; his eyes were dancing with excitement, he wanted this woman so much. She was his addiction and he wanted to bang her brains out, make her want him. Larry Watson could have had any woman he wanted. He was sexy, firm and toned and he had a way with the ladies too, the gift of the gab. But Larry never did anything by the book, no way. He wanted Dawn at any cost. He knew his girlfriend would be missing him soon and he was eager to get this over with. Linda Mellor was on the ball and she didn't miss a trick, a proper nosey cow she was, nothing ever got past her. Larry flicked his eyes to his wristwatch knowing time was ticking away. "Hurry up then, for fucks sake Dawn," he moaned, desperate to get inside her.

Dawn rolled her black lacy knickers down over her slender thighs slowly; they looked like silk in the moonlight. Expensive they were, not that Primark shite everybody was wearing, top of the range - proper silk, or so she said. Dawn's eyes switched one way then the other looking for any signs of danger; he was right, they didn't have long. Larry was all over her; his hand disappeared up her skirt as his steamy red lips suckled on her ripe breasts. "Open your legs wider then, come on for Christ's sake. I can't get it in. I'm going to explode in a minute, just open your legs." Dawn groaned as she felt him enter her, she was moist and ready for him, gagging for it she was.

The lovers were in a dark alley at the back of The Foresters Arms. The Human League song, "Don't You Want Me", pumped from inside the boozer covering up the lover's sexual groans. The DJ was cheap and cheerful and his song choices had a lot to answer for; cheesy tunes that eventually would have everyone up on their feet dancing the night away. These were fun songs, crowd pleasers - the type that uncle nobhead would be up dancing to by the end of the night with his tie hung around his head. Dawn's facial expression changed and she rolled her eyes to the back of her head as Larry penetrated deeper inside her. Her fingernails sunk deep into his flesh causing the skin to turn white. Larry's penis was big and the girth of it took her breath away. Legs hung around his waist she thrust up and down making sure she pleased him. This was the last time this was happening and she wanted to leave him with a smile on his face, for him to remember her, always still wanting her, never forgetting their time together. Taking his unshaven chin in her hand she made sure she had his full attention, she squeezed hard at his cheeks making his lips touch together at the sides. Her voice was low and she was struggling for breath as he pounded her body up against the wall.

"Promise me that you'll never come near me again Larry. If Jud ever finds out about this he'll kill you stone dead and me for that matter," she stuttered as her body slowed down. Her words fell on deaf ears though. Larry was concentrating and he was nearly ready to finish off. Jud was Larry's elder brother and a force not to be messed with, he was the main man in the area. Jud was a complete nutter who had no mercy for his enemies. If only he knew what was going on with his woman and his brother, Larry would be a dead man. He would cut him up into a thousand pieces and feed him to the pigs at the local farm. Jud never took anything lightly; he was lethal, a proper head the ball. He liked his victims to beg for mercy, to plead with him, to know he could end their life at any time. Dawn gripped Larry's head in her hands as he pushed her back up against the cold brick wall. "Promise me," she mumbled as he thrust hard inside her. Larry's head wasn't with it and all he wanted to do was to fuck her brains out. He didn't love her; no way, she was just forbidden fruit, his brother's fruit.

Larry was a good looking man and he could have had the pick of any woman he wanted. All the Watson brothers were lookers, heart-throbs that always had the women chasing after them. Jud was over six feet tall and towered over his younger brothers. He tipped the scales at a lean fourteen stone, pure muscle and with a body to die for. He had to be trim, he had to be fit. His lifestyle demanded it. It was only a matter of time before some new wannabe gangster made a play for his title in the area. This was a dog eat dog world and nobody gave a shit who they hurt to get where they wanted in life. Jud was the main man in Collyhurst and he ran a lot of the crime scenes there. He was ruthless; a sick, twisted bastard who took no prisoners. Everyone feared him and they had every right to, he was fucked in the head, not all there. Larry Watson had always lived in his brother's shadow and he rarely got a look in when his brother was around. He hated that he wasn't respected like his brother. Larry loved control and he craved respect from the men he worked with. He would never get that though, he was disliked by a lot of the men and it was only by the skin of his teeth he was allowed into the circle. Nobody trusted Larry, there was just something about him. He was double agent, a grass. Ever since the Watson brothers were kids Jud ruled the roost and he never let his younger brother get a sniff in. It was his way or the highway. Well, until now.

Behind them there was rustling and the sound of crunching gravel, somebody was watching them from the shadows, listening to their heavy, struggled breathing. Dipping her head low Michelle Buckley covered her mouth with her hand as she watched. "Well, you dirty bastard," she whispered under her breath. "Oh, you just wait Larry, you slimy cunt." Michelle was as quiet as a mouse as she hid away out of their view. She stood gawping at the lovers, her mouth was wide open. You could see the whites of her eyes. She wished it was her Larry was fucking, she wanted him so much, she always had. "Oh, let's see you talk your way out of this one Larry Watson," she sniggered as she moved closer to get a better look. Larry could sell sand to the Arabs, he was quick-witted and could always think on his feet, he was good like that. He always had an answer to everything. A smart-arse he was. The corners of her mouth started to rise. Michelle Buckley licked her lips slowly as she twiddled the piece of hair dangling near her cheeks. She was turned on by what she saw and her nostrils flared as she watched Larry Watson have sex with Dawn. She wanted this man so much that she would have done anything to have him, anything. Cracking her knuckles slowly she carried on watching the lovers with eager eyes. This was hot gossip and something she would keep close to her chest. For now anyway…

Dawn yanked her knickers up and straightened her red mini-skirt. She loved this skirt and always thought she looked like a model when she was wearing it. It was cheap and tacky though, just like she was. "Do I look okay or what?" She giggled as she grabbed him back by his arm as he moved away trying to catch his breath. "Oi," she snapped. "Will you look at me? Is my hair alright? Do I look respectable?" she flicked her fingers across her blouse removing the grit and the dust from her. "If I go back in there with my hair all over the show people will be suspicious. Bleeding hell, do I look alright or what?" Dawn's bobbed hairstyle was backcombed beyond belief and full of hairspray; there was no way it was moving about, not even after Larry had just banged her brains out.

Larry sighed and pulled his strides up. He lifted his eyes up and gave her a quick once over. If the truth was known he wasn't arsed how she looked anymore, he'd got what he wanted, he had no further use for her. He'd emptied his sack and that was all he cared about. "Yeah, yeah, stop flapping, you're fine. You're sorted. Just check me out for any lipstick marks on my neck. You know what you're like for biting me." She gave him a quick once over and carried on straightening her hair. Scouting about the alleyway Dawn found her missing red shoe near an old sofa someone had flung out. She shoved it back on her slender foot with haste and flicked a moth from her blouse that had settled there. Larry inhaled deeply and rubbed at his crotch. His eyes met hers and he knew he'd satisfied her. "That was the dog's bollocks that was. You can't beat a good old knee trembler can you?"

Dawn shook her head; she loved this guy's sense of humour and couldn't help herself when he was about, she was butter in his hands. It's just the way it was, he excited her. Larry sniggered and tucked his crisp white shirt down the front of his pants. He grabbed his grey suit jacket from a nearby rubbish bin and dusted it down before he casually slung it over his shoulder. This was his favourite and he always thought he looked the main man in it. He thought he looked like Jud.

Larry walked to Dawn's side with a smirk on his face. He was playing with her now, full of himself as per usual. "How can you say you don't want any more sex like that? You're tapped in the head if you ask me. My body's much sort after you know? Top of the range it is." He opened his eyes wide and he pushed his pigeon chest out in front of him as he continued. "Ask anyone if you don't believe me. Larry Watson is sex on legs."

Dawn walked towards him and stroked her long fingernail over his plump lips slowly. There was no way she was listening to his bullshit any longer. Yes, it was true what he was saying but there was no way she was admitting that to him. His ego was big enough. "Larry, I said I'm done. It's over. Call that," she jerked her head back and paused, "one for old time's sake. I love Jud and I'm going to be his wife. You have to back off now and forget about us and what we've been doing behind his back." Dawn was as bad as him though, they were both playing a dangerous game. A game where people got hurt, lost their lives. In her heart Dawn loved Jud and she wanted to be his wife but it was in her blood, she was a dirt bag, she just couldn't help herself. Who was she kidding? She could never be faithful, she was a tart and always would be. She loved the chase, she loved having secrets, dark secrets that kept her awake at nights. A leopard never changes its spots.

Larry pulled a cigarette from his packet and popped it into the side of his mouth, he passed her one too. He flicked his lighter and sucked hard on his fag to get a light. Blowing the smoke over at her he growled. "You don't even love him, Dawn. Why are you even marrying him anyway, the guy's a waste of space?" He went nose to nose with her, he hated losing to his brother. His warm breath tickled her cheek. "Is it his money?" he raised his eyebrows high as he continued. "Because, if it is. I can earn cash too you know? I'm no dick-head. Things are on the up for me, you just watch." Thick grey smoke circled his face as he blew it from the side of his mouth. "I know you think Jud rules everything around here but things are changing, trust me, things are turning around. It's just a matter of time."

Dawn retaliated and bent her head into his. "It's not the fucking money. Why do you always say that? Stop winding me up Larry, you know I hate it when you say stuff like that." Dawn sucked hard on her cigarette. Blowing the smoke into his eyes she continued. "He's your brother Larry and that's the end of it. Can't you get that into your thick head? Me and you should have never happened, it was a mistake," her eyes dipped and she looked like she was filling up. Did this bitch really have a heart or was it just for show? "It was my mistake Larry, and it won't be happening again. It's over. I'm done with all this."

Larry held his head back and sniggered. He clicked his jaw slowly making large smoke hoops. There was no way he was backing down, this fight wasn't over, no way. "We'll see about that Dawn. We both know you can't resist my charms. You'll come begging for my cock just like you always do when you're feeling unloved and lonely." He knew he was right and smirked at her. Dawn gritted her teeth tightly together, he was winding her up. And, yes, he was right about her, she did get lonely, but Jud was always out until late, grafting and Larry always seemed to be around when she needed a shoulder to cry on. So what if she just phoned him for a booty call, she was a woman with needs. A noise from the end of the alleyway made Larry jump; Dawn's mouth was wide open and she was about to scream.

Larry pressed his finger up to his mouth and snarled at her. "Shut it, big gob, somebody's out there. For fuck's sake. This is all I need. Just stay there and keep still." Larry sprinted to the end of the cobbles and saw the back of a woman walking back inside the pub; she was too quick for him to see her identity. "Fuck, fuck," he mumbled under his breath. Now somebody knew their secret. He had to find out who it was, he had to silence her.

Dawn was at his side now and tapped him on the shoulder. She was serious. "Goodbye Larry. Like I said, it's over, just leave me alone to get on with my life. It was fun while it lasted, just let's keep it like that."

Watching her walk off into the distance he stubbed his cigarette out on the floor. "We'll see about that. Nobody says goodbye to Larry Watson, nobody."

★

Jud Watson stood at the bar talking with his mates. His loud laughter echoed throughout the pub, everybody knew when he was in the building, he was such a gobby fucker. Jud was a well-built man and looked as hard as nails. He was dressed in a dark grey suit, it was expensive too, not one of them cheap ones off the market stalls. It was the real McCoy. His look was everything to him and he always made sure he was in tip-top condition. From the corner of his eye he clocked Dawn coming back into the room. He didn't trust her and he always kept a close eye on her. She was a devious bitch who needed watching twenty-four-seven. Yeah, he'd heard a few rumours about her sleeping around but once they were married that would all change. If he heard one more whisper about her playing around, she would be going to an early grave, he'd end her life for sure.

Clicking his fingers above his head rapidly he tried to get her attention. Dawn was stressed, as he watched her from across the room and he was sure she was having second thoughts about marrying him. Watching her playing with her hair he whistled over to her. "Dawn," he shouted at the top of his voice. "Get your arse over here for a minute while I show you off to my boys." Hearing his voice she turned her head slowly and came to join him. She was trembling inside but hid it well. She was good at that, she could always put a brave face on when she needed to. Dawn raised a struggled smile and wiggled across the room towards Jud; she was gorgeous, a real head turner. A ringer for Dusty Springfield people said.

"Hi babes, I was just in the toilet talking to my old mate Wendy. Bleeding hell, she can't half gab that woman. I couldn't get away from her," she was lying through her teeth and he sensed she was trying to have him over. Dawn twisted a piece of her honey blonde hair dangling down at the side of her face and smiled at Jud.

She was a prize catch for sure and he knew he was punching above his weight from the moment he met her. Of course he'd been told she was a slapper but he had ignored the rumours and made her his woman anyway. "Look at my girl here boys. Just think, in two days time this woman will be my wife."

Jud was watching her like a hawk, waiting for her reaction, looking for any signs that she was backing out, she never flinched. A firm hand landed on Jud's shoulder and he turned his head quickly to see who it was. He was always edgy, always on his guard. He had to be in his line of work, people were out to hurt him and take over his empire. It was just something that came with the job. 'Trust nobody and never let anyone get close to you', was his motto and he lived by this rule every day.

"Correct, Jud you're a lucky man. You've done well for yourself. Dawn's going to make you a great wife." Larry held a cunning look in his eyes and smirked at Dawn. He was being sarcastic as he licked his bottom lip. He was such a tease and Dawn knew he was playing with fire, she snarled at him letting him know he was dicing with death.

"A very lucky man indeed," Jud replied. He draped his arm over his girlfriend's shoulder and whispered into her ear softly. "I'm going to make you so happy sweetheart, me and you forever, ay?"

Larry picked his pint of lager up from the bar and went to find Linda. Jud was knocking him sick, he was a right pussy where Dawn was concerned and he could never see beyond her tits and her firm shapely arse. Larry Watson knew Linda would be on the war path and he prepared himself for a mouthful from her. He could hear her big trap from the other side of the room shouting his name out. He'd only been seeing her for a few weeks and he knew if she went over the top he would kick her to the kerb at the drop of a hat. She meant nothing to him, she was just another notch on his belt. Larry was ruthless with the ladies and only ever thought about himself. He was a lady's man for sure. The best looking man in his family, his mother always told him and she was right, he was drop-dead gorgeous. His thick black hair flicked across his forehead but it never hid his deep blue piercing eyes. Come to bed eyes the ladies called them and they were right too; sexy, smoky enchanting eyes. It only took one look into them and women were hooked; they were putty in his hands. Larry jiggled across the pub looking for Linda. He was a lively soul and always up for a laugh. As he walked into the crowd of people he bumped into Michelle Buckley, face first. She was the sister of one of the grafters he worked with in the area. Michelle had the hots for him. She was drooling from the mouth as she looked deep into his eyes. She was always flirting around Larry, trying to catch his eye but he never batted an eyelid, she was a fat mess, a dirty grease ball, 'a pig in a fit' he liked to call her. Larry had shared one drunken kiss with her though, but he kept that to himself, it was nothing to write home about, 'taking one for the team' he called it, and he was pissed out of his head at the time so it didn't count. That was his excuse anyway. This woman was a minger in his eyes and she always seemed to be around him no matter where he was, like a fly around shit she was.

The woman gripped him by his shirt at the front and pulled him to the side of the dance floor away from prying eyes. Her stale breath tickled his cheeks. She'd taken him by surprise and he was unsteady on his feet. "Whoa, you crazy bitch what are you doing, get your dirty hands off me," he screamed.

"How are you Larry? We've not had a dance tonight have we? Are you up for it or what?" Michelle Buckley had loved Larry Watson for as long as she could remember. Even from being a small child it was him she dreamt about, the one she wanted to spend the rest of her life with. Larry had never given her a second look though.

His face creased at the sides and you could see he wasn't impressed. He laughed right into her face. "Me, dance with you? Are you having a laugh or what? I've got no rhythm anyway," he lied as he tried to move her out of the way. Michelle moved closer to his ear and spoke in a low voice, her breath tickling the side of his ear. There was no way he was getting one over her this time, not now she knew his seedy little secret. She looked him directly in the eye and got ready to deliver the killer blow. With a single finger she slid it over his bottom lip.

"You had rhythm before though didn't you, when you were down the back alley with Dawn?" His face dropped, he was gobsmacked. So, it was her who had been watching them, the crafty cow.

Making sure nobody could see him he gripped her by the waist and sank his fingers deep into her blubber, he was hurting her, digging his fingers deep into her ribs. "You didn't see jack shit, did you?"

Michelle's eyes were popping out of her head and she was in pain. Dragging herself away from him she growled. She was bright red and she snarled at him. "I know what I saw Larry Watson, so don't you come all the innocent with me. I mean, if your Jud ever found out that you were slipping his bird one, what would he have to say about that ay. Yeah, he wouldn't be a happy bunny would he?" She had him by the bollocks and he knew it. Michelle was calling the shots now and he knew her big mouth could get him into deep trouble. He had to make amends and fast before she told everyone in the pub about his secret. And, she would have you know, she was a right trouble-causer. Michelle was a ticking bomb and he had to keep her quiet.

Michelle Buckley was highly respected among the grafters in the area and she was always the first to come up with money making ideas for the lads, she was as bent as a nine bob note and she was always up for a quick earner. She had money too, plenty of it.

Larry chuckled trying to make light of the matter. There was no way he could show her she had him rattled. "I'm only joking, Michelle. Where's your bloody sense of humour gone? Come on then, let's get you to the dance floor and see what moves you've got." She bought it, she was smiling from ear to ear, she was actually dancing with Larry Watson.

Michelle was as proud as a peacock and barged past the other people on the dance floor; she cleared a space for them to dance. This was her time to shine and nobody was going to ruin it for her, nobody. Yanking her pink skirt up high she sucked her pot belly in and placed her handbag on the floor in front of her. She was dancing with him and she loved every second of it. Her eyes never left him, she was savouring every moment.

At that moment Linda marched towards Larry from the other side of the room but he didn't see her as he was pretending to enjoy the dance with Michelle, shaking his arse and rolling his hands about. Linda's face was like thunder and she was ready to kick some arse. She held her drink above her head as she pushed past the other people in the pub, she was a woman on a mission. Stepping to the side of the dance floor she placed her hands on her hips and gritted her teeth together. There he was, right in front of her eyes, the liberty taking bastard. How could he humiliate her like this? He'd always told her in the past that he couldn't dance and never once had he hit the dance floor with her, she was livid. What did fat Michelle Buckley have that she didn't? Her voice was loud and she made sure he heard her. "Where the hell have you been Larry? I've been looking for you for ages? We're out on a date remember. What the hell are you doing dancing with this porker?"

Michelle was dragging at his hands. She didn't care if he was Linda's boyfriend or not, this was her time to shine and nobody was going to spoil it for her, not even Linda Mellor. Michelle bent forward and went nose to nose with her. "Oh piss off you bean pole; he's having a dance with me. Stop moaning and leave him alone. Can't you see he's having some real fun here?"

Linda snapped, she was ready to fight, her fists curled into tiny balls at the side of her legs and she was unclipping her large gold hooped earrings out of her ears ready for action. Linda dropped her handbag to the floor and stepped forward pointing her finger into Michelle's face. This was war. It was going off big time. "Ay, you cheeky fat cow. That's my boyfriend you're dancing with. Take your dirty mitts off him and go and find a man of your own, this one belongs to me. If you can find a man who's daft enough to have you that is."

Michelle stood tall and jerked her head forward slowly. This girl could fight and everybody was waiting on her next move. She was well known for being a hard case and she always left her opponents with scars. Michelle was built like an Irish navvy and she would have thought nothing of head-butting this tart, knocking her right out. Larry's girlfriend was playing with fire and it was only a matter of time before she would be flat on her arse nursing a busted nose. Linda's friend nudged her in the waist and darted her eyes at her, she bent over and quickly whispered something into her ear. Linda paused, unsure of her next move; whatever her friend had just told her made her change her mind very quickly. Looking at Larry for some kind of response Linda backed off slowly trying to keep her pride. Walking away she shouted over her shoulder. "Larry, come and see me when you've finished dancing with that slob. We need a serious chat me and you. I'm not putting up with your shit anymore, it needs sorting out."

Michelle was ready for action, she was ready to scratch Linda's eyeballs out but Larry held her back with a firm grip. "Leave her be. I'll deal with her later, she doesn't bother me." His eyes looked demented as he stood grinding his teeth together. Michelle Buckley would have slaughtered his girlfriend in seconds and he knew it. Perhaps he should have let Michelle go and saved him the job of doing it later on. He was like that, he would never have thought twice about giving a woman a slap, he had no respect for them whatsoever. He was a woman-beater.

Larry sniggered to Michelle as they watched Linda retreat from the dance floor, she wasn't a happy bunny. "Come on then, let's have that dance," Larry chuckled. His face creased at the sides as he rested his head on her shoulder. She stank of sweaty arse and he heaved as she dragged him closer to her. The lights were low and other couples joined them on the dance floor for the last dance of the night. Michelle rested her head on the top of Larry's chest as a George Michael track, "Careless Whisper" played. This woman was knocking him sick and he couldn't wait until the dance had finished so he could get rid of her. She wasn't doing his street cred any favours, everyone was sniggering at him from the corners of the room, laughing as her hands caressed his body.

Jud was dancing with Dawn at the side of them and Larry could see his brother singing into Dawn's ear. His head sank; his heart was beating ten to the dozen and you could see his chest rising. He thought Dawn was just a bang but as he looked at her he realised she was much more than that, he had feelings for her.

Michelle held the man of her dreams in her arms and she was inhaling his body scent. He smelt of "Fahrenheit" aftershave. It was a sweet, sexy aroma. The fragrance tickled her nostrils and she inhaled deeply enjoying every second of him. There was no way she was letting him go; not now she knew the secret that could keep him by her side forever. Her fingers gripped his body tightly and her eyes closed slowly, she was lost in the moment. He was her happy ending, the man she'd been searching for all her life, her Prince Charming.

CHAPTER TWO

DAWN PRITCHARD STOOD in the full length mirror admiring her ivory wedding dress, she was twisting and turning. It fitted her like a glove and showed off her curvaceous body shape. Jud had bought the dress of course; there was no way she could have afforded it, she wasn't even working, she was a kept woman. Dawn was penniless. She'd been out of work ever since leaving school and it had never entered her head to find employment even though she was only twenty. Let's face it though, she didn't need to work when she had the men falling at her feet. She was lazy and bone idle. Dawn Pritchard had men wrapped around her little finger. She very rarely paid for anything, she was a freeloader who used her body to get what she wanted.

Maureen, her mother, walked to her side as if she was floating on air. She held a proud look in her eyes and she was tearful. She was the one who had been pushing Dawn to marry Jud for ages now; he was the answer to her daughter's prayers, her meal ticket. The answer to her own prayers too if she was being honest with herself. Maureen came to her daughter's side and touched the side of her daughter's cheek. "You look stunning love. I tell you what Dawn, you've landed right on your feet marrying that Jud Watson. You'll never want for anything again while he's by your side."

Dawn stamped her foot; she'd heard enough of her

mother's bullshit. Day after day she was always reminding her of how lucky she was bagging a Watson brother. "Mam, why are you always talking about money? Have you ever thought to yourself that I might just love Jud? You know, actually love him, with all my heart?"

Maureen held her head back and laughed out loud. She knew her daughter of old and knew more than anyone that she was a gold-digger. Like mother, like daughter or so the saying goes. The facts were there for everyone to see, Dawn would have never have gone near Jud if he wasn't loaded, it just wasn't her style. She never looked twice at a man who had no money. Jud wasn't the best looking man in his family and Maureen knew her daughter could have done a lot better for herself, looks wise, but this guy was wealthy and he ticked all the boxes in that department, so nothing else mattered. Jud was smart and lived the high life and that was enough for him to win her over. Maureen held her own and answered back. "Stop being so bleeding defensive you moody cow. I'm just saying that's all. Shoot me for even caring why don't you?"

Dawn's face was bright red as she wafted her hand across her body. Small beads of sweat were forming on her forehead and she was getting flustered. "Well, keep it to yourself then, mother. I don't want people talking behind my back thinking I'm only marrying Jud for his money. I bet it's you who started the rumours, you and your big mouth. I wouldn't put it past you."

Maureen zipped her mouth shut and rolled her eyes. What a joke! Did Dawn not know everyone was saying it behind her back anyway, she was the talk of the town!

The bedroom door swung open and in walked Sally, Dawn's best friend. She was dressed in a silk lilac dress and didn't look happy, she was pulling and tugging at it. She was furious. She walked straight up to the mirror and dragged her hands up and down the dress. "Dawn, please don't make me wear this bag of shit. I feel like an actress in that film 'Gone With the Wind'. Honest, I feel a right nob-head."

Dawn held the bottom of her stomach and giggled. Sally always dressed in more boyish clothes and rarely ever wore a dress; she was a tomboy, she always wore hoodies and tracksuits bottoms. Dawn smirked trying to hide the fact that Sally was right, she did look like a nob. She just didn't suit dresses. It was the way she stood, back arched over and legs bent slightly. "You look amazing Sally, honest to God, on my life. I wouldn't lie to you, cross my heart," she shot her eyes to her mother who couldn't contain her laughter. "Mam, doesn't she look beautiful?"

Maureen stood up to get a better look; she held her hand over her mouth to stop herself from laughing. Maureen was a straight talker and never held anything back. Sally snapped and marched about the bedroom in a strop. "Maureen, will you tell her I can't wear this bleeding dress. Look Dawn," she pointed over at Maureen. "Even your mam knows I don't look right in it. Don't make me wear it, please."

Dawn growled at her mother and shook her head; she wasn't helping the situation at all. Maureen was in stitches now and she was giggling loudly. "Just take no notice of her Sally; she's been on the gin again, she's pissed up."

Maureen roared laughing and her eyes were watering.

Dawn was right, she had been on the lash and her cheeks were bright red, she was wrecked. Maureen sniggered and tried to contain her laughter. "You look great Sally, stop being a mard arse. I'm only laughing because of your face that's all. Come on, get a drink down your neck and you won't be bothered what you look like. Get a swig of gin, it'll soon sort you out." Dawn walked back to the mirror and took one last look at her wedding dress. She looked pure, untouched, and special. Maureen was right about one thing though, she'd hit the nail right on the head when she said she was only marrying Jud for his money. Plus, Jud made her feel safe and that was something she'd never felt before in her life. Her upbringing had been chaotic and she'd watched so many men come in and out of her mother's life. There was no way she could have stayed living in poverty for a minute longer, she had lived on the breadline all her life and struggled for even the basic things when she was growing up. Jud had saved her in more ways than one. He was her hero.

Sally gulped a large shot of straight Gin and wiped her mouth with a swift movement. Maureen was right, it did take the edge off her anxieties. Dawn and Sally had been friends ever since primary school and they were inseparable. "Hinge and Bracket," their friends nicknamed them. They were very close and shared a lot of secrets. Sally paced the room trying to get used to her bridesmaid dress, she didn't look comfortable and the fabric was itching her neck. A bright red rash was appearing with every second that passed. "I hope Jud's invited some good looking mates," she said flicking her chestnut brown hair over her shoulders, "I'm sick of all his ugly friends now, I want some fresh meat."

Dawn turned her head away and smirked. Sally had slept with almost all of Jud's friends in the past and now she was on the hunt for some fresh eye candy. She was a hopeless romantic and was never lucky in love. She was always looking for the one, her Prince Charming but he never came along, she just always picked the dead legs, men who wanted nothing more than a quick leg-over. "Don't you worry Sally; I'll make sure I hook you up with a good one this time. There should be some good lookers there today. Jud said Larry has invited the Morgan lads down from Langley and believe me them guys are class. I've seen them with my own two eyes. They're fit as fuck."

Sally stood up and waited until Maureen had left the room, she was hovering about waiting to speak. Checking the door again she kept her voice low. "Did you finish it with Larry last night then or what?"

Dawn stuttered and made sure her mother was gone. Maureen was always eavesdropping, she was a right nosey cow, she was always hid around some corner trying to listen to any gossip. Closing the door slowly, sadness fell over Dawn, her heart was low as her eyes clouded over. "Yeah, stop worrying. I told him last night that it's over. He wasn't having any of it though; you know what he's like, he just made a joke out of it."

Sally gripped Dawn's hands tightly, she knew her best friend was dicing with death and she wanted her out of the situation as quickly as possible. "Dawn, it has to be finished with you and Larry. You should never have slept with him in the first place, you should have known better.

Fuck me, the guy is bad news. A car crash waiting to happen."

Dawn stroked her neck with her fingers slowly and seemed in a deep trance as she thought about the days gone by; the lust, the wanting, the need for him to touch her body one last time. "I know, but, he just turns me on so much. I can't say no to him, he just does something to me. I know what you think, but you've never felt what I've felt before with a guy. He just gets me inside and out. I suppose we're both the same in a way." She looked at Sally with a serious face as she cradled her body in her arms. "Jud's crap in bed compared to his brother you know? He gets breathless just walking up the bleeding stairs, never mind performing in the bedroom. I've told him to cut down on the fags but he's a chain-smoker he's never got one out of his mouth. Sex is shit with him. I'm a woman with needs you know?"

Sally sighed shaking her head. Was this girl on drugs or something, she just wasn't getting it? "For fucks sake Dawn, get him on an E-cig or something, or better still, buy a vibrator. Sex isn't everything, you know. You'll just have to train Jud in the 'Karma Sutra' or something like that. But for now, leave Larry Watson well alone. Are you listening to me or what? Larry's a complete nutter, he's tapped in the head. A couple of butties short of a picnic. You'll be sorry if Jud pisses off with someone else trust me."

Dawn didn't reply, she was in a world of her own. What did Sally know about love anyway, she'd never known how hard it was to walk away from someone who turned you on so much. Dawn felt her heart sink and her heartbeat change. Even though she'd told Larry it was over she was already missing him, missing his phone calls, missing the daft texts he usually sent her, missing his daft sense of humour. She just missed everything about him.

Maureen raced into the room shouting and screaming like she'd won the lottery. She was hysterical and holding another glass of gin in her hand. "The cars are here. Come on, hurry up. Let's get our arses into gear. You don't want to be late, do you Dawn?" Maureen walked to the mirror and checked herself over. Her royal blue hat was held on by two clips at the side of her head and every now and then you could see her scratching at her scalp, it was irritating her head. This was the best Maureen had looked in a long time. Usually she was still sat in her housecoat at this time of the day watching daytime TV. Well, that was if she'd paid her electric bill. She was always behind with her rent and crap at anything that involved money. She lived from hand to mouth most days. Maureen owed a lot to Jud; he'd saved her family in more ways than one. He'd personally threatened the loan sharks who were constantly hammering at her door for overdue payments and he was always bunging her a wad of cash to go and treat herself, he was a good lad Jud and she liked him, she liked that he looked after her. Maureen never told her daughter about the treats she got though, no, that was her little earner and she was keeping that to herself, no one was pissing on her parade and stealing her thunder. If Dawn had found out about the money she was getting she would have called her a scrounger and put a stop to it. She hated anyone else having anything, she was right a selfish bitch.

Spencer, Dawn's brother, stood at the bedroom door looking smart in his grey suit and his black brogues. A good looking man with a cheeky smile, he had lovely white teeth and a beaming smile. He was giving Dawn away today. Their father had walked out on his family years ago and nobody knew where he was. Maureen always said he was dead but she was a heartless bitch who was still bitter towards her ex-husband. Dawn knew, in her heart, that she still loved him but she could never forgive him for what he'd done, she could never let it go, no way.

Dawn's father, Ben, had slept with his own mother-in-law. He had denied it until he was blue in the face but Maureen knew he was lying, she'd seen the evidence with her own eyes. Betty, Maureen's mother, had also denied it all but she had a gut feeling she was right, there was just too much evidence against them both. Maureen had found them in when she'd called to her mother's house out of the blue. Ben came up with some cock and bull story and she never for one second believed him. She knew what she had seen and since that day she could never look at him in the same light again. The marriage was over and she made him pack his bags and flung him out. Maureen missed Ben, she missed the closeness they'd once shared in the years they were together. But, that was in the past and she didn't give him a second thought. Life was too short to sit about crying about how things could have been. She was living for today.

Spencer smiled at his sister as he touched the top of her shoulder. "You scrub up well sis, who'd have thought it ay, my baby sister marrying one of the Watson's boys," he sniggered. The Watson brothers had always been a big name on the estate where they lived, even as children the Watson boys were running the crime scene in the area. They sold weed and anything else they could get their hands on to earn a quick few quid. Day by day they were getting bigger and nobody ever messed with them, they were ruthless. If you fought one of them, you fought them all. The Watson's had family values and no matter what, family came first. Spencer looked up to Jud and he would have done anything to make him happy. He was his hero, his saviour. Jud could do no wrong in his eyes.

Sally stood up dragging at her dress; she was in two minds whether or not to rip it off her back and fling it across the floor, she hated it with a passion. It just wasn't her. Spencer clocked her from the corner of his eye and chuckled. "You look very pretty Sally. I might even slip you one later if you're lucky." Sally playfully punched him in the arm; the two of them loved flirting with each other, she was blushing. There was definitely some chemistry between them, a twinkle in both their eyes. They'd been friends for a long time but nothing had really happened between them.

Dawn chirped in and stopped the banter there and then. "Ay, she's my best friend Spencer; so don't be speaking to her like that. She's no slapper you know, so back off."

Sally loved the attention he was giving her and jumped into the conversation. It wasn't every day she had any male attention and she was making the most of it. "No Dawn, let him carry on. If Spencer thinks he's got what it takes for a woman like me, then let him bring it on. Let's see what he's got." Sally walked to his side and grabbed his crotch with one hand, a good handful she had, his face dropped. She'd overstepped the mark this time. He was howling out in pain as she carried on talking. "Otherwise mate, keep it shut," she giggled. "I want a man, not a boy who thinks he can. Do you hear me, nipper nob?"

Spencer's cheeks were on fire; he was beetroot and tried to bounce back with his banter. Sally was always quick with her mouth and he knew he would never get the better of her. "Oh, I'm a man alright Sally, don't you worry about that. I'd break you in two with this monster between my legs, trust me." The room was filled with laughter. Spencer and Sally hugged each other and looked into each other's eyes for longer than they should have.

Maureen was running about like a headless chicken, she was searching for something. "Where's my bleeding gin gone? I'll have a quick tipple before we go the church, my nerves are shattered. Do you want one Sally?"

Maureen was looking underneath some clothes on the table, she was getting desperate. "Dead right I do Maureen," Sally answered. "I need something to numb the pain of wearing this dress. Make mine a treble when you find it."

Spencer lifted the net curtain back from the window. He could see all the neighbours gathering outside waiting to get a glimpse of Dawn in her wedding dress. He knew there would be some snide remarks about his sister, she was a bitch and had lots of enemies. Spencer looked over at Dawn and smiled softly. "Jud's done you proud with these cars. Come and have a look, two white Rolls Royce he's sent over for you," he lifted the curtain right up from the window to get a better look.

Dawn perked her lips together and slid the light pink lipstick over her lips slowly. She never looked at him as she spoke, she was concentrating. "I'm not arsed what he's sent for me Spencer as long as I get to the church on time. I would walk there if I had to. What time is it anyway, shouldn't we be going now or what?"

Spencer rolled his sleeve up and checked his wristwatch. The watch was a gift from his new brother-in-law and it was his pride and joy, he cherished it. The Rolex was expensive and Dawn had questioned Jud on why he was treating her brother to big gifts like this. Jud never really gave her an answer and she just took it on the chin. "Yep, it's time to make a move Dawn. Shall I get us a quick drink before we go or what, something to steady your nerves?" He rolled his eyes as he continued in a sarcastic tone. "Well, that's if those two piss-heads haven't already drank it all."

Dawn was worried; her heart was racing inside her ribcage, she was anxious, she had a dry mouth and sweaty palms, she was having second thoughts. "No, I'm fine Jake. I just need to get this over and done with now. My stomach's in knots. I'm shitting myself to tell you the truth. Oh, for crying out loud, why did I ever agree to getting married? We could have just carried on the way we were." Spencer nodded his head slowly and left the room. Dawn needed some time to herself, he could see in her eyes that she was petrified. He knew all about her affair with Larry too but kept schtum, there was no way he was getting involved in her seedy little secret, no way in this world. He had enough with his own problems. Jud would have snapped him in two if he thought he'd been lying to him, ruined his life, wiped him right out, made him pay. No, he turned a blind eye to it all and pretended he knew nothing. But how on earth did he know about the affair? Dawn had never told him, that was strange, so strange.

CHAPTER THREE

JUD SAT AT the kitchen table with his brothers and swigged the last bit of whisky from the bottle. The men were laughing and joking and all in high spirits. Jud's three brothers Larry, Paul and Sean, sat with him keeping him calm. Mary Watson stood at the kitchen sink watching her boys with a proud look in her eye. She was the backbone of the family and she was feared by her sons, she was a right snapper. Her husband Tony had died a few years before and raising this mob hadn't been easy. At one point she actually thought about putting them all in care and running away because she couldn't cope. They were a handful, always up to something, they never kept still. The police were always knocking at her door in search of one of her offspring and she stood by them no matter what.

Mary Watson had a plump round figure, middle age spread she called it. She hated that her once slim figure was now hidden away beneath mounds of blubber, gone forever. She had such a bad temper too and when she blew everybody knew to keep out of her way. She could switch at any time and her moods were so unpredictable. She was lethal and never thought twice about launching objects at her son's heads. Shoes, ornaments, she threw the lot when she flipped. If she needed to be heard they all knew about it. Mary was a tall woman with thick grey hair. Her fingers were like bunches of bananas and some of the neighbours said she looked like a transvestite, not to her face though, no, they said that behind closed doors where nobody could hear them. Mary would have throttled them if she'd have heard their comments.

The Watson family were always the talk of the neighbourhood and there always seemed to be something happening with them. If the magnolia painted walls of the kitchen could speak, the family would have been locked up for years, the lot of them were bent and they would have done anything to get the upper hand on anyone they were dealing with. Jud raised his glass in the air and cheered, his cheeks were red and he was half-cut. "Here's to married life then boys, no more single life for me. I'm on the ball and chain from now on."

Larry slammed his empty glass on the table and bolted up from his seat, his nostrils flared as he scarpered from the room. He was finding it hard to control his emotions and every now and then he looked like he had something to say to his brothers but stopped at the last minute before he caused World War Three. Mary was watching him like a hawk, she knew he was up to something; he was always the same from being a kid, wherever there was trouble Larry was never far behind it. He had something on his mind, she was sure of it. Following him out of the room, she closed the door softly behind her, her voice was low. There was no way she wanted the others to hear her. "What's up with your kite, you've got a face like a smacked arse," she poked her finger into his chest pressing for an answer. She was laying the law down for sure. "Our Jud's getting married today and it's supposed to be a happy day for all of us. So sort your miserable face out, do you hear me, sort it out now, before I straighten it for you."

Larry sat on the bottom stair tying his shoe laces, he was wobbling about, he was pissed as a fart and he was trying to focus as he snarled at his mother. "Just piss off will you. I've got a banging headache that's all, just leave me alone. Why do you always think I'm up to something, just give me some space and leave me alone."

Mary nodded; she knew he was up to something, he wasn't having her over, no way. She rammed her crooked finger into the side of his head with force, this time she made sure he was listening. Her eyes were wide open and she meant business. "Don't you be spoiling this day for our Jud. Sort out whatever it is that's nagging at you and straighten your bleeding mush." Mary trudged back into the kitchen to join her other sons. She was wasting her breath talking to Larry. When he was in this frame of mind she knew to leave him well alone. It was like banging her head against a brick wall, he never listened. He was a stubborn fucker when he had a bee in his bonnet and nobody could get through to him.

Larry rammed two fingers in the air behind her. If he had done this in Mary's face she would have knocked his block off. "Fuck off," he mumbled under his breath. "Just leave me alone and stay the fuck out of my life."

★

Dawn sat in the wedding car with Spencer at the side of her. There was silence, not a word was spoken between them during the journey. Before long they pulled up outside the church. Dawn gazed out of the car window and she seemed in a world of her own as the colour drained from her cheeks. It was show time. There was no going back now. Sally waved her hand above her head in the distance; she was smoking at the side of the church, getting a last blast of nicotine before the service began. Watching her flick her cigarette butt away, Dawn held her dress up to get out of the car.

The weather was fine today and just a few white fluffy clouds filled the blue skies above. Maureen's face squashed up against the window, her nose splattered against the glass and she smiled. "He's here love, Jud's already here. I thought he might have stood you up, but no, he actually turned up." Maureen blew a laboured breath, everything was going to plan, all she needed now was to get her daughter down the aisle, she'd drag her down it by the hair if she had to. There was no way she'd let her get away. Dawn raised a wry smile and opened the car door. Standing tall she straightened her dress and inhaled deeply. Spencer came to her side and linked her by the arm.

Sally ran to her side looking flustered, she stunk of stale tobacco and her hair was wind swept. "Bleeding hell Dawn, are you really going to go through with this or what? This is your last chance to run, girl. Make sure you know what you're doing before you go into that church. There's no turning back after that."

Maureen was spitting feathers and punched her clenched fist into Sally's arm. A proper punch it was that sent her flying. "Of course she's bleeding going through with it, you clown. Stop freaking her out will you, she's nervous enough without you spooking her too. Just keep it shut and let her get on with it. Anyone would think you didn't want to see her happy."

Sally rubbed her arm and chewed hard on her bottom lip. If that would have been any one else she would have belted them, knocked them right out. Maureen was lucky. Dawn was speechless, every step she made towards the church doors seemed like she was debating her next move. Her head twisted from side to side checking the area. She was definitely looking for someone. Maureen marched inside the church and took her seat at the front; this was a show not to be missed, the proudest moment of her life. At last her daughter was getting a ring on her finger, being made respectable. The church was packed out and Sally too was nervous as she clocked all the people sat inside. Her neck was bright red, it had spots all over it and she was constantly scratching at her skin.

The organist started playing the music and Dawn took her first step into St Patrick's church in Collyhurst. All heads turned to face her, it was time to get married. Dawn's face was bright red and she was wafting her hand out in front of her, struggling to breathe. Her chest was rising rapidly. "Just take deep breaths," Spencer whispered into her ear. "It will be all over soon," he said in a gentle calming voice. The clicking of her heels made the congregation aware she was ready to make her entrance. They all wanted the first glimpse of the bride. Jud stood at the front of the church and smiled softly as he watched his bride glide down the aisle towards him. He straightened his jacket and nudged his brother in the waist. "I told you she would turn up, didn't I tell you," he chuckled. Dawn froze as she clocked Larry sitting with his brothers. His head twisted towards her and she could she by his sunken eyes that he was drunk, he was a ticking bomb. Small beads of sweat appeared on Dawn's forehead and her chest was rising with speed. Her heart getting ready to leap from her ribcage. Her palms were hot and sticky and she was constantly wiping them on the side of her dress.

Spencer squeezed her hand tightly, he could see how stressed out she was and he feared she was about to turn and run out from the church. "Nearly there now, just breathe, come on Dawn, deep breaths." Spencer was panicking but his job to get her down the aisle was nearly over. Dawn's heart was racing and when she reached the front of the church her legs looked unsteady, she wobbled to the side and nearly fell over. Jud gripped her hand just in time and he pulled her to the side of him. "You look amazing Dawn, stunning." The full Watson family filled the church, rows of them filling each bench. There were loads of them, cousins, uncles, aunties the lot. They were dressed in the top swagger and the expensive scents they were wearing filled the air. Dawn only had a few close relatives in the church and they were sat on the opposite side, the bride's side was mostly empty. Maureen twisted her head back over her shoulder and waved to her younger sister and her husband. She was as proud as punch that her only daughter was finally getting a wedding ring on her finger. The service began and you could still hear Dawn's heavy breathing. Jud kept trying to calm her down, but still her heart pumped inside her ears.

At last, the couple were ready to exchange vows and everyone was sat forward eager to hear the words "I do". Dawn's voice was shaky and low and at one point the priest passed her a drink of water to moisten her lips. Larry sat forward in his seat, he was twisting his fingers rapidly and he was unsure of his next move. He kept stretching his neck to get a better look. The priest continued talking and he knew it was now or never. There was no way he could let Jud marry the girl he loved. Standing to his feet he coughed loudly and made sure he held everyone's attention in the congregation. The spotlight was on him now and he couldn't turn back, it was show time. His hands gripped the bench and his knuckles turned white as his head started to lift. Dawn was white and her eyes were desperate as she turned to face him, what the hell was he doing? Larry's brother Paul pulled at his brother's legs. "Sit down you bleeding nutter, they've not said 'I do', yet. Just sit back down and stop making a show of yourself." Larry made his way out of the pew. He pushed past everyone, not caring whose feet he stamped on. Larry stood facing Jud and Dawn was unsure of her next move. She shook her head at him and tears filled the corner of her eyes, surely he wasn't going to ruin her big day.

Mary was trying to get out of her seat too but Sean held her back down by the back of her dress. This was true life drama and he didn't want to miss a second of it. "Mam, sit back down will you, just leave him to it. Jud will sort him out." Larry began speaking and he wasn't bothered who was listening.

Mary closed her eyes and made the sign of the cross across her body. "Jesus, Mary and Joseph," she whispered under her breath. Larry held everyone's attention now. The ball was in his court. He smirked and held his head to the side.

"So Dawn, are you really going to marry him or what?" He held his hands up in the air and shrugged his shoulders. "Come on Dawn, who are you kidding here. We both know you don't want to marry him."

Dawn blew a breath and wafted her hand in front of her, her mouth was open but no words were coming out, she was speechless. What the hell was he doing? Sally was biting her fingernails from where she stood, she couldn't believe her eyes and she knew that any second now the shit was going to hit the fan. Jud let go of Dawn's hand and turned to face his younger brother. How dare he piss on his parade and try and ruin his big day, he was having none of it. Jud stepped forward, he tried to make light of the matter. He kept his cool. "What's going on Larry, go and sit down while I marry this woman. This isn't the time or the place for you to start being a dick-head. Go on, go and sit back down before I knock you down. Do you get me or what?"

Jud meant business, it was a look Larry had seen so many times before. The look he gave just before he went in for the kill. Larry edged closer; he was dicing with death but he didn't seem to care. As he stood facing Jud you could smell the alcohol on his breath. Larry was a man on a mission and there was no way he was stopping for love nor money, he'd come this far now, it was do or die time, there was no turning back. Sally ran to his side aware of the secret he was about to reveal. She yanked at his jacket, pulling him to her side as she kept a close eye on Jud. Jud was getting ready to launch a punch right into his brother's face, he'd had enough. Sally took him by the arm and tried to move him from where he stood. "Come on Larry you crazy fucker, you're pissed. I'll take you outside for a bit of fresh air. Come on, don't be doing this now, you'll regret it when you're sober." Sally realised that she'd just swore in the house of God and hunched her shoulders at the priest who was stood growling at her. "Sorry about that father. I forgot where I was, sorry God" she said as she raised her eyes to the ceiling. Sally had never been a churchgoer and this was the first time she'd set foot inside a church in years. Her mother was a devil-dodger and there was no way she was following in her footsteps, she didn't believe in God and there was no way she was starting now. After all, if there was such a thing as God why had he never listened to her when she needed him most? No, she didn't believe in the big man in the sky. She made her own luck, nobody was there to help her.

Larry dragged his arm away from Sally and moved closer to his brother, he was cocky, ready to deliver the blow. He was game for anything and ready to pounce. Taking a deep breath he draped his arm around Dawn's shoulder. He made sure she was looking at him. Larry was scared of nothing. The whisky had seen to that. "Go on Dawn, tell him. Tell him that you love me."

Dawn was unsteady on her feet and her legs buckled. Her face was blank and she hunched her shoulders as if she didn't have a clue what he was talking about. Maureen bolted up from her seat and faced her relatives at the back of the church. Her voice was loud and she was trying to keep a smile on her face. "Don't worry Sylvia, our Dawn's still getting married; this is just a little hiccup. It will be all sorted out soon, don't you worry. Just wait and see." Maureen flicked the invisible dust from the arm of her jacket and raised a smile to the woman sat next to her.

"Our Dawn will make a lovely wife, she loves Jud with all her heart she does. That's his brother there kicking up a fuss. Families ay, who'd bleeding have them?"

The woman smirked and knew Maureen was talking out of her arse trying to smooth things over. She could see there was going to be no wedding today or any other day for that matter of fact, this man was making sure of that. Whatever it was he was saying he had the congregation on the edge of their seats. Jud went nose to nose with his brother and this time he meant business. He gripped Larry by the neck and flung him across the church. The vein in the side of his neck was pumping with rage and everyone was about to see what he was all about. "Sit down you dick-head and let me get fucking married. This isn't the time or the place for you to start performing. Like I said, if you have a problem with me then let's sort it out after I've got married."

Jud backed off and walked back towards the priest who was now getting agitated. He wasn't going to tolerate much more of this behaviour, he'd heard enough. Larry spoke in a loud voice and this time nobody was keeping him quiet, nobody. "Dawn loves me Jud. Ask her if you don't believe me. Go on, fucking ask her."

Dawn collapsed and her mother ran to her side in a state of shock. Jud ran back down the aisle and gripped Larry by the scruff of his neck and jerked his head back. The head-butt knocked Larry for six and he fell to his knees with a loud thud. Scrambling to his feet Larry wiped the blood that splurged from his eye, he was dazed. Not really sure if he was seeing straight. "It's the truth Jud, like it or not. For months she's been sleeping with me, she loves me, not you."

Jud froze. Dawn was in her mother's arms crying. Maureen was hysterical; she stood up and left Dawn for Sally to attend to and ran at Larry Watson, she was ready to scratch his eyes out. There was no way he was ruining this big day, no way in this world. She grabbed him by the cheeks and went nose to nose with him. "Listen you spineless life wrecker, this is my daughter's wedding day, so don't you dare try and spoil it for her, she's waited ages for this you selfish get. Don't you dare begrudge her a bit of bleeding happiness."

Mary Watson was in the middle of it now and she was pleading with her sons to stop fighting, they were swinging at each other. She grabbed Larry by the scruff of his neck and pinned him up. "Will you turn it in?" she stressed. "Go home and sober up you're a drunken bastard. Just you wait until I get you home, you selfish bleeder. How dare you try and destroy our Jud's big day. What on earth are you playing at?"

Larry wiped the blood from his forehead and held a shaking hand out towards Dawn. He was desperate. "It's now or never sweet cheeks, come on, do you really want to be married to Jud, you've said yourself you don't love him."

The whole congregation was stood up now and there was no way they were missing any of the drama. They were whispering to each other and eager to hear every word that was spoken. You could have heard a pin drop. Maureen's sister moved to the front of the church with her husband and she couldn't believe what she was witnessing. She knew her niece was an out and out slapper, she'd said it in the past to her husband and now she was being proved right, she knew you could never polish a turd. Maureen had always defended Dawn of course and tried to make out that she was a good girl but she had a gut feeling Dawn was just like her mother, an out and out slut. Sylvia shot a look at her sister and growled. There had been rumours that Maureen had slept with Sylvia's husband over the years and even though she knew in her heart it was true, she could never prove it. Yes, Dawn was just like her mother and she for one was glad she'd been uncovered for the cheap dirty trollop she really was. All eyes focused on the bride to be, she stood to her feet and tried to regain composure, her whole body was shaking and a piece of hair was dangling at the side of her cheeks, she quickly flicked it back and looked around the church. Sally was by her side and she whispered into her ear but whatever she said to Dawn, she disregarded it and pushed her away.

Dawn edged closer to her fiancée. She swallowed hard and touched the side of his arm. "Jud, I never meant to hurt you. It just happened. I'm sorry, I'll do anything to make this right." What was she doing, Jud was her meal ticket to a better life, this girl must have lost the plot to ever think Larry could give her the life she'd grown accustomed too. He was an out and out arse-hole.

Maureen gripped the edge of the wooden bench and blew a laboured breath. "You silly, silly cow," she mumbled. She shook her head and growled at her daughter. "Fancy bleeding, admitting it. You've blown it now my girl, you're up shit street. What a bleeding fool you are, fancy admitting it. You should have taken that to the grave. Have I never taught you anything?"

Maureen's sister shot a look at her and it looked like she wanted to pummel her fists deep into her face. Years of frustration were coming to a head. This was definitely getting worse by the minute. Sylvia moved forward and she was just about to speak when her husband dragged her back by the arm. "Stay out of this love, it's Maureen's business not yours." Sylvia stopped dead in her tracks, he was right, this wasn't the time or place to bring up the past.

The priest had finally had enough, he was bright red and his ears were twitching at the top. How dare these people act like this, in this sacred place? "Can I ask you all to leave please? This is the house of God and I think you should all respect that. Can you all just leave now, please? Come on, all head towards the exit, there is going to be no marriage here today or any other day for that fact."

His arms were held out fully as he marched towards the guests forcing them down the aisle towards the exit. Mary stood frozen, her eyes were welling up. This was so humiliating. All her family were here today, what would they think of her family and the perfect picture she'd painted of her life? Jud's marriage was ruined before it started - what a sham, what an utter disgrace! Mary ran at Dawn and poked her finger deep into her chest. She was getting a mouthful now, why should she hold anything back now it was all out in the open? "Well, you dirty scrubber. How could you? Jud gave you everything you ever wanted and look how you have treated him. You dirty tart. I hope he kicks your skinny arse right to the curb. I told him you know, I said you were nothing but trouble right from the start." Before Dawn could reply Mary ran at Larry. "And you, you big lump of shite, how could you betray your own flesh and blood for a bit of skirt. Because, that's what she is you know, a no good trollop who'd drop her knickers for anyone. You deserve everything that's coming to you Larry, you're a shower of shit."

Mary made the sign of the cross across her body and closed her eyes as Paul and Sean came to her side. Jud stood tall and his eyes were menacing, this was the quiet before the storm and everyone was waiting on his next move. He was never going to walk away from this, he wanted blood, his brother's blood. Running at Larry with full force he dragged him out of the church doors, swinging him like a rag doll. Jud was like a man of steel and Larry didn't stand a chance. He was done for. Mary shrieked as she covered her eyes. "Paul, Sean, go and help Larry. Our Jud will kill him stone dead if you leave him any longer, you know what he's like when he gets that red mist, he's a bleeding maniac." Mary covered her face and shook her head as she peeped through her fanned fingers. She watched her sons trying to control this mess. Paul left his mother's side in a hurry but Sean remained with her. He hated violence but Larry deserved what was coming to him; it was about time someone put him in his place. He had got above his station. Mary pushed her hand into Sean's waist with a distressed look. "I said go and help Larry. We don't want our dirty washing airing in public do we? Go and make sure Jud doesn't kill him." Sean made his way out of the church, he was in no rush to get there either, he took it all in his stride.

Sean Watson seemed calmer than his other brothers, a bit feminine in his actions so to speak. He wasn't really a fighter either, he preferred to sit back and watch the action, never get involved. If the truth was known he hated the family he was born into, he'd much rather have had had a proper job and kept his nose clean. A nine to five job, in sales probably or something dealing with the public. His father had always said he was the runt of the litter and hated that he wasn't as feisty as his other sons. "A fucking throwback," was the way he described him and he was right. Sean was a coward, a yellow-belly. Mary Watson always protected her son though and she told her husband that her son would step up to the mark when he was older. But, he never had, something was missing in him, he had no backbone. Mary was aware of her son's yellow streak and tried her best to ignore it, in the hope that one day he would stand by his family's name, he never did. This life wasn't for him.

The fight outside the church was like two gladiators fighting in the arena, punches were being thrown, people were shouting. Larry was trying to fight back but he didn't stand a chance, Jud was destroying him. The spectators covered their eyes as Jud threw a final punch into his brother's stomach. Blood surged from Larry's mouth and Paul had to find his inner strength to pull Jud away, he was going to kill him. His brother was so strong. Paul screamed down his brother's ear as he tried with every bit of strength in his body to drag him away. "Leave him now Jud, he's had enough, for fucks sake you're going to be on a murder charge if you carry on like this."

Jud jumped to his feet and screamed with rage. His

clenched fist banging on his bare chest. "I'll fucking finish you Larry, trust me, this isn't the end, watch your back because the next time I see you, you won't be as lucky. You're a dead man walking, you cunt."

Paul dragged Jud away with the help of the other men. He was like a caged animal, thick white saliva hanging from the corner of his mouth, eyes bulging. Larry lay still with a pool of thick red blood around him, he wasn't moving, he was in a bad way. Every now and then his body shook and his legs lifted as bubbles of blood steamed from his nose. Sean stood over his brother and lit a cigarette. His brothers half killing each other was something he was used to and he didn't seem bothered about it one little bit. It was everyday life in his household. Once he'd stubbed his cigarette out he bent his knees and lifted his brother's head into his hands. "I'll ring an ambulance Larry. Fuck me, you've really gone and done it this time haven't you. Why didn't you just keep your big trap shut? You always have to go over the top don't you?" Sean shook his head slowly and bit hard on his bottom lip as he dipped his eyes low. Larry never answered him, his eyelids were flickering rapidly and his breathing was shallow.

Michelle Buckley came screaming over towards them. She was horrified when she saw her true love lying in a pool of blood. She covered her mouth with her hand and knelt down on a bended knee. "Larry, it's me Michelle, you're going to be fine. An ambulance is on its way, just try and keep still. I'm here with you now, you're going to be fine, just try and breathe." Michelle was holding his hand as if her life depended on it. She kissed the end of his fingers as the tears streamed down her cheeks, big fat bulky tears. Dawn was screaming as she ran towards the gathered crowd. Once she saw Larry lying on the floor she folded in two and screamed like an injured animal. She ragged her fingers through her hair, pulling the clips out and launching them at the crowd of onlookers. "Why Larry, why?" she yelled at the top of her lungs. "You should have just left me to marry Jud. Look at the mess you've caused now. It's all ruined, everything fucked up because of you and your big ego."

Maureen kicked her foot into her daughter's legs. She held her hands firmly on her hips and hissed. "You silly bitch, you had it all and you fucked it up. Men like Jud don't come along every day. What's Larry going to give you, think about it," she rammed her long slim finger into her daughters head at the side. "I'll tell you what he's going to give you shall I?" Her voice went higher and she made sure everyone heard her. "Fuck all, and plenty of it too. He's the lowest of the low, fancy ever thinking he could get away with sleeping with his brother's woman. He deserves to rot in hell for what he's done, the life wrecking bastard."

Dawn lifted her head up and she was aware all eyes were on her, she clenched her teeth together tightly. "Mother just do one, you're only arsed about the money anyway. What is it, are you scared you will have to pay all your own debts off now? Go on, tell everyone that's the real reason you wanted me to marry Jud in the first place." The crowd was hanging on her every word as she continued. Maureen folded her arms tightly across her chest, she was livid as Dawn continued. "It was so that you didn't have to pay the loan men off. You're going to have to sleep with them again now, aren't you mother, just like you used to. Go on, piss off you cheap whore."

Maureen shot a look at the crowd of people and her jaw dropped. This was a low blow, she went beetroot and was stuck for words. Her daughter was right in what she was saying though, she did sleep with the loan men she owed money to but there was no way she was ever admitting that in public. So what if she'd slept with a man to pay off her debt, lots of women did it, it wasn't a hanging offence. It was the only way she could get by! Gathering her wits, Maureen retaliated. "Mark my words Dawn, you'll regret this day for the rest of your life. You silly cow. Don't you come crying to me when that pile of shit has left you," she pointed her finger over towards Larry. "And, he will you know, men like him never change, he's a womaniser, he always will be."

Maureen marched off in a strop, she kept her eyes low and sprinted off in the distance. Her reputation was worse than ever now. How could she ever hold her head high again? Michelle Buckley met Dawn's eyes and she smirked at her. She made sure Dawn could hear everything she had to say. "Every dog has its day, slut, and you'll keep for some other time. Trust me Dawn Pritchard, somehow, someway, you'll pay for this. Larry is the love of my life and you knew that. I'll teach you to play about with other people's hearts." Dawn had heard enough of the bullshit and Sally was by her side now watching her back. There was no way she was taking anymore crap from anyone.

Dawn stood tall and shrugged her shoulders. She made sure everyone was listening to what she had to say. There was no way she was leaving here without saying her piece. "Listen Michelle, get your facts rights before you start judging people. Larry has never loved you, so take your head from up your arse and smell the coffee. He kissed you once," she chuckled and held her hands out in front of her. "Does that make you his wife?" The crowd were loving every minute of the drama and edged closer as Dawn continued. This was a cat fight and the claws were out. "And, from what he's told me he was pissed out of his head and doesn't remember a thing about it, so fuck off home, you stalker and get over it. He's never been your man and never will be." Michelle was bright red, her eyes were nearly popping out of their sockets. The kiss did mean something. It was sweet and caring and lasted forever. How did Dawn know what it meant to them both, she was just jealous. Larry must have remembered it too, just like she'd always remember it until her dying breath. It was the first kiss from her true love, a kiss she'd never forget. She growled and lifted her head up slowly. "Like I said bitch, watch your back. This is far from over." Michelle walked away. There was no way she was discussing her private life in front of all these people, they didn't know about her relationship, they didn't know how much Larry loved her. Michelle knew the truth and that was all that mattered. Larry would always remain in her heart, no matter what. He was her man and always would be.

Mary Watson watched Larry being stretchered into the back of the ambulance. Sirens blazing, medics were running about trying to keep him alive. Mary's make-up had run all down her cheeks, she was a mess, she was sobbing her heart out, inconsolable. This would be the talk of the town for months, how could she ever hold her head up high again? Her family had been shamed, thrown out of the local church, could things get any worse? She was a broken woman. Mary passed Dawn and spat at her, wiping the side of her mouth with a swift movement. "You hard faced cow. I'll tell you what Dawn Pritchard, if I was a few years younger, you'd feel my foot right up your bony arse. I'd rip your bleeding head off." Mary was serious and she actually looked like she was going to fight. At one stage she was rolling her sleeves up and unclipping her earrings.

Dawn was about to reply but Sally stopped her just in time, this wasn't the time or the place for a bust up. She was just adding fuel to the fire. Sally held Dawn in her arms and stroked the top of her head. "Don't make things any worse than what they already are Dawn, just button it will you and let her go. Come on. Let's get you home. You need to get that dress off. You look a mess." Dawn's wedding dress was in tatters; it was ripped and torn, just like her heart. Her life was a mess and she had nowhere to run, everybody had turned their back on her. Spencer shot a cunning look at Sally and smirked. He went to his sister's side and snarled. The look on his face told her he wasn't happy either. Jud had helped him out in the past and now the shit had it the fan, his handouts were just a distant memory too. What a disaster this day was. There was no wedding, no best man's speech, nothing.

Sirens filled the air, the police were swarming the area. Team-handed they were running about the crime scene, searching for the man who had put Larry Watson in hospital. Everybody scarpered; there was no way any of them were ever going to give a statement to what they had just witnessed. This was the Watson family they were dealing with and everyone knew grassing would be more than their lives were worth. Grassing was the lowest of the low and the unwritten law on the estates where they lived, everybody kept schtum. Nobody broke the code of silence unless they were looking for trouble. Nobody was willing to talk.

Michelle Buckley made sure the coast was clear, she ran one way then another checking she was safe. There was no way she wanted to be branded a snitch. When she was sure nobody was about she approached a police officer. Michelle was singing like a budgie, she wouldn't shut up. She gave them all the evidence they needed to make an arrest, she wanted her identity kept a secret though and made sure she got witness protection before she started to talk. Jud Watson was well-known to the police and this was just what they needed to get this dangerous man off the streets. Michelle smirked as she watched the police car drive off. She kept her head low and held a cunning look in her eye. The deed was done, Jud Watson was going to get slammed for this attack for sure.

Dawn stormed into her mother's house and dragged her dress from her body as if it was carrying a lethal disease. Grabbing her pink housecoat from the side she wrapped it around her shaking body. "Open a bottle of gin Sally, my nerves are shattered, look at me I'm shaking like a leaf."

Sally went to walk into the kitchen but paused as she got to the door. She turned her head slowly and rubbed at her arms as a chill passed over her body. "You'll need more than gin Dawn to sort this mess out. Jud will be gunning for you now. What the fuck are you going to do? He'll kill you stone dead when he gets his hands on you."

Dawn paced the front room aware of the consequences of her actions. She was living on borrowed time and knew Jud would be planning her downfall. "I know, I know. I need to think about this. Why the fuck didn't I just deny it! I could have said Larry was lying. He's lied in the past, we all know how much of a bullshitter Larry is don't we?" Dawn sank to the floor, her head was spinning. What a bleeding mess this was. Anything that could have gone wrong had, it was a complete disaster.

Sally left the room and went to get the drinks. Maureen stormed in like a whirlwind. Hands on her hips she looked directly at her daughter, she was fuming. "So, what now ay? You've lost it all, and for what? A quick knee trembler with Larry Watson."

Dawn knew she was right but stood her ground well. Who was Maureen to preach to her anyway, people who lived in glass houses shouldn't throw stones. "Oh, so you've never made mistakes in your life have you Mrs Perfect? It is what it is. I can't change it can I? I'll just have to deal with it. So, back off getting on my case about it. I don't need the extra stress of you ballooning too."

Maureen lit a cigarette and popped it into the corner of her mouth. She sucked hard on it, needing a fix of nicotine to steady her nerves. "I suggest you go and see Jud and tell him you've made a bad mistake. It's your only chance if you ask me. That's what I'd do if I was you anyway."

Dawn was livid. Why did Maureen always talk out

of her arse? She knew Jud more than anyone and knew he would have her guts for garters the moment he set eyes on her. She didn't need anyone else telling her what to do, she had a mind of her own. "What, do you think Jud needs an apology? Do you seriously think he would listen to me? Mother, you don't understand what he's like. Do you think he's going to welcome me back with open arms because let me tell you, he will make me pay for this. I know him of old, he's a dangerous bastard, he'll try and kill me."

Maureen sat down. She was blowing thick clouds of smoke from the corner of her mouth. Sally was back in the room sipping at her drink listening to everything that was being said before she voiced her opinion. "Yep Maureen, she's right. Jud won't stop until Dawn is six foot under. Do you remember when he thought she was seeing that guy from the other estate?" She raised her eyebrows and blew a laboured breath as she continued. "Maureen, he threatened to cut Dawn's hair off. In fact, he was going to shave all her hair off and leave her bald. The man's a head the ball, trust me, he's not to be trusted. I've heard some sick stories about him and he's not to be messed with. He's a crank."

Maureen sighed and rubbed her cold hands together. "What if I speak to him, surely, he'll listen to me?" Nobody answered her. She was clutching at straws trying to find a solution. Dawn and Sally sat staring at the four walls, both of them in a world of their own. They both knew without a shadow of a doubt that Jud would be hatching a plan to make her pay. It was only a matter of time before her time was up. The clock was ticking.

CHAPTER FOUR

Jud cracked his knuckles as he sat at the kitchen table in his mother's house. "Oh, I'm going to kill him stone dead. Who the fuck does he think he's messing with?" His chest was rising frantically and he looked like he was going to have a heart attack. His fingers were bruised and sore and dried blood was stuck to his knuckles. Grabbing a bottle of brandy from the kitchen he roared with rage from the pit of his stomach, banging his fist onto the kitchen side. "Why didn't I see this fucking coming? I mean, how long has this been going on? I bet they were at it like rabbits, the dirty bastards. Why, why, didn't I see it? I'm a right daft twat".

Mary shook her head and offered her hand out to comfort her son. He just moved her out of the way with a quick flick of his wrist. He didn't want any sympathy; he was a man and wouldn't let his vulnerable side show, not even to his mother. His heart was broken and every now and then he dipped his head low and he held back the tears. Paul sat down, he was hoping his brother was calming down, praying this was over. Watching Jud swig the brandy down like it was water, he knew this was only the start of things to come. The quiet before the storm. Jud was a man on a mission and he knew he wouldn't rest until justice had been done. He was like that Jud, he always finished what he started. If it had a beginning then it had an ending. Once Jud had a bee in his bonnet he never settled until the problem was sorted out. That usually meant taking some fucker out, destroying everything they had or loved.

Sean was by his mother's side, his head resting on her shoulder as she was stroked the top of his head. He was a right Mary Helen, soft as shit he was. The other brothers just ignored him, they were used to his demand for attention. Sean coughed to clear his throat. He was part of this family too and wanted to voice his opinion, he was sick of treading on eggshells. "Just take it on the chin Jud. Larry has always been the same. You live and learn don't you our kid?"

Mary slapped Sean on the side his head. He was a right gobshite and he was adding fuel to the fire, he never knew when to keep his mouth shut. Jud gripped his glass and his knuckles turned white as he squeezed at it. "He's a dead man walking, so shut the fuck up Sean. Mother," Jud ranted. "I swear to you now, this is far from over. I loved Dawn with all my heart. She was going to be my wife for Christ sake, what the fuck did he think he was playing at?" Jud bit hard onto his bottom lip. It was true, he did love her, she made him feel special. She made him feel loved.

Paul agreed and patted his hand on his brother's shoulder to offer some comfort. "You live and learn Jud, he's a dirty rat and we should banish him from this family."

Mary was distraught; this was her son they were calling, what the hell was he talking about, Larry was part of this family no matter what. She swallowed hard as she tried to get her words out. Mary knew she should have held back but she just couldn't help it, Larry was her flesh and blood no matter what he'd done. Mary rubbed her hands together and held her shoulders back. "I don't care what's happened, we're a family and we should stick together," she pleaded with her eldest son in hope he would calm down. "Jud, you've half killed him already, surely it should end here? What more can you do, he's had enough."

Jud chuckled, he shot a look to Paul and spoke in a sarcastic tone. "Is she on this planet or what? Does she not know me? Does Larry not know what happens to people who cross me?" He stood up and looked out of the kitchen window. His fingers played with the side of the net curtain. "Mother, he's a dead man, end of. I'd order his coffin if I was you. If he knows what is good for him he needs to get on his toes and move away from around here because if he doesn't, like I said, he'll be in a body bag, family member or not." Jud jerked his head back from the window, he was white. His heart was racing and his eyes were wide open, he panicked. "It's the fucking dibble. Somebody must have bubbled on me. Quick! Paul! Sean! Keep them talking while I try and get out of here."

His brothers knew the script where the police were concerned. This was second nature to them. The police were always raiding their house looking for knock-off gear and drugs. It was everyday life to them. Paul made sure Jud had left the room before he opened the back door. Four officers barged past him and they were quickly on the scent of Jud. "Where is he, where's Jud Watson?" they ranted. Paul stood tall and tried to calm things down. He was stood ragging his fingers through his hair, this wasn't good and he was trying his best to buy a bit of time so his brother could make his getaway.

Mary Watson was gasping for breath as she stood wafting her hand in front of her. Her lips were purple and the stress was showing on her face. She ran at one of the officers ready to attack him. Sean pulled her back. "Piss off, you no good bastards," she screamed as she tried to get her breath back.

Paul stood in front of his mother and held a cocky look. "Whoa, hold your horses, eager beavers. What do you scumbags want here anyway? Have you got a warrant to search, you know the score and so do we, so no warrant, no searching?" A male officer came to talk to the family but the screams coming from the hallway made him halt and turn around to assist the other officers.

The hallway was narrow and the lighting was poor. Jud was twisted up and he was fighting for his life, there was no way he was going down without taking a few of these bastards with him. It wasn't his style, he had to give all he had. Jud was solid and he was like an attacking lion as he rolled about with the rozzers. Paul ran to his brother's side trying to calm things down, help his brother break free. He knew the show was over as he saw the handcuffs being hooked on his brother's wrists. There was no way he was getting involved now, he knew better than anyone to tackle the arm of the law, he was outnumbered. Paul Watson was already up for an assault charge and adding another crime to his record would have almost certainly landed him in the nick.

Jud was handcuffed. As they brought him to his knees he was still trying to fight them off. Spitting at them, jerking his head to the side hoping he would connect with one of them. "You lot think you're smart don't you.

It takes a team of you to take me down, watch later on when these cuffs are off. We'll sort the men out from the boys then, just you wait and see, you bent bastards."

Mary ran to Jud's side and placed her two palms on his cheeks. He was twisting his head frantically as she spoke to him. "Just calm down Jud, don't make things worse than what they are already. We'll have you home before you know it, just go with them." Mary knew she was fighting a losing battle and backed off with her body quivering as she stood up against the wall. Jud spat at the officer at the side of him and smirked. "Dirty scum, that's all you lot are. Fucking have a go heroes, get a real job you wankers."

Paul spoke in a firm tone; he knew the law and knew Jud had rights. "What's the charges anyway officer? Come on, you can't just come in here and arrest him for fuck all. What's he being charged with?"

The police officer read Jud his rights. He'd been arrested for the attack on his brother Larry Watson. Mary stood back and watched as her son was taken from the house, she was heartbroken. Once the front door was closed she sank to her knees and lifted her eyes up to the ceiling. "Who's opened their big mouth? This is a family matter that we could have sorted out behind closed doors. Nosey bleeders they are whoever stitched us up."

Sean flicked the switch for the kettle as they all headed back into the kitchen. Paul helped his mother up from the floor and guided her to a chair, she was a bag of nerves. A cup of tea was the only remedy Sean had to offer his mother, hot sweet tea was what she needed to calm her down. It usually always did the trick and he was hoping the dash of brandy he added to it was enough to keep her calm for now at least.

Paul plonked down on his chair, he was fidgeting about, out of his head with worry. "This is bad, Sean; Jud will get slammed for years if Larry presses charges against him. I'm going to go down to the hospital to make sure he keeps his mouth shut. Sean, you stay with my mam, I'll be back soon. If anyone comes, tell them fuck all, say we don't know what they are talking about, we need to keep this on the low," he blew a laboured breath and looked directly into his brother's eyes. "If the Morgans get wind that our Jud is out of the picture, we're done for. Fuck me, that's all we need is them lot on our back." Sean kept his back to his brother, he wasn't interested in all this palaver, he'd much rather have been sat down with his mother watching "Cash in the Attic" on the telly. It was on at this time and he wasn't missing it for anybody, not even Jud. Paul left in a hurry and the house shook as the door slammed shut behind him.

Larry was on the critical list. His heart had stopped beating a few times and the medical team had just about stabilised him. He was hooked up to lots of machines and it was touch and go as to whether he'd make it through the night, his injuries were severe. His head was swollen like a pumpkin. The doctor left the room and came to talk to Michelle Buckley. She'd been there for hours and she'd told the medical staff that she was Larry's girlfriend, they never questioned her. Sitting down in a small room just off the corridor the doctor looked at Michelle with sympathetic eyes. He read from his notes. Once he'd told her all the medical details about Larry's injuries and his chance of survival he left the room in a hurry. He could see she was about to break down and cry so he went to get a nurse to sit with her and help her come to terms with her heartache. Michelle was sobbing her heart out, the next twenty-four hours were crucial for the patient and if Larry didn't respond to treatment he was definitely a goner, that's what the doctor said anyway.

Paul walked into the room and shot Michelle a look. He was surprised to see her sitting there. The receptionist had told him it was Larry's girlfriend who the doctor were speaking to and he half expected Dawn to be sat there not Michelle. Placing his hands on her shoulder's he prepared himself for the news, he knew it wasn't good. Michelle lifted her head up and sobbed her heart out, tears rolling down her cheeks, the flood gates had opened. "It's not good Paul, the doctor doesn't think he's going to make it through the night."

Holding back his own emotions Paul tried to remain strong and positive. "Our Larry is a fighter; you know he's not going anywhere."

She nodded slowly as she wiped away the tears as snot dribbled down her nose. "I hope so Paul. I love him with all my heart. I may as well be dead without him here next to me, he's my life."

Paul studied her further, was he missing something here or what? Had his brother really been sleeping with this slob, this social reject? He delved deeper, he wanted answers. "I didn't know you and Larry were an item. Since when have you two been seeing each other?"

Michelle was edgy; she had to think on her feet. Her web of deceit started to unfold and she was giving a performance any actress would have been proud of, she deserved an Oscar. Sat up straight she played with the cuff of her blouse, picking at the stitching slowly. Her eyes were low and she gave him no eye contact. "I've been with Larry for months, Paul. Nobody knew this except me and him, that's how he wanted to keep it. He told me about Dawn and told me she meant nothing to him, in fact, he'd finished with her lots of times and she just kept coming back to him threatening him she'd tell Jud. He had no other option than to tell Jud himself," she sat forward in her seat and held a serious look. She was actually believing her own cock and bull story, what a lying bitch she was! Why was she saying this when it wasn't true? "That bitch was blackmailing him, Paul. She was out for what she could get from him. I told Larry I would deal with her but he made me promise him that I would keep my mouth shut. I should never have listened to him, I should have dealt with her once and for all."

Paul held his head in his hands as the plot thickened, this was all getting out of control. He had no reason to doubt Michelle and he believed every word she was telling him. After all, he'd seen her around Larry and he knew how much she loved his brother, she always had, for as long as he could remember. Everyone knew.

★

Jud was in the holding cells in the police station. His body lay flat on the wooden bench at the back by the wall. Eyes focused on the ceiling he looped his hands above his head.

The police had nothing on him, fuck all. Who would give a statement against him anyway? He knew he was safe, he was untouchable. Jud started to relax and close his eyes. Keys jingling outside the door made him stir. The cell door opened and a police officer stood looking at him. He was aware that Jud could switch at any moment and approached him with caution, always checking the door behind him, making sure he could see the exit. Jud was calm and sat back with his back pressed against the wall. They had nothing on him and his manner was confident. "How long am I going to be in this shit-hole, boss? I'm a busy man as you know. I've got things to do and places to go; you know how I roll, officer. What time am I leaving?" Jud chuckled and stretched his arms above his head. He loved the power he held and smirked at the dibble.

The male officer loved that he was going to wipe the smile right from Jud Watson's face. He'd met this man before in the past and could never make a charge stick, well, until now that is. Coughing to clear his throat he was ready to deliver the killer blow. He leaned forward and sniggered. "You're going nowhere, pal. So get yourself comfortable, you're here for the long haul. No bail, straight to jail, or so the saying goes."

Jud was used to being inside the cells and knew his solicitor would be working his magic as they spoke. He'd paid him enough backhanders in the past to see to that, and he'd never let him down as of yet. Money always got you the service you desired. "Yeah whatever pal, you and I both know I'll be out of here before the night's over, so do yourself a favour PC fucking plod and fuck off out of here pecking my head."

The officer popped his head out of the door and made sure nobody could hear him. He knew he shouldn't be acting in this manner but this man had got right under his skin and he wanted to break him in two. Dig the knife in, knock him for six. "Not this time smart-arse. We've got a statement and a witness. A statement might I add that will make sure you're banged up for a good few years."

Jud turned his head slowly, was this guy blagging him or what? He wasn't sure, he maintained eye contact with him and licked his lips slowly, he was calling his bluff. "Yeah whatever mate, go and fucking arrest some real criminals instead of wasting my time. Ay, I bet while you're out at work your wife is getting banged by some random guy," Jud nodded his head slowly; this always got the dibble's back up. The officer knew the script and he wasn't biting. Correct, he'd heard it all before, this behaviour was normal from the criminals who he'd arrested and it was just part of normal life in his line of work. Jud lay flat on his bed and as soon as the door closed he bolted up and paced the floor. With a swift kick he booted the bottom of the door. "Bastards," he groaned.

Sean lay across his mother's plump thighs as they both watched the TV. She was stroking his head softly, twisting bits of his hair. Paul had just phoned and informed them about Larry's health. Mary wanted to go straight up to the hospital to see her son but Sean had told her to stay put until they knew what was happening with Jud. That was all he needed, his mother talking to the old bill. And, she would have you know, given half the chance Mary would have told them all about what had happened between her sons. She didn't understand the law anymore, in her day if two men had a fight that was it; they shook hands and walked away, no charges or anything. She still thought that's how things happened today. How wrong could she be? Mary was staring into space; every now and then she blew a breath and lifted her eyes to the ceiling. "Please Lord, let my Larry be okay," she prayed.

Sean's cheeks creased as he listened to her, she was a right bible-basher and he hated that every time the chips were down she prayed to God. Nudging her softly in her waist he turned to face her looking deep into her eyes. "Mother, stop being so upset. Larry will be fine, just you wait and see. Anyway, stop snivelling now that programme's coming on where they surprise people who haven't seen each other for years." Mary dabbed the crumpled tissue in the corner of her eyes. She chewed on her bottom lip and closed her eyes as the tears fell. She made the sign of the cross across her body. Sean rubbed his hands together as the theme tune started to the show.

★

Paul opened the door and crept to Larry's side. The heart monitor was beating rapidly and he knew now how serious his brother's injuries were. Speaking in a low voice he made sure nobody could hear him. "Larry, it's me Paul. If you can hear me, blink your eyes twice?" Paul lifted his head up and studied his brother's face, there was nothing. Larry's eyes were firmly shut. He tried again. "Larry, stop fucking about. I know you can hear me, this is serious, our Jud could end up in the slammer if you don't wake up and sort this fucking mess out." Larry remained still; Paul watched carefully from the side of the bed and checked his brother for any movement.

Michelle came into the room and she was in a hurry to get to the bedside. "Has he woken up yet, the doctor said he might if we keep talking to him. To tell you the truth I bet he's sick of hearing my voice. I've not shut up talking to him. He knows everything about me now. Every secret I hold, every dream I have."

Paul played with his fingers and dipped his head low. "He needs to wake up and sort this shit out. Our family is falling apart because of this. Michelle, I need you to stay with him as long as you can. If he wakes up I want to be the first to know. Phone me if there is any change."

She nodded her head and played with the end of her chin. "I'll stay with him don't you worry about that. I'm going nowhere. I want to be the first person he sees when he wakes up, Paul, I love this man with all my heart. If he dies, then my life is over too. I'm nothing without him, he's my world."

Paul turned away from her, he cringed thinking that his brother could ever have a relationship with her; she was a minger, a fat porker. How on earth they had ever became an item was beyond him. She stank of stale sweat and her hair was stuck to her head, she was hanging. Paul sighed and checked his wristwatch. "Right, like I said, if he wakes up, ring me." Paul left the room and closed the door behind him. Michelle stood to her feet and walked to the top of the bed. Making sure nobody was watching she bent over and placed her chubby lips onto Larry's. She was kissing him, not just a little peck either, she was actually opening her mouth for a full on snog, she was one sick twisted woman.

CHAPTER FIVE

DAWN PRITCHARD opened her eyes slowly. This wasn't a dream; this was reality, her reality, her nightmare. Her eyes were swollen and heavy; she'd barely slept a wink all night. She was tossing and turning and unable to sleep, who could blame her though, she had a lot on her mind. Sally was at her side and she was snoring her head off. Loud, grunting noises, like a balloon being deflated. The bedroom was as depressing as ever, wallpaper hung from the ceiling and black fungus crept along the edges of the wall gripping the ceiling, spreading further every day. It was damp and cold just like her heart. Dawn sat up and reached for her cigarettes. Nicotine was always the answer to her problems; it calmed her down and made her relax. Eyes staring about the room, she folded her pillows up behind her head and tried to get comfortable. Thick grey smoke circled her mouth as she sucked hard on her fag. Eyes scanning around the bedroom she focused on Sally. She was a pretty thing in her own way, kind of a rough diamond. With a quick swift movement of her hand she nudged her in the waist, she needed somebody to talk to. Somebody who would listen to her. "Will you wake up; I'm having a nervous breakdown here. Please, I need to speak to you, to clear my head before it bursts?"

Sally stirred; her eyes were still closed as she sat up, she opened them, yawned and fell back onto the bed pulling the duvet back over her head. "Orr leave me alone, I'm knackered. I've not long got to sleep. I need some shut-eye."

Dawn kicked her again but this time she used more force. "Sally, are you taking the piss out of me or what, will you just wake up and talk to me? My head's doing overtime here and I can't think straight. Where's the support. I thought we were best mates?"

Sally spun on her back and her head reared from under the covers. Her hair was stuck up all over the place and her lips were dry and cracked. She rubbed her knuckles into her eyes and yawned. "Give me a drag of that cig will you? What time is it anyway?"

Dawn passed the cigarette over and sat back with her arms folded tightly in front of her. "It is sort my life out time Sally. I'm going to see Jud today. I'm going to try and smooth things over. If he fucks me off, then he fucks me off, at least then I will know one way or the other won't I?"

Sally inhaled deeply and sucked hard on her lips. She was alert now, listening to her every word. "Have you tried ringing him?"

"Yeah, but his phone is switched off," Dawn moaned. "You know what he's like, he's a stubborn bastard. I'm just going to have to front him and go around to his house. I hope he's in because I don't fancy facing Mary Watson. She'll swing for me if she sees me, she's a bleeding nutter."

Sally agreed and sat forward to flick the ash from her cigarette. "Do you want me to come with you? You don't want to be going there on your own. You'll be a lamb to the slaughter if mad Mary gets her hands on you. She's a wild woman. She'd eat you up for breakfast and spit you out of her arse."

This was music to Dawn's ears, Sally was right though, Mary was a battleaxe and she knew she wouldn't have thought twice about lashing out at her the moment she saw her. Dawn kicked the covers from her and sat on the edge of the bed. "Get ready then. I want to do this as soon as possible. I can't stand the not knowing. If it's over, then it's over isn't it? I'll just have to deal with it?"

Sally sat smoking, she never answered, but going by Jud's previous record she wasn't holding her breath. He was a crazy man and she didn't trust him as far as she could throw him. He was a loose cannon who could switch at any time.

Maureen sat in the front room with her housecoat fastened tightly around her waist. There were no lights on and the place was cold and dark. Dawn knew the electric had gone as soon as she walked into the room and as per usual Maureen didn't have an electric card to put in the meter. Jud had previously told her he was going to get the electric wired up, but that was before Dawn had broken his heart, there was no chance of that now, she was fucked. Sally sat shivering; her teeth were chattering together, she pulled her t-shirt over her knees and sat with her head resting on her lap. "Put the bleeding telly on then Mo, there's some good talk shows on at this time. Dawn bang the kettle on too, my mouths like a camel's arsehole. "

Maureen sniggered and kept her eyes low. There was no way she was looking at her daughter; she would have only given her a lecture about spending her benefit money again. "I'll put a card in the meter then shall I, mother," Dawn hissed. "It's a good job I always have a spare one isn't it?" Dawn spoke in a sarcastic voice as she walked to her mother's side. She bent over slightly and went nose to nose with her. "Don't tell me you've spent your money again. You're a disgrace you are mother, how can you just sit here with no electric or gas, where's your morals, your dignity?"

Maureen never answered and watched as Dawn searched in her purse for the electric card. Once she slid it into the meter she walked back into the front room. She had an announcement to make. "I'm going to see Jud, mam," she sat down and waited for her to answer.

She didn't have to wait long, Maureen was ready to voice her opinion. "And, so you bloody well should. I bet he's heartbroken. Mind you, can you blame him?"

Dawn snarled and the usual arguments between them began. They were like chalk and cheese, Sally just sat listening, there was no way she was getting involved. "I know what's gone on mother, for fucks sake you don't need to keep reminding me of it. I've just said I'm going to see him haven't I, so wind your neck in."

Maureen stood up and spoke directly to Sally. "You better go to the funeral directors and get Dawn measured up for a coffin, she thinks Jud's just going to have her back with open arms. Is she for real or what?"

Dawn sat forward in her chair. "I don't think that at all. Will you give me some bleeding support please? I'm heartbroken here too. It's not just Jud who's hurting. I am too."

Maureen left the room to make a drink, she didn't buy her daughter's story for one minute. Who the hell was Dawn trying to kid> Maureen loved a strong cup of coffee in the morning and most days that was all she had to keep her going for the rest of the day. Her diet was coffee and fags and gin, she didn't need anything else to make her happy. Today was Monday and Maureen knew more than anyone that Jack the loan man would be knocking at her door shortly. Her purse was empty as usual and she knew she would have to offer him sex to let her payment go unnoticed. He'd done it before, lots of times, so she was hoping today was no different. Sex meant nothing to her anyway; she would just lie back and think of England as she always did. Jack the loan man was a big fat slob, and just the thought of him made Maureen's skin crawl. He was a well known loan shark in the area and he always preyed on the poor and the single parents who were having a tough time. Maureen had always had loans in the past, it was just something she classed as normal and everyone did it. Jud had paid a lot of the loans off that she owed and this was the last debt that Maureen had going, well, what she was admitting to anyway.

Sally sat playing with her toes in silence. Maureen walked back into the room with two cups of coffee looped on her fingers, she passed one to Sally. Dawn was alert and watched as her mother sat down. She coughed to get her attention. "Where's my drink, don't tell me you've just brewed up for just you and Sally?"

Maureen nodded her head as she sipped on her black coffee, the steam circling her face. "You didn't ask for one, bleeding hell I'm not a mind reader. Go and make yourself one if you want one. The kettle has just boiled."

Dawn was in a strop and threw the cushion over at her mother. "No, shove it up your arse. I'm sick of your attitude towards me. I'm going to get ready anyway so you can stick your drink right up your arse. I'll do without. I hope you choke on it. Sally, when you've finished your brew come upstairs and get ready. I want to get round to see Jud before he goes out." Dawn left the room and Maureen sniggered, she reached for her cigarettes and sparked one up. "Jud will knock ten tons of shit out of her you know that don't you Sally, she deserves it too. She's always been the same that one has, she thinks everyone owes her a favour. She'll come to earth with a bang when Jud pisses her off."

Sally smirked and made sure Dawn couldn't hear her. "I'm going with her to see him, but if he starts, I'm getting off. I'm not being funny Mo but I don't want to get involved with it all, there's no way I want The Watson boys on my case, my life's hard enough without adding Dawn's problems to it too." Sally sat slurping her hot drink. Her life was in bits at the moment, her parents had told her straight that she had to find her own place to live before the end of the month and after that she was going to be homeless. Sally needed help or a miracle to get her back on her feet, she'd hit rock bottom. Yeah, she was seeing somebody, a fuck buddy she called him, but nobody ever saw him, she very rarely spoke about him too. There was something fishy about it all, something not right. Sally wasn't telling anyone everything.

All of a sudden there was a hammering on front door. Maureen bolted up from her chair and ran to the window, she peeped from behind the grey net curtains. "Oh, that's all I bleeding need. It's our Sylvia and her husband. She's a right nosey cow, she's only here to gloat." Maureen banged her clenched fist onto the window. "Stop bleeding banging will you. I'm opening the door now, you impatient fucker."

Sally placed her cup on the table and left the room, she was going to get ready. "Good luck Mo, you tell them how it is, don't let her get to you, just stay calm."

Maureen walked to the front door and giggled at Sally. "Don't you worry love, if she starts with her lectures she's getting slung right out, arse first." Sally ran up the stairs.

Dawn was nearly ready, her hair was done and she was sat in front of the mirror applying some bright pink lipstick. Candy floss pink was her favourite colour and she always had it to hand when she was going out anywhere. She puckered up at the mirror and slid the lipstick slowly over her lips. Sally plonked onto the bed and rolled about slowly. "Dawn, do you think you're doing the right thing here. It might just be worth leaving him alone for a while. I mean, let things calm down and all that. You have to remember what's happened, you need to let him calm down."

Dawn puckered her lips together and turned her head from the mirror. "Sally, do you think I can carry on living in this shit-hole with her downstairs. I'll just end up like her if I do. I realise now that I've fucked up, but ay, it's got to be worth a try hasn't it?"

"I know Dawn, but I'm really scared of what he might do to you. He's pure evil and even if he did forgive you he would make you pay somewhere along the line.

Could you live with that?"

Dawn thought about what she'd said for a few seconds, she could live with it, she had to and anything would be better than the way she was feeling at this moment in time. "Are you coming or what, I need to go now. You can follow me on if you want?" Sally agreed and you could see she was more than happy for Dawn to go it alone. If the truth was known, she was petrified of the outcome. Part of her was happy though, it was about time her friend got some bad luck. She was sick of her always landing on her feet.

Dawn stood across the road facing the Watson household. She was taking two steps forward and one step back. This wasn't easy. Biting her fingernails she finally plucked up the courage and crossed the road. It was show time. A car honked its horn and it had to swerve to avoid hitting her. Dawn was flustered and rammed two fingers up at the driver. "You crazy crank, watch where you're going next time, you prick," she shrieked at the top of her voice. There it was, the front door was staring at her. Taking a deep breath she flicked her hair back over her shoulder and started to walk down the garden path. She pushed her breasts out and pulled her red top down so you could see her cleavage. Jud loved her breasts and she knew one look at them and he would be putty in her hands. Dawn was breathing heavily and she was forever licking at her lips, she was nervous. She knocked at the letterbox several times in hope somebody would open the door. She knew any second now the door would open and she would have to explain her visit there; standing back she prepared herself for her fate.

Sean Watson opened the door and he swallowed hard as soon as he seen her trying to get his words out. "What the fuck do you want Dawn, you better do one before my mam gets a grip of you, she's gunning for you, do you know that?"

Dawn stood her ground, and spoke in a confident manner. So what if all the family hated her, she wasn't bothered. It was Jud she'd come to see, nobody else. "Is Jud in? I need to sort this mess out. I'm not here for trouble Sean, I just want a quick word with him."

Sean chuckled and closed the door behind him as he stepped out into the garden. A Magpie sat on the fence at the bottom of the garden and it was hopping about squawking. Sean began to speak. "Dawn, Jud got nicked last night, someone grassed him up. Do you know Larry's in hospital too? The doctors think he's going to kick the bucket. My mam's in bits in here, she'll string you up if she knows you're here. I suggest you leave before she gets wind you're here."

Dawn came to his side and went nose to nose with him. Sean was always telling lies and she didn't trust him as far as she could throw him, he was a wind-up and loved that she was eating humble pie. "Just go and get him Sean, stop fucking about. I know he's in. This is serious. I need to speak to him."

Sean didn't get chance to answer her, the front door flew open and Mary Watson ran at Dawn like a charging bull. "Do you have no shame? Get out of my garden before I drag you out of it head first." Sean pulled at his mother's arm; she was fighting hard to get away. "Let go of me Sean, she's getting what's coming to her. I should have done this a long time ago. She's a boot, a dirty slut."

Dawn backed away slowly; she was watching her back as she knew Mary would land one on her given half the chance. Hands on her hips she stood facing them both, cocky as ever. "Mary, I just want to talk to Jud, just a few minutes is all I need, then I'll go. I'll be out of your hair."

Mary spat from the back of her throat and it landed on Dawn's arm. "Our Jud wouldn't piss on you if you were on fire you're nothing but scum. Sean, will you get off me will you, while I rag that tart about."

Sean was screaming for Dawn to leave as he held his mother back. Paul ran outside and he lunged for Dawn. Once he had a firm grip of her he dragged her out of the garden head first. He pinned her up by the scruff of the neck, he was nose to nose with her. "Get back to whichever rock you crawled from underneath you dirty bitch. I swear to you now Dawn, if you don't go I'll do you in. Do you hear me?" Dawn was struggling for breath, her feet were dangling in the air, she was turning purple. He was trying to kill her. Paul flung her to the ground and quickly scanned the area and made sure nobody could see him. His hot stale breath was in her face. "If our Jud goes down for this, I'll make sure you pay for it, that means, you and all your family, including Spencer, do you get me?"

Dawn was trembling inside and managed to scramble to her feet. She had to fight back, there was no way she was bowing down to him, she couldn't be weak, it wasn't in her nature. "What's my family got to do with all of this? It's between me and Jud, nobody else. Do what you want to me but leave my brother out of it."

Paul stood tall and walked away slowly, he shouted over his shoulder. "Like I said you bint, the lot of you will pay, mother, brother, they all count, so be prepared."

Dawn picked her handbag up in a panic and ran down the street, she was sobbing and the black mascara from her eyes was running down her cheeks. She was a walking wreck. This was not how she'd planned it. Her mission to smooth things over had failed. What was she going to do now? This was war.

Sally walked down the main road, she was in no hurry to get to the Watson's and if she knew Dawn, she would be sat with Jud pleading for his forgiveness, begging him to have her back. Sally looked sexy, she'd borrowed some of Dawn's clothes and she was forever admiring herself in the shop windows as she plodded along. This was the way she wanted to be dressed but her budget would never allow it, she was on her arse and jobless. A "Primark" bird she was, cheap and cheerful. It made a nice change to see her dressed as a woman. She looked sophisticated, classy. A silver car pulled up at the side of her and for a moment she didn't know who it was, she jerked back from the road in a panic. The music from inside the car was deafening, the baseline was pumping as she watched a head bob from out of the window. "Are you alright Sally, long time no see," the voice said. Dipping her head low she studied the man sat in the driver's seat. It was the one and only Danny Morgan. Her jaw dropped and she had to pinch herself. Danny was a big name in the area, up and coming some people said. A man with power, somebody who was calling the shots.

Sally was in shock, perhaps he'd mistaken her for somebody else. She'd met him a few times in the past but not that they were good friends or anything like that. Sally blushed and patted her hair down. This guy was hot and there was no way she was crumbling in front of him. She pushed her breasts out in front of her and puckered her lips together. "Alright Danny, what you up to?" Sally replied in a shy low voice. Hoping he still remembered her and this wasn't a mistake.

"Nothing much darling, just the usual stuff. Where you off to anyway? Do you want a lift?" Sally couldn't believe her luck; this guy was actually offering her a lift. She shot her eyes around the area looking for the jokers, surely this was a set-up, a prank, but there was no one in sight, nobody peeping around any corners watching her.

Sally cautiously opened the car door and sat in the passenger side. "I'm just going to the Watson's house. Dawn's already there. I'm going to meet her, well, that's if she's still alive."

Danny looked at her in more detail, she'd let the cat out of the bag and once he flicked the engine over there was no stopping her from talking. She was telling him everything that had happened, every little detail about the betrayal. Danny held a cunning look in his eye; this was music to his ears. Something to smile about. He tapped his fingers on the steering wheel and held his head slightly to the side. "So, let me get this right in my head. Larry was actually banging Dawn?"

Sally nodded, she was smiling, teeth showing. "I know it's bad isn't it? I told her time and time again that it would end in tears, but did she listen?" she bit onto her bottom lip and turned her head out of the window as she continued. "Did she hell, she thought she knew it all, but knew fuck all. It was only a matter of time before Jud got a whiff of it. I mean, you don't piss on your own doorstep do you?"

Danny pulled over and clicked his seatbelt off. He wanted every scrap of information on this affair. Jud was at a low and this could be the ideal time for him to strike, for him to take over his criminal empire. "So, what's happened to Larry, is he still breathing. I mean, Jud is not someone to mess with is he? The guy's a crank. I've seen him destroy men for less."

Sally was caught up in the moment and her fist punched into the air as she acted out a few of the scenes between the two brothers. "He was in a bad way when we left him. I swear, if he's still breathing he's a lucky man. Jud left him for dead. Honest Danny, as true as I'm sat here Jud wanted to kill his own brother."

Danny rubbed his hands together; he looked at Sally and licked his lips slowly. "Do you fancy a drink later on? I'll pick you up if you're up for it?"

Sally opened her mouth but no words were coming out, did she hear him right, did he say he wanted to meet her? This was her lucky day for sure. Danny Morgan was a top catch and there was no way she was wasting a second more, she answered him. Her cheeks blushed slightly. "Yeah, I'll come and meet you later if you want. Give me your mobile number and I'll ring you later." They swapped numbers and Sally's heart was beating ten to the dozen, she tried to remain calm but her chest was rising faster than normal. "I just hope Dawn's okay, you know what Jud's like. I bet he's holding her captive or something, he's tapped in the head he is!"

Danny nodded his head slowly and you could see his mind was doing overtime. Sally was just what he needed at the moment, a spy in the camp. She could keep him updated on everything the Watson brothers were up to, keep him two steps in front of them. Bending over slightly he kissed her on the cheek. "Right, I'll see you later on then."

Sally opened the car door and got out; she was smirking and tried to hide her excitement. "So, see you later then," she said.

"Yep, you sure will." Danny chuckled as he gave her a cheeky wink. Sally watched him drive off and she was still in shock, she was bouncing on the spot. Checking her hair in a wing mirror on a nearby car she smiled from ear to ear. Sally headed off with a spring in her step, she was singing. What a great start to the day! Dawn was never going to believe what had just happened. Sally's bad luck was starting to change; Danny Morgan was the answer to all her prayers. At last she'd found a decent man who would look after her.

★

Dawn stood outside the hospital and chugged hard on her cigarette. She walked one way then the other ragging her fingers through her hair. She knew beyond the hospital doors Larry was there and she couldn't make up her mind if she should go and see him or not. Dawn froze and flicked her fag to the side of her. Flicking her hair back over her shoulders she started to walk through the main doors. This was it, she was going to see Larry. What did she have to lose anyway, fuck all?

Michelle Buckley was sat next to Larry's bedside. One of her hands was under the bed covers and you could see the blankets moving rapidly. The dirty bitch was wanking him off! Standing to her feet she bent over and started to kiss him on the lips, she was snogging him. Her tongue was out and she was kissing him passionately. Michelle's hand jerked up and down with speed under the blankets and her eyes were rolling. Her head disappeared under the covers and sexual moans could be heard. Larry was still unconscious, his face was unshaven and he looked dead to the word. Michelle pulled the covers from her head and at that moment you could see the truth of her obsession with Larry, she was sucking him off. She reached her hand up and stroked Larry's dry lips with her finger as she pulled her knickers to the side and straddled him. She seemed in a world of her own, not on this planet. "See, Larry, this is how it could be with me and you. I only need a chance and I'll show you how good I can be. Me and you need to be together." Michelle's nostrils flared as she caressed her hands all over his body. "I need you inside me Larry, I want you so much," she mumbled under her breath.

Dawn spoke with the receptionist and found out which room Larry Watson was in. Searching in her handbag she saw her reflection in a window and applied some lipstick. Puckering her lips together she walked along the busy corridor. The hospital made her feel sick inside, just the smell of the place made her stomach turn. This was where she had been brought when her grandfather was dying and ever since then she associated the place with death. The hospital was depressing and everyone she looked at had that gaunt look about them, that waiting for God look, waiting to die. With a deep breath she opened the door slowly.

Frozen to the spot she watched Michelle Buckley panicking, she was straightening the blankets and pacing around the bed in a fluster. "What the fuck are you doing here?" Michelle snarled at Dawn and coughed to clear her throat. She didn't speak straight away.

Michelle smoothed over the blankets but wouldn't make eye contact with Dawn. "I'm here because I care about Larry, and that's more than I can say about you. We are together now you know. He loves me, he's told me. So, turn your skinny little arse around and leave us to get on with our lives. Just leave us in peace."

Dawn walked towards the end of the bed and her fists curled into tiny balls at the side of her legs. "Are you having a laugh or what?" She placed her hand on the bottom of the bed frame and gripped it tightly and spoke directly to her. "Michelle, you need to sort your head out. You will never be with Larry, so just get over it you lunatic."

"I am with him Dawn, he told me to keep this a secret but now he's on his death bed why should I? He said he loves me and we're going to get married. It's true, he loves me and I love him."

Dawn studied her face, she knew she was lying, she was always a bull-shitter and some of the tales she'd spun in the past had got her in serious trouble. She had mental health issues for sure and needed sectioning, "Michelle, just go home will you. You're just making a show of yourself, everyone's laughing at you. Larry loves me, everyone knows that. Why do you think he stopped the wedding, come on think about it… it's not rocket science, work it out?"

Her words stabbed deep into Michelle's heart, she was gasping for breath, she looked faint. "Fuck off Dawn. You've always been the same around men. You don't love anyone but yourself. Why don't you give me and Larry a chance, ay? You can have any man you want. Just leave Larry alone he belongs to me."

Dawn went nose to nose with her and she could feel her warm breath on her face. "Larry's mine and always will be. Do you think I've gone through all this for fuck all? Jud is going to kill me when he gets his hands on me because of this. I love Larry, end of." Dawn was lying through her teeth. She was so mixed up and didn't know if she was coming or going, but she knew one thing for sure, there was no way in this world she was coming second best to Michelle Buckley, she would have been a laughing stock.

Michelle stood and looked Dawn up and down. She could have broken her in two if she wanted to, scratched her eyes out. Dragged her heart from her chest. She gritted her teeth tightly together and walked to the chair at the side of her. Picking her coat up she shot a look back over her shoulder. "I'm going home for a rest, you or no one's army will keep me from my true love's side. I'm here for the long haul, love. So, just get used to it. I'll be back soon. Don't you be here when I do."

Dawn watched her carefully and she was aware Michelle could strike at any minute. She was cunning like that, unpredictable. "Fuck off home you dick-head. You need to give your head a shake if you ever think Larry will pick you over me."

Michelle picked her bag up from the end of the bed and started to walk to the door. Looking back over her shoulder she spoke to Larry. "I'll be back soon babes, make sure this tart is gone before I get back."

Dawn shook her head and ignored her comment, this girl needed serious medical help, she was off her head, away with the fairies. The door closed and Dawn sat down fidgeting with her thumbs, she gazed about the room looking at all the machines. "Fucking hell Larry, why did you have to open your big mouth? We could have still seen each other. You've just fucked it all up now. What am I going to do?" She turned her head and looked at Larry half expecting him to answer her, he never did. Sat alone with just her thoughts Dawn sat wallowing in her own self-pity. The sound of the heart monitor at the side of her was all she could hear.

CHAPTER SIX

JUD LAY IN HIS PRISON CELL. This was not how he thought things would have turned out. He'd been set up, had over for sure. He was now on remand at Strangeways prison in Manchester. The place was a shit- hole and he hated every minute he was in custody here. He needed out of this gaff as soon as possible, back on the streets of Manchester. Looking over at his pad mate he snarled. He had to stand his ground and show this convict he was no prick. One word out of him and he was getting it big time, there were no doubt about it. The man sat facing him was a smack head. He could tell that just by looking at the track marks on his arms. The addict was still craving the drug, every minute of every day the inmate was searching for his next hit. Deep purple bruises were visible all the way up his arms, his complexion was yellow and his teeth were brown stumps rotted away with the use of drugs over the years. All night long Jud had listened to this guy rattling his balls off and spewing his ring piece up, the inmate was a disgrace.

Norman Jennings was an older man in his late forties and he was serving a twelve month sentence in the jail for burglary. A shit and a shave sentence some might say but to Norman, it felt like twelve years. He didn't mind who he told either about his criminal activities, he was proud as punch that he was a grafter. For two days Jud had been padded up with him and as soon as the cell door opened that morning he was going to cart the low life as far as he could. Heroin addicts were the lowest of the low in the prison system and there was no way he was having this scrote in his cell a minute longer than he needed too. Just watching this junkie made his blood boil. He was always fidgeting about, never still, always had his head to the window shouting out to other inmates. Norman was desperate and he would have done anything to score some brown at this time, including selling his arse. He'd done it before on his last sentence and he had no shame in the lengths he'd go to get his next fix. It's just how it was, he had no morals. The drugs had seen to that. He had no self-respect.

Jud was on his first visit today. Paul and Sean were coming to see him and his mother Mary. He'd told his mother straight that jail was no place for her but she still insisted that she wanted to come and see her son. She said she had to make sure he was alright, see him with her own eyes. The cell door opened slowly and the screw stood there looking smug. He held a bunch of keys in his hand and the sound of them jingling could be heard. "Morning ladies," he chuckled. "Come on, get ready and go and get your breakfast." Jud growled at him, this screw had it in for him and from the first moment he'd set foot on the wing he had seen that he was gunning for him.

Norman ran to the door and pleaded with the screw. "Boss, I need to see a doctor today. I'm roasting my nuts off here. I need some medication. Something to stop the pain. Some strong painkillers. Look at me, I'm fucking dying here."

The screw, who the inmates nicknamed Hitler,

stepped inside the cell and chuckled loudly. He stood tall and held his head back. "Listen, you raging bag head, do your rip and stop fucking crying like a baby. You can go and see the doctor later but for now man up, and face it. You bleeding big Mary Helen." The screw walked over to the window and stretched his neck through the steel bars. "That's the trouble with the world today, men have no balls anymore. Back in my day, men were men and we all stood tall. None of this 'I can't do it' malarkey."

Norman's face dropped and he turned to Jud for some support. "Jud, have you heard this tosser? Who the fuck does he think he is, fucking Sergeant Bilko?" Norman walked up to the screw and bent in towards him, they were nose to nose. "I have human rights you know, stop being up your own arse and sort me out. I need to see a doctor, do you get me or what?" The screw gripped Norman by the throat and tossed him back onto his bunk with one swift movement. Norman looked like he was flying, his body nearly snapped in half. Jud was watching from where he stood and he was unsure of his next move. He knew if he attacked the officer he would have been twisted up and flung down the block for weeks, he never flinched. This was Norman's beef not his. The addict tried to get back up, his body was shaking. As he scrambled to the top of the bed he stood up and his bowels opened. He'd shit himself, wet brown patches all over his grey tracksuit bottoms. The stench was rancid. Norman's face was distraught as the warm brown liquid ran down his legs and seeped out through the bottom of his tracksuit bottoms. Jud's eyes shot to the floor and he was retching, the cell stank like manure.

The officer inhaled and once the stench hit his nostrils he ran from the cell, he was green in the face and gagging. "You dirty bastard," he shouted back inside the pad. "You can get that cleaned up before you go anywhere".

Jud ran to the door and covered his mouth with his hand. "Boss, you need to get me moved out of here. I can't be banged up with him any longer. I'll end up doing the cunt in."

The screw marched forward and went nose to nose with Jud. "Where the fuck do you think you are lad, a hotel? This is a prison not a fucking holiday resort, you'll stay put laddo." Jud pushed his hand against the officer's chest; he was snapping and getting ready to strike.

Norman's screaming from inside the cell was the only thing that stopped him knocking this man to kingdom come. Jud ran back inside and his jaw dropped. Norman had covered himself in shit and he was running about the room like a mad man. "I need medical help, if I don't get it, I'll do myself in, trust me, you fucker. You'll have a death on your hands if you don't sort me out."

The screw whose name badge said John pressed a red button outside the cell and within minutes the pad was swarming with officers. Loads of the fuckers all ready for action, tooled up, ready to fight. Norman was not taking this lying down, he ran at the screws with shit all over his hands, he was smirking at Jud and he knew exactly what he was doing. "Come on you cunts, let's have it. I'll show you what I'm all about. I'm a junkie yeah, but don't treat me like I'm some kind of prick. I'm a human being." Jud backed off and watched the heroin addict being twisted up, he was screaming and shouting at the top of his voice.

"Human rights, I have fucking human rights. Can you see this everyone? I'm an ill man and this is how they are treating me. Fucking liberties, cheeky cunts the lot of them."

The prison was in uproar, other inmates were on the landing and they were shouting abuse at the officers. So what if this guy was a junkie, he was still one of them. "Bastards, leave the man alone, you pricks," an inmate shouted from across the landing. This was just another day in prison life, the screws dealt with the incident quickly and without any further commotion. The other convicts stood on the wing watching with eager eyes. They all held that hard look and some of them looked menacing. Jud walked along the landing slowly after Norman had been removed. A few of the inmates nodded at him as he slowly passed by them. He was well known to them and whispering amongst them could be heard. Jud was the new kid on the block now and he knew he would have to prove himself before the day was over. This was a dog eat dog environment and every inmate knew that the moment their backs were turned someone would stab them in the back for a quick earner. They would have his eyes out of his sockets given half the chance. This was a bad, dark place where only the strong survived. Jud walked down the staircase, he could feel all eyes on him. Standing tall he puffed his chest out and gritted his teeth tightly together. Just a quick look over his shoulder at the inmates to let them know he meant business. This was his manor now and he would bring down anyone who tried to tackle him.

The noise was deafening as Jud walked into the

canteen area. Walking up to the serving hatch he picked up a white tray from the side. Jud had been in prison before but only for driving offences, a shit and a shave sentence he called it, nothing much. He stood holding his plate out and gave the server a nod of the head once his beans had been put on his plate, his hand never flinched. "Bang some more on there for me pal, I'm a growing lad."

The server was used to this and let out a laboured breath. "Fucking hell mate, I'll do it this time but I'm not doing it again. I'll lose my job here if I do it for everyone."

Jud smirked as the extra portion of food was slapped on his plate. "Nice one, you'll be doing it every time for me mate, do you understand?" Jud kept his eyes fixed on the prisoner just long enough to let him know he was the boss. Jud chuckled as he walked along the line. He loved the power he felt over the men.

"Jud, Jud," someone shouted from across the room. He turned his head quickly and spotted a man pushing in the queue next to him. "Alright pal, I thought it was you, when did you land in here then?"

Jud shook the man's hand firmly and spoke. "Just the other day Jim, how long have you been in here?"

Jimmy Walsh shrugged his shoulders and held a proud look in his eyes. "I'm just finishing a three year stretch off, mate. I got stitched up for an armed robbery didn't I?"

Jud was interested and finished getting his food. "Who grassed you up then?"

Jimmy bit down on his bottom lip and you could see he was angry. "Danny Morgan and his crew bubbled on me. I don't have the proof yet but I know that bastard set me up."

Jud waited for Jimmy to get served and they both went to sit down together. Anything concerning Danny Morgan, Jud wanted to know about it. If he was ever going to get rid of him he needed to know exactly what he was dealing with. He needed to know what made him tick. Once they sat down Jud wasted no time in getting down to business. "So, tell me again, why do you think it was Danny Morgan who got you nicked?"

Jimmy made sure no one was listening and moved closer to Jud. "He was the only one who knew the times and dates. And, I saw him on the day of the job just floating around clocking us. He's a snidey cunt Jud. He's not to be trusted. Anyway mate, enough about me, what you in for?"

Jud swallowed the food in his mouth and looked Jimmy straight in his eyes. "I've done our Larry in. He was fucking my bird, you know Dawn?"

Jimmy slurped on his hot mug of tea. Of course he'd heard this information from the outside but he was cracking on daft. "No way mate, that's bangers that is. I mean, that's so wrong. He deserved his arse kicking if he's playing it like that."

"I was marrying the bitch too," Jud chirped in feeling sorry for himself. "There we were, all stood in the church ready to exchange the vows and that rat stood up and said he'd been shagging her."

Jimmy patted Jud's arm and shook his head. "That's bad news mate. So what have you been charged with then?"

Jud scraped the last few beans from his plate and

spooned them into his mouth like a starving animal; he was a right pig when he was eating and the red bean juice was dripping from the side of his mouth. "I'm not sure yet but Larry's on a life-support machine in the hospital. He could snuff it at any minute. I suppose it will be a murder charge if he pops his clogs, won't it?" Jimmy was lost for words, he'd known Jud for years and was aware how dangerous he could be, but to nearly kill his own flesh and blood, this was in a league of its own. Jud knew he needed some back-up in the jail if he was ever going to take over things on the wing. Looking at Jimmy he made sure he had him on board. "Who's running things on the landing then?"

Jimmy checked no one was listening and spoke in a low voice. "It's a kid from Blackley. Beanhead he's called. He's a fucking muppet mate if you ask me. He's got fuck all on you. A quick arse kicking and he's a goner. He's a plastic gangster. You know the type, king of the seesaw."

This was all Jud wanted to hear; he smirked and made Jimmy his wingman. "Right show me his pad and let's get the ball rolling. It's time for Jud Watson to start calling the shots around this jail. It's showtime." Jimmy stood up and waited at Jud's side until he'd finished drinking his tea. They were brothers in arms now ready to waste anyone who stepped in their way.

Minutes later Jimmy Walsh boomed the cell door open and Beanhead sprang to his feet looking shocked. He was covering his head as Jimmy smashed the tins of tuna he'd put into a pillowcase over his head. Beanhead's pad mate ran to the corner of the room shivering like a scared animal. He was keeping out of this and wanted no trouble. Jimmy ran at him and dragged him out by the scruff of his neck. There was no way he wanted any witnesses to what was about to happen. Jud ran at Beanhead like a raging bull, his face was bright red and his nostrils were pumping with rage. Once they got him to quieten down he pummelled his clenched fists into his body stopping at nothing. "I'm fucking running things from now on, is that alright with you?"

Beanhead was spitting teeth; blood pumping from his mouth. He was trying to fight back but Jud was too strong for him. The battle was over within seconds and the inmate knew there and then that his days as top dog were over. Jimmy came back in the room and stood behind the closed door. "Get the fucking drugs from him Jud, and I know he's got a mobile phone plugged too."

Beanhead fell to his knees as Jud whacked him in the face again. "Get me the gear now," Jud ordered. Beanhead crawled under the bed, he could hardly move. He was rummaging around at first, papers rustling. A few minutes later he came out with a bag of white powder and some pills. It wasn't a big parcel but it was enough to keep Jud going for a while. "And, the phone. Where the fuck is the blower?" Jud ranted as he kicked the man within an inch of his life.

"It's up my arse. You'll have to let me get up so I can get it out." Jimmy dragged Beanhead up and launched him against the cold brick wall. "We haven't got all fucking day, come on then, get it fucking out." This was humiliating to watch. Beanhead dropped his pants as Jud chuckled. "You can fucking wash it before you give it to me too. You dirty rat, hurry the fuck up I've not got all day." There was banging on the cell door and Jimmy was doing his best to keep the door closed. Once Jud got what he wanted the door was opened and in ran three lads. Once they saw Beanhead twisted up they shot a look at Jud, they were weighing him up and ready to strike.

Jimmy came to Jud's side and they were both ready for action again, teeth gritted and fists curled. "Come on then if you want some. I swear, the first one of you who comes near me is getting mashed up, come on then, let's have it." Not one of the inmates moved, they were like statues. The colour drained from their faces. Beanhead's men backed off slowly, the show was over for them. The injured convict was coughing up blood up in the corner of the room and he needed urgent medical help. His chest was rising frantically and he was gasping for breath. No one was helping him. Jud was now the main man on the wing, he held the power, called the shots. As he left he smirked at Beanhead. "One word out of you about this and I'll be back. Do you hear me prick? I'll be back."

When visiting time came around, Jud was looking forward to seeing his family. Not that he needed anyone, he was doing fine on his own. He'd never needed anyone to hold his hand and he never asked anyone for help, he liked riding solo. Jud looked thinner than usual and his pants were baggy on him around the waist. Family visits were all prisoners lived for. Seeing their loved ones was all that kept some of the inmates going mad. One hour a week to see their loved ones, this was precious time, the best part of any week. Once Jud was in the visitor's room he sat down at the table and watched the door like a hawk. Some of the inmates were getting drops today and Jud knew exactly what was coming in from the outside. If these drops paid off he was well on his way to be becoming top dog in all of the prison, not just the wing. Smiling at the inmates he nodded his head slowly as he watched them prepare to meet their families. A quick wink was all it took to let them know he was watching them.

"Can you see him yet," Mary shrieked at the top of her voice as she pushed through the door. She was pushing and shoving the other visitors out of the way trying to find her son. She really thought she was royalty and deserved to be treated better than anyone else.

"Mam, will you calm down, you're making a show of yourself. Fuck me, just hold your horses and wait like everyone else." Paul ranted.

"Oh, there he is sat over there. Look, can you see him Paul? Oh he looks so bleeding thin. I bet the bastards aren't feeding him enough." Mary moaned then waving her hands above her head. Everyone was looking at her as if she'd lost the plot. She didn't care though; she rushed towards her son with open arms. "Jud," she screamed as she got closer.

Sean pulled Mary to the side as they walked to where Jud was sat. "Mam, stop acting like a nobhead will you. No wonder our Jud didn't want you to come here with us, he's in prison mother. He's not in a bleeding Christmas pantomime. So, just tone it down will you. Stop showing us up?"

Mary walked with speed to her son's table as Paul went to the canteen to get some food. Sean sat down first and it was only seconds before Mary joined him, she was sobbing her heart out. She reached over the table and stroked her son's hands. "Oh, Jud, look at the bleeding state of you, you're all skin and bone. Are they feeding you in here or what?" She shot her eyes over to screw and clicked her fingers over her head. She was getting this sorted, there was no way the officers were treating her son like this. She'd seen it on the news how some prisoners were badly treated and there was no way in this world it was happening to her boy, not over her dead body. "Excuse me, excuse me," she shouted.

Jud was livid and dragged her arm back down. His face was white, what the hell was she playing at? She was embarrassing him. "Mother, what the fuck are you doing?"

Mary sat back in her chair and her cheeks were flushed, beetroot she was. "I'm going to tell this shower of shite to start feeding you proper. You're not an animal. They need to make sure you get all the food you need."

Sean hid his face behind his hands and chuckled. His mother was such a funny character, she didn't realise what went on behind prison doors. She was living in cloud cuckoo land. Jud shook his head and raised his eyes to the ceiling. "Mother what fucking planet are you on? This is a jail, things don't work like that in here. You get what you're given, and if you don't eat, then it's hard bleeding luck. So, keep quiet will you before I get Sean to take you outside. Fuck me, I've got a reputation to uphold in here and here's you smashing it to pieces in seconds."

"I can bake you a meat pie and bring it in next time I come to see you. I'll do you my special apple pie and custard too, you like that don't you?"

Nobody answered her. Both her sons just looked at her in disbelief. She thought she could actually bring food into the jail. Sean shook hands with Jud as Mary sat with her arms folded in front of her, she had a face like a smacked arse and she'd definitely spat her dummy out. Paul placed a red tray on the table and it was filled with chocolates and biscuits and two sandwiches. He reached his hand over and patted his brother's shoulder. Paul knew from his own experiences how hard jail could be and had pity for all the inmates who sat here. This slammer was a shit-hole, there was no denying that. "How you bearing up our kid?"

Jud stretched his arms above his head and yawned. "I'm alright for now, but that solicitor better sort this shit out and get me out of this nick."

Mary was at it again, she placed her hands on the table and banged them softly. "This needs sorting out once and for all. Jud, I've been to see Larry and let me tell you now, you've half bleeding killed him. Whoever grassed you up must have known you would get arrested for this. I'm not being funny though, but you do deserve it Jud. If Larry doesn't make it. I'll never speak to you again."

Sean nudged Mary in the waist. "Mam, why don't you go and wait outside. Jud will end up throwing you out of here if you don't keep it shut."

Mary had seen her arse, she was on one now. "No one is keeping me quiet anymore. I'll say what I have to say and that's it. I'm sick of holding everything in, it's making me ill," Mary stressed. Paul tried to calm things down and a quick look at his mother let her know she'd overstepped the mark. She was right though, the stress was killing her, she'd had pains in her chest all day and every now and then her heart skipped a beat.

"Dawn came the other day to sort things out with you. I carted her though. Who does she think she is just walking back into your life as if nothing has happened? If you want her sorting Jud, just say the word. I'll have her removed, never to be seen again." Paul sighed and lowered his voice as he continued. "She didn't even know you'd been nicked. I told her straight to sling her hook. The dirty slut."

Jud was confused and sat thinking for a minute. "So, if Dawn didn't know I was banged up then who the fuck phoned the dibble?"

Mary just couldn't do it, she just couldn't keep her big trap shut for one second. "Of course she bleeding knows where you are. Don't let her fool you. She's a crafty cow that one is, don't let her pull the wool over your eyes, Jud. See her for what she really is and kick her to the kerb once and for all."

Paul growled at his mother and his voice was loud. "Will you wind your neck in and keep out of things that don't concern you. What have I told you about our business, ay? Keep your nose out."

Mary snarled at him and gripped her knees tightly. She was at boiling point. Jud cracked his knuckles and one name kept floating about in his mind. "It's fucking Danny Morgan. I know it. It all makes sense now. I've just been speaking to a guy in here who knows Danny and he told me he grassed him up too. Paul, I want that tosser sorting out. I want him in a body bag. I don't trust him as far as I can throw him. You know he's after taking over our patch don't you?"

Sean chirped into the conversation and made sure he held Jud's attention. "Why are you thinking its Danny? He wasn't even there, Jud. You're barking up the wrong tree if you ask me. It's someone much closer to home, it has to be."

Paul turned his head quickly and gritted his teeth at his younger brother. "Fuck me, will you shut up, you fucking fairy. If Jud says its Danny Morgan then we'll sort it out. Why would anyone else grass him up? This has got the Morgan lads stamp written all over it. It all makes sense now they're after our patch, thicko. Can't you see that? Just fucking think about it before you put your mouth into gear. If Jud is off the streets they know they have a better chance of moving in on us. Devious bastards they are the fucking lot of them."

Sean dipped his head. He'd never felt part of this family and anything he ever said was always swept under the carpet, so what, he couldn't fight, but he was still a family member with an opinion. He sat sulking. Mary comforted him as she always did when his brothers ganged up on him. She cradled her arm around his shoulder, kissing the top of his head. "Oh, just leave them to it Sean. They think they know it all, but they know fuck all." Mary stood up and grabbed her coat from the back of the chair. Everyone was looking at her now and she wasn't shutting up. She was saying her piece no matter what. "Jud, I'm going. I can't listen to this bullshit a minute longer. This family needs to be strong. Our Larry is on his death bed and you're not even arsed how he is. He's your own flesh and blood for crying out loud, surely that should mean something to you. Blood is thicker than water."

Jud kept quiet, he just wanted her to leave, she was winding him up. The vein in the side of his neck was pumping and the tops of his ears were blood red. Mary started to walk off slowly, she was waiting for him to call her back, but he never did. "Bastard," she muttered under her breath. "Fucking heartless cunt." There were no kisses exchanged, Mary just marched off and left the visiting room. Sean followed closely behind her, he couldn't let her leave on her own, she was livid and ready to blow. He shook his brother's hand before he left and ran after his mother. Paul sat with his head in his hands, the stress was showing and he knew without Jud by his side the Morgan's would be on his back soon like scavenging hyenas scrounging for food.

A screw circled Jud's table, he was hovering. The officers were aware of the disturbance between the woman on the visit and kept a keen eye on her as she left. Jud twiddled his thumbs and his voice was low. "So Dawn came to see if she could sort things out?"

Paul blew a laboured breath and banged his fist onto the table. "Jud, don't tell me you still want her after this. Look at what she's done to this family. We could lose it all because of that dirty slag."

"I know Paul, but," he hesitated. "I still fucking love her don't I? I can't just switch off my feelings for her at the drop of a hat. I want you to get her on a visit to see me. I need to hear what she has to say."

Paul was up in arms. "I don't believe what I'm hearing here Jud. Are you right in the bastard head? The woman is nothing but trouble, for fucks sake she's been sleeping with Larry. What does that tell you about her? Nar, leave her to rot the scumbag."

Jud raised his voice and bent over the table looking directly into his brother's eyes. "I said, I want to see her. Fuck me, do you not think I'm stressed out enough without you adding to it?"

Paul backed down, he always did when Jud was on the war path. He'd learned a long time ago that his brother's word was gospel and he would never change his mind once something was in his head. They both sat looking about the room. Paul sat tapping his fingers on the table, his mouth was moving but no words were coming out. Jud broke the silence. "I've got it boxed off in here already. See that guy over there?" Jud shot his eyes to an inmate not far from where he was sitting. "Well, he's got a parcel coming in today, should be a good one too, he's expecting some brown and white and some steds." Paul was impressed. Heroin and cocaine were like rocking horse shit in the jails lately and as soon as it came inside the prison the inmates were like flies around shit for it. They'd do anything to get their hands on it. The steroids were for him though, nobody was getting a sniff at them. Paul admitted defeat and backed down. Jud spoke with excitement. "Right, I'm going to ring Dawn later on. I've got a mobile phone stashed so it will be when we get banged up and the landing is quiet. I'll sort a visit out with her, so wind your neck in. You don't have to speak to her. My main concern now is the Morgan's. Get down to the pub and make sure you move any cash from there. We need to be two steps in front of them. Anything we're doing now make sure it's only our lads that know.

There's that wagon coming in tonight from Scotland full of electrical, so carry on as if I'm still there. Let's get back on our feet now and watch each other's back. Paul, are you listening to me or what?"

Paul was rolling his eyes to the back of his head. His heart was low and he'd hoped Dawn would have been out of the picture now for good. Life was a bitch. Even from inside these prison walls his brother was still dictating to him, still calling the shots. He hated that he never had the balls to say no to him. "I'm on it," Paul stuttered. "Me and the lads will sort the wagon out and as for Danny Morgan," he flexed his biceps and kissed the top of them. "Let him try and mess with us and he's going on the missing list. It's time for me to step up to the bar now and show them all what us Watsons are all about. We can all be sick cunts, can't we Jud?"

"Now you're talking, let's start as we mean to go on. We rule Manchester, not some fucking crowd of muppets who think they can handle us. I put my trust in you Paul. Make sure it all runs smoothly." The men shook hands and the bad atmosphere had lifted. Jud shot his eyes to the inmate getting a parcel in and he could see the exchange taking place. It was quick and just like they'd planned. "Right our kid, you get going and get that mother of ours out of the cold. Do me a favour ay," Paul was waiting for him to continue with a smirk on his face. "Don't bring her again, she does my bleeding head in. I know she means no harm but fuck me, she presses my buttons. And, get that gay fucker on the wagon job too. He always sits back and reaps the rewards. It's about time that runt started pulling his weight. Tell him to keep his big trap shut too. You know what he's like when he has a few beers, he sings like a fucking budgie."

"A fucking pink budgie at that," Paul chuckled. The men sat laughing, Sean had never admitted that he was gay but both of them knew that he was batting for the other side. All the signs were there, he was a poo-poker for sure. The visit came to an end and Jud watched his brother leave. His head sank low on the table as he ragged his fingers through his thick crop of hair. Tonight was the night he was going to phone Dawn and end the torment he felt deep in his heart. The woman was a tart yeah, but Jud still loved her.

CHAPTER SEVEN

DAWN WATCHED SALLY getting ready with eager eyes. She was nursing her bruised eye, dabbing a cold flannel on it. It was changing colour by the second, deep purple with yellow at the side of it. Paul had really gone to town on her, she was in a bad way. There was no need for the force he used on her, he'd taken liberties. Once she'd dabbed some witch hazel on her injury she turned to face Sally. "So, enough about me. Why has Danny Morgan asked you out on a date? You hardly know him. I mean, if it was me he was asking I could understand it. I know him more than you don't I?"

Sally was upset and you could see the anger in her eyes. Who did this woman think she was? "Dawn, I've told you what happened a million times over. It's not my fault if he finds me attractive is it? And, what the hell has it got to do with you who I date anyway. I'm a grown woman not a kid?"

Dawn sat thinking, she held a puzzled look. "Yeah that's it, you were wearing my clothes so what do you expect," she played with her hair slowly, she was still in deep thought. "No, there is something not right here. I smell a rat."

Sally shot a look at Dawn and her teeth were gritted tightly together. Why was she being such a bitch with her, she was sick to death of the way she was treating her? "What is it with you lately Dawn? Don't you think

I deserve a bit of happiness? Stop being a misery guts just because you have been caught with your knickers down. Don't be taking it out on me. I'm sick of it."

Dawn launched a cold wet sponge across the room towards Sally and stood to her feet, she was holding her waist and her face was bright red. "Listen gobshite, since when have you become so gobby. Do yourself a favour and zip it before I twist you up. I don't need to listen to your bullshit anymore. Don't you think I've been through enough without you adding to it? I thought you were my best friend, where is the shoulder to cry on ay?"

Sally backed down, she knew she'd put her mouth into gear without thinking. Dawn was a hard nut and although at times she thought she could take her, she started to have second thoughts. She wasn't ready to tackle her yet. "Dawn, just wind your neck in. For fucks sake we're best friends. We need to stop arguing about men. I'm going on a date with Danny no matter what. It's not the end of the world is it? It's not like he's asked to marry me."

Dawn plonked back down on the sofa and picked up the sponge from the floor. Pressing it on the side of her face she snivelled. She was crying. "I'm sorry Sally, just ignore me. I'm a bit hormonal at the moment. I can't believe Paul treated me like this. It just goes to show you that blood is thicker than water doesn't it?"

Sally shook her head and was relieved the argument was over. "I know love, Paul is out of order. I thought he was an alright guy too, but after this I'll never speak to him again. He's taken liberties with you. I bet Jud doesn't know he's belted you?"

Dawn rubbed at her arms, she shivered. "Jud probably told him to do it. Anyway, he's locked up now. I'll be the last person on his mind. I've fucked up big time haven't I? I'll just have to ride it out."

Sally came to her side and patted the top of her shoulder. Dawn was a bitch, but beyond the hard surface she did have a heart in there somewhere. It just took a lot to find it. Sally let her guard down too and tried to comfort her. She was like that Sally, anything for a quiet life. "It will all turn out for the best. Just, let the dust settle. Jud loves you and I think after he's calmed down he'll speak to you again. Just try and be patient."

The living room door swung open and Maureen barged in holding a bottle of gin in her hand, she was pissed as a fart, swaying about. "Before you start, I've only had a few. I've danced my bleeding legs off I have. I only went to the afternoon bingo session in the legion and before I knew it everyone was buying me drinks. I'm totally pissed."

Dawn snapped and her fist pounded the arm of the sofa causing a large cloud of dust to rise up from it. "Fucking bingo! Have you even bought any bleeding shopping. There is fuck all in the cupboards to eat. What, do you think we can all live off gin?"

Maureen staggered across the front room, she was smirking. "Well, I could. I don't know about you. A gin diet sounds great to me. What do you think about that Sally?"

Sally hung her head and sniggered. She knew Maureen was on the wind- up and tried to stay out of the slanging match between mother and daughter. She'd been in the crossfire many times before and learned the hard way not to get involved. Sitting down she hid her face behind a cushion. It was all going to kick off now for sure. Dawn raised her hands above her head. "It's always something with you mother. When are you going to start acting your age instead of your bleeding shoe size? You're a raging piss-head, nothing else. You're no mother."

Maureen screwed her face up, she sucked hard on her gums, there was no way she was backing down, the gin had seen to that. "Well, look who's bleeding talking here. She was jilted at the altar because she couldn't keep her legs shut and she's got the cheek to preach to me about how I should live my life. I tell you what Dawn, you're my daughter but you're one moody cow. Look at me, you don't see me crying over men do you? I just bounce back up and get on with life. Every time I look at you lately you're bleeding crying. It's you who has the problems not me. I'm the happiest I've ever been," she sniggered and did a little dance across the room. "So what, I like a little tipple ever now and then, it's not the end of the world is it."

Dawn shrugged her shoulders and raised her eyes. "Oh fuck off mother, you're doing my head in now. Go to bed or something. I can't stand you when you're pissed."

Maureen danced across the front room lifting her skirt up, showing her baggy knickers. Sally was giggling when Maureen caught her eye. "You know I'm right, don't you Sally. You don't have to answer me, but you know I speak the truth."

Sally stood up and revealed her outfit, she had to change the subject quick before they both scratched each other's eyeballs out, and, they would have fought, yes they would have exchanged blows. There was no respect in this household. Sally spoke in a loud voice. "Check me out Mo, I'm out on a date tonight. You're never going to guess who with. Go on take a wild guess?"

Maureen loved a quiz, she sat down and slurped hard on her bottle of gin, draining the last few mouthfuls from it. Sitting forward in her chair she wiped the side of her mouth. "Let me see, is it Jona from the pub? No, no, you're too good for him he's a right minger. Errrmmm..... I'm fucked if I know. Go on tell me."

Sally licked her lips slowly and prepared to say her date's name. As she spoke her cheeks blushed and you could tell she was already smitten with Danny Morgan. Maureen sat thinking, she knew the name. She'd heard it a few times before. "Is he the one who Jud hates? Dawn, is he the one you pointed out to me weeks ago in the Asda car park?"

Dawn nodded. She hated not being the centre of attention. "Yeah, he's the one who said I was looking good when we walked past him." Dawn chewed on her lips. That would put Sally back in her place. Who did she think she was anyway? One date with Danny Morgan and she thought she was the bee's knees, the belle of the ball.

Maureen clapped her hands together in excitement. She shot a look over at her daughter and smirked. "Oh, he's bloody lovely him. He's got a few quid as well. Oh Dawn, "she turned her head to face her. "We have a new girl on the block now. I mean, here's you having it all, and Sally was just a passenger. It's all turned around now hasn't it? Now you're her passenger. It's bloody swings and roundabout isn't it?"

Dawn was beetroot, she jumped up from her seat and went nose to nose with her mother. Who did she think she was, shooting her down like this? "As if that's going to happen mother. I'm not being funny or anything Sally, but come on, can you ever see me just being a normal working girl. I attract men with a few quid, I do. I always have and I always will?"

Sally snarled and walked to the mirror, you could tell by her expression she wasn't happy. "Dawn, we'll both be happy one day. Your mam is just winding you up. Aren't you Mo? Go on tell her you're only joking?"

Maureen was not backing down. She wobbled as she stood up. Her eyes were trying to focus. "I say what I see. Dawn will just have to deal with you getting all the gifts and the money from now on, just like you had to sit back and watch her. Let's see how the brat acts now the shoe's on the other foot."

Maureen left the room, there was an eerie silence and both girls were lost for words. It was all true though. How was Dawn going to cope now she was back to square one? Sally bent down to put her shoes on and Dawn spoke to her. "Fuck me, she's hard work that woman. Do you see what I have to put up with every day? She's a crank, a fucking nutter. I'll be glad when I've gone from this house. Let's see how she survives then."

Sally was in no mood for the usual drama with Dawn, she let out a laboured breath and paced the living room floor in her outfit. It was Dawn's clothes Sally was wearing and Dawn was looking at her with envy. "Make sure you don't ruin that dress. It cost a bomb you know. I know what you're like when you have a few beers down your neck, you're ruthless. If you decide to have a leg-over then take the dress off. I'm not having spunk marks all over it. Remember the last dress you borrowed from me. It looked like you'd been dragged through a hedge in it backwards."

Sally froze, her lips were moving but no sound was coming out, her nostrils were flaring and her chest was expanding. She was actually going to rip the dress off and tell her to stick it up her arse but stopped at the last minute. "Okay, okay. I'll look after it. For fuck's sake Dawn you're going on like I get shagged every night or something. Yeah, I admit the last dress I borrowed from you was in a bit of a state, but I did take it to the dry cleaners didn't I?"

Dawn never replied, she grabbed a magazine from the corner of the sofa and started to read it. Sally picked up her handbag and looked for one last time in the mirror. "Right, I'm off to meet Danny, wish me luck then?"

Dawn was struggling to speak, she was so jealous, she just couldn't hide it. "Are you coming back here tonight or staying at your house?"

Sally giggled and flicked her hair back over her shoulder. "With any luck I'll be staying with Danny, so don't wait up for me. I'm off to show this dress a good time."

Dawn waved her off and as soon as she heard the front door close she stamped her feet hard on the floor like the spoilt brat that she was. "We'll see who's laughing soon Sally, just you wait and see. I'll be back to normal soon. I'll get back on my feet. It's just a matter of time."

★

Sally waited patiently for Danny Morgan to come inside the pub. She was fidgeting and biting her nails nervously. She looked stunning and the four hours she'd taken to get ready had paid off, she was gorgeous. A voice from the bar area made her turn her head. It was him, it was Danny Morgan. He had a few men with him and each of them looked as hard as nails, solid. Waving his hand above his head he acknowledged Sally.

"One minute love," he shouted across to her. "What are you drinking?"

Sally sat up straight and replied. "A white wine please." Usually Sally was a lager drinker but she wanted to act sophisticated in front of Danny and tried to order a ladies drink. Her heart was beating faster than normal and small droplets of sweat were visible on her brow, she was so nervous. She'd been on dates lots of times before but this was different, this was a date with the one and only Danny Morgan. He was gorgeous. Grabbing her handbag from the side of her she quickly applied another coat of lip gloss. Smacking her lips together she was ready to meet her date.

Danny walked across the pub as if he owned it. As he got closer to her he started to smile. "Fuck me, you scrub up well. It's amazing what a bit of soap and water does isn't it?"

The ice was broken and Sally started to relax. "Ay, you cheeky bleeder. I'm always clean and tidy."

Danny sat down next to her and pecked her on the

cheek. As he did she inhaled hard and smelt the fragrance from his body, he smelt good and if she would have had her way she would have had sex with him there and then. He was good enough to eat. He smelt of success and money. He smelt of power. "We'll have this drink in here and then go for a scran. Do you want Indian or Chinese?"

Sally shrugged her shoulders. "I'm easy love, whatever you want to eat is fine by me."

"I'm glad you're easy Sally that might come in useful later when I get you into my bed," he chuckled. Sally blushed and shied away from him but inside she was excited and couldn't wait for the night to finish so she could feel his hot sexy lips all over her body. She was finding it hard to keep her hands off him. His perky pecks were visible through his white shirt and he had a body to die for. Sally usually ended up with porkers. Lazy men, the couch potato type, the type that's not done a day's work in their lives. Danny's mobile phone started ringing in his hand, clocking the number of the caller he picked his phone up and walked away from the table. He held one finger up at Sally and smiled. "Back in a minute, it's a call I've been waiting for."

Sally look flustered, she was constantly playing with the hem of her dress. Watching Danny in the distance she could just make out what he was saying. She listened carefully. "Right, just watch the fucking van. You know what to do next. Fuck me, am I working with clowns or what? Just sort it out." Danny ended the call and Sally sprang back to her original position. Looking over to the bar she could see Spencer perched at the end of the bar, he gave her a cheeky wink and carried on supping his pint.

Danny walked back to her and remained on his feet. Reaching for his bottle of beer off the table he necked it in one gulp. "Come on then sweet-cheeks, let's go and get something to eat. I don't know about you, but I'm starving." Sally finished her drink and followed him outside to his car. Most of the women in the pub were watching her leave with envy in their eyes. They all wanted a piece of Danny Morgan, but tonight he was hers, all hers, and she wasn't sharing him with anyone. Spencer nodded his head at her as she passed him, he never said a word though he just let her walk on by as if they were strangers.

Dawn rolled about on the sofa, she was restless. She thought about going to see Larry again but decided against it. She needed time alone, time to think of her next move. Paul could have been at the hospital with Mary and she didn't need the hassle of the Watson's on her back again. Flicking through the channels she let out a laboured breath. Her mobile phone started ringing, an unknown number. Taking a few seconds to look at the screen she answered the call. Dawn swallowed hard and her jaw dropped as she sat up straight. "Jud, I'm so glad you have rung me. I came to your house to sort this mess out but Paul battered me and launched me out of the garden." Dawn was alert, she was nibbling on the loose skin at the side of her thumb as the conversation continued. Dawn pulled the cushion in front of her body and squeezed it tightly. As the conversation came to an end Dawn whispered in a low voice. "Jud, I love you so much. I hope we can sort this out. I'll come and see you soon then. We can talk more then." The phone call ended and Dawn was much happier than she'd been earlier. She grabbed her coat from the sofa and buttoned it up tightly. The sound of the front door slamming shut could be heard. Dawn was gone.

★

Sally was drunk, her words were slurring and she was finding it hard to stay focused. Danny was holding her up by one arm. She'd drunk too much and she was wobbling about. "I was alright until the fresh air hit me," she lied. "I'm wrecked, sorry about this; usually I can take my beer." Danny chuckled and helped her into the car.

Sally was all over him like a rash, desperate to feel his body. As soon as he started driving she was up for having some fun. Her hand reached across to the driver's side and she was rubbing at his crotch. "Whoa.... come on, you're going to make me crash woman, just hang on while I pull over," Danny sniggered. Sally was going for gold and she was up for anything. Pulling over at a nearby alleyway, he turned the engine off and pulled his seat back. Arms above his head he sat back and licked his lips slowly. Sally was in full control and she ravished every inch of his body, she was licking and stroking his firm chest before her head met the tip of his penis. Looking up at him she smiled before she began oral sex. The windows steamed up and their sex began, hot, steamy lustful sex. Sally yanked her knickers down and straddled him, there was no way she wasting any time. Dawn's dress was the last thing on her mind, she was like a woman possessed and she didn't give a shit about any stains landing on the garment. This was her time and she was enjoying every second of it. Danny was inside her and her face became serious, she grinded hard on top of him and sexual groans could be heard. This guy was well hung too and at one point he struggled to get it inside her, what a lucky girl she was. Sally sat up straight and flicked her hair back over her shoulders, she was riding him hard, fast and furious, passionately. Danny held her hips with a firm grip and grinded his teeth tightly together, he was ready to come. Sally was moaning with pleasure and any time now she too was going to reach climax. Her body was stiff as the final waves of pleasure surged through her veins, breathless. Falling back into the steering wheel she tried to regain her breath, chest rising frantically. Danny pressed the button at the side of him and opened the window slightly, his face was red and his body had small droplets of sweat dripping from it. She'd worn him out. He was such a dish, a handsome guy. In the moonlight you could see every ripped muscle at its best.

Sally turned green, scrambling to the other side of the car she fumbled to open the door, she was puking her guts up. Danny watched her as he pulled two cigarettes from the packet. Popping one in the corner of his mouth, he lit it with confidence. He shouted outside after her. "Go on girl get it all up. You'll feel better once it's all out. That's what you get for being a smart- arse drinking too much." Sally never replied, she held her hair back from her cheeks and carried on vomiting. Projectile vomit that stank of sour cheese. Once she was finished she blew deep breaths and inhaled deeply. The cold circling wind on her face was refreshing and helped her sober up.

Wafting her hand in front of her rapidly she turned to Danny and you could see she was embarrassed. "It's the wine, I don't usually drink it. I'm always like this when I mix my drinks. I should have known better. I bet you think I'm a right idiot now don't you?"

Danny lit the other cig and passed it to her. "Here, this should sort you out. Sally took it from him and he was right, the colour started to return to her cheeks. "Do you want to come back to my house then or what?" Sally was surprised that he'd even asked her. Now that she'd just had sex with him, she thought she'd blown it with him and he would just drop her off at home. Usually, once she'd dropped her knickers the man she was dating would just cart her off home. What a result this was, an overnight pass, a bed buddy for the night. Her voice was low and she tried to act calm when inside she was bursting with excitement. She took a few seconds to answer him, not being too eager. "Yes, I will do if you don't mind. I can't go waking Dawn up at this time of the night can I, she'd go off her rocker."

Danny paused, he held a cunning look in his eye. Leaning over to where Sally sat he twisted a piece of her hair slowly. "So are you and Dawn close or what?"

Sally was thinking about the question longer than she should have. She always thought Dawn was a good friend but lately she was being such a bitch, a self-centred cow, everything was about her. Sally answered him. "We were close once, but if I was being honest to myself she's changed so much lately, she's a cocky cow. Out for herself and all she can get."

This was music to Danny's ears. "So, is there any news on Jud then? Is he getting out of nick or what?" Sally was spilling the beans and she filled him in on what Paul had done to Dawn. The cracks were appearing in the Watson Empire and Danny was loving every minute of it. For years he'd been waiting to take over the crime scene in the area and now Jud was out of the picture it was just a matter of time before the Morgan's were the new kids on the block. "Me and you could do well together Sally. You're just what I'm looking for in a woman. You're like me I suppose. You take what you want at any cost."

Sally stroked her long finger over his wet lips and smiled. She didn't see herself as a ruthless person but if he was saying she was who was she to argue with him. "And, what do you want Danny? Do you even know?"

Danny looked at her and studied her for a few seconds; he knew he had her where he wanted her, he could see it in her eyes, she was besotted by him. Here it was, the bullshit, the lies the deceit. "I want you Sally. I mean, I've never felt like this about a woman before, you tick all my boxes," he was chatting shit of course but she seemed to be buying it. What a fool she was, could she not see he was having her over? Sally leant over towards him for a kiss. Nobody had ever come within an inch of loving her like this before and any sex she'd had was just a one night stand, this was love for sure. He wanted her like she wanted him.

Danny swallowed hard; he was ready to put his cards on the table. Taking her hands in his he looked her directly in the eyes. "Help me take over the Watson's Empire. Why should Dawn have all the glory? You deserve some too don't you?"

Sally was alarmed but she hid it well. She knew she had a choice to make and Danny was pressing her for an answer. Could she sell Dawn out and betray her in the worst way possible? Thinking for a few seconds she stared out of the window at the night sky before she turned back to face him. "You're right Danny, Dawn's always had the good things in life and perhaps it is my turn to have a taste of it too."

Danny knew he had her where he wanted her, she was like a lamb to the slaughter. He kissed her passionately to seal the deal. Getting her on side was a lot easier than he first thought, this was child's play. Patting her knee slowly, he chuckled. "I can see we're going to be good together Sally. Me and you can go all the way if we play our cards right. We can have it all." Sally turned her head towards him and the corners of her mouth started to rise. He was right, they could have it all.

CHAPTER EIGHT

PAUL AND SEAN WATSON were hidden in a lay-by waiting for the lorry to pull up at its destination. It was late and the sky was jet black, the low clouds looked like they were nearly touching the ground and it was drizzling. The men were nervous and Sean was having second thoughts about seeing this job through, it just wasn't his scene. He sat cracking his knuckles and blowing his breath out in front of him, this shit was going down and he didn't want to be here. He'd been on jobs before but never as big as this. Sean was more the errand boy, dropping money off, picking parcels up. This was way out of his league by his own admission. Sean quivered and grabbed Paul's shoulder. "I'm not sure about this lads. I've got a gut feeling this is going to go tits up."

Paul snapped and gripped him by the scruff of the neck. He went nose to nose with him as the other men watched. Paul hated grafting with Sean at the best of times and it was only now that he was a man down that he let him come on the job. "Listen, you fucking Jonah, just do your job. Why the fuck I let you come on any graft with us is beyond me. You're always the same, you fucking muppet. Just relax and do what I've told you to do. Fuck me..."

Paul let go of Sean's neck and he watched the white articulated lorry pull up. There was a driver and a driver's mate just like they were told there would be, the information they received was bang on. This was a shipment of electrical goods; TV's, stereos, microwaves. There was a right few quid to make off this lot, a right good earner. Paul dug his hand down the front of his pants and made sure the gun was safe. He wasn't planning to use it but if he had to step up to the mark he would, just like he'd done in the past. He'd shoot someone's fucking head off, blow their fucking brains out if he needed to. The gang were ready to strike. Paul pulled his scarf up over his nose and you could only see his eyes. With a quick nod of his head, the men sprang into action. Like ninjas, they were fast, quiet and deadly. The night was cold and the car park was deserted. Paul led the men to where the attack would take place. His voice was low. "Right, let's fucking have the fuckers."

It all happened in what seemed like a few seconds. Paul jumped up and dragged the driver from his seat and rammed the silver pistol deep into his mouth. The guy was gagging and he was clearly petrified. "One word out of you dick-head and I'll blow your fucking brains out. Do you hear me, wanker?" The man was struggling but with a quick belt over his head he knew Paul meant business. The driver's mate was yanked out of the van, there was no fight in him whatsoever. Before they knew it they were bound and gagged lying face down on the floor. Paul grabbed the keys to the lorry and passed them to his wingman. "Right Simon, get the fuck out of here before it's on top."

Sean was frozen, he was shaking from head to toe as he watched the two men lying on the floor trembling. He hated violence, he hated watching men beg for their lives, he hated being a Watson. Sean's head bent over near their captives, he was deeply concerned and stroked the top of one man's head trying to calm him down. What the hell was he doing, this was a heist not a coffee morning? "Paul, are they going to be alright?" he shouted behind him. "We can't just leave them here like this, its freezing cold. Can't we put a blanket over them or something?"

Paul ran at his brother and growled. He was sick to death of hearing his whining voice. "Will you keep your big mouth shut? What have I told you about using names when we're on a job?" Paul dragged Sean behind the lorry and made sure he was out of sight. Everything was going to plan. All they had to do now was drive the lorry away. They were minutes away from a successful mission. Paul was just about to the get into the lorry when he was struck from behind, a lethal blow. He fell to the floor straightaway. He didn't stand a chance. Two men jumped into the van and you could see one of the Watson's gang taking a beating in the distance. Paul's body was lifeless, blood trickled from the corner of his mouth and every now and then he shook from head to toe. He was in a bad way, he would be lucky to come out of this alive. The men drove off and screeched from the car park. They'd been ambushed, double-crossed, had over.

Sean twisted his head over his shoulder, he could see the driver and his jaw dropped. Head searching for his brother he could see a large mound lying on the floor in the distance. He waved his hands to the other men from their cars. "Hurry the fuck up, we've been had over." Sean sprinted to his brother's side. He bent down and held him in his arms. "Paul, it's me Sean can you hear me or what?"

Simon was there too now and two other men. Simon was in a bad way too, blood pouring from his nose. As Simon was talking his eyes seemed to be bulging out from their sockets. "It was the Morgan's. I'm sure of it. The dirty, low life cunts. I swear, this is war. How dare they step on our turf?"

Paul was mumbling and he was trying to focus, trying to stand up. "Get me the fuck out of here before the dibble comes," he croaked. The lads carried Paul to the car waiting nearby. He was helped into the back of it. As soon as the door closed the driver put his foot down and they all headed home. Sean sat in the front of the car and he kept turning his head around patting his brother's leg. "You're going to be alright our kid. It's just the blood that makes it look bad. Just try and keep still, we'll be home soon." Paul was lay in the back staring into space, he was shook up and in shock. This was bad news. Jud was going to go sick when he got wind of what had happened. The money from this graft was supposed to get them back on their feet. This was devastating for all those involved. No wages, no fuck all.

The car pulled up outside the Watson's. There was a bedroom light on that meant Mary was still awake reading. She loved a good book, it kept her calm and took her somewhere nice and peaceful. Away from her worries and the family trauma she faced every day. Sean jumped out of the car and dug deep in his pocket for his front door key. He waved the others to bring his brother in when the coast was clear. Once they were near the front door he held a single finger up to his mouth. "My old queen's still up, keep the noise down, she'll be like Sherlock Holmes on whizz if she sees the state of Paul." The men plonked Paul down on the sofa in the front room. They didn't stay long, they were in and out once they knew he wasn't dying. Sean yanked his coat off and ran inside the kitchen. Coming back holding a small bowl of hot water he sat down at the side of his brother. "Paul, it's me Sean can you hear me?"

Paul tried to sit up but his body was weak. His voice was low. "Of course I can fucking hear you. I'm not dead yet. My head is pounding though, they must have knocked me out."

Sean pulled some cotton wool balls from a packet and sank them inside the scorching hot water. "I'm going to clean you up. Once all this blood has gone we can see what we're dealing with."

Sean dabbed the first cotton wool ball on his brother's head. He screamed out howling in pain. "Fuck me, what are you trying to do, finish me off you muppet? Take your bleeding time ay, just take it easy, and don't press too hard?" Sean shook his head. Paul was always the same he would never accept help from anyone. He thought he was untouchable and no one could ever get to him. Sean started to wipe the deep gash on his head slowly, as he studied it further, the corners of his mouth started to rise. Something had amused him. The living room door swung open and there she was like a preying lioness.

Mary was stood there with her mouth wide open. "What's all the bleeding noise I can hear down here? I was trying to get to sleep. I've told you before, if you're pissed, you can stay out. It's not a party gaff this, you know.

I won't stand for all this."

Sean carried on bathing his brother's head. Mary could see the blood and panicked, she was hysterical. She ran to his side. "What's up with him, does he need stitches," she peeped at the wound through her fanned hands, scared to look, scared to see any more blood oozing from the hole in his head. "Jesus, Mary, and Joseph. I'm phoning an ambulance. I can see his skull. Look Sean, it's there I can see the bone."

Sean stood up as Mary pulled him away from Paul. "Let me have a closer look. Oh my God, what the hell has happened? You're going to need a few stitches in this cock, its deep, very deep."

Sean was about to spill the beans about what had happened. He could never hold a secret, he was a right blabbermouth. Paul rolled on his side and shut him up just in time before he told her everything. "I fell over mother, you know what I'm like when I've had a few too many. I'm sorted now, just go back to bed. I'll be fine after a good kip."

Sean's eyes were wide open and Mary knew he was hiding something, eyelids flickering rapidly. Even from being a small child he could never keep a straight face when he was telling lies. His eyebrows twitched and he was constantly licking his lips. Mary knew she would have to get him alone, he would never confess in front of his brother. Mary stood up and shot a look at Paul. "I'll get to the bottom of this you know. I don't believe this cock and bull story for one minute. Do you think I came over on a banana boat? Like I said, I'm onto you two and I'll find out what really happened here."

Paul struggled to his feet, he was wobbling, trying to focus. "I'm going to get cleaned up. Mother stop fucking stressing and get your arse back into bed. Like I just told you Columbo, I was pissed and fell, just leave it at that." Paul growled at Sean and nodded his head slowly, that was all it took to let him know to keep his big trap shut.

Paul left the room and Mary plonked down on the sofa. Here it was, the sympathy vote she always looked for, after she'd been shouted at. "What's the world coming to ay Sean? I've done my best for you boys and this is how you treat me. Did you just hear the way he spoke to me then, no bleeding respect whatsoever."

Sean sat at her side and rested his head on her shoulder. She knew he couldn't hold his own piss and waited for him to tell her what had gone on. It was just a matter of time before he confessed; he was just waiting for the right moment. Mary continued, she pulled out the card she always played when the odds were against her. "If your dad was alive he would have demanded some respect in this house and he would have got it too. You know as well as I do that he wouldn't have stood for all this shit you lot are giving me. I don't know where I went wrong. I worked two jobs and always made sure there was a meal on the table. Shoot me for even caring why don't you?"

Sean gripped her wrinkled hand and stroked her fingers softly. He realised just how hard she'd had it over the past few months and felt sick inside when he thought about how long she had left on this earth with him. His mother was his life, his heartbeat. He would never survive without her. Feeling his heart sink deep into his chest he sighed. Mary knew she'd said enough now to play with his heartstrings. "Mam, we do treat you with respect. Well, I do anyway. Paul's just upset that's all. Take no notice of him, he talks out of his arse when he's pissed. He just stressed because Jud is putting the pressure on him that's all."

Mary knew she would have to up her game if she was ever to get to the bottom of this. He was holding back, she was sure of it. She carried on stroking his head. "I mean, if I knew what was going on I could help but you always keep me in the dark. I'm your mother, you shouldall trust me, not keep stuff from me."

That was it, Sean was ready to tell her the truth. He sat up and checked the door and made sure no one was listening to him. Lying back down in his mother's arms he spoke in a low voice. He was telling her everything, the snitch. "We were on a job and we were Shanghai surprised. Double-crossed I mean. Somebody knew exactly what we were up to and they must have been waiting for us. The crafty bastards."

Mary stopped the tears and wiped her nose on her sleeve. "Who knew what you were up to? Come on, you must have an idea?"

Sean scratched his head and chewed on his bottom lip. "I've not got a clue mam, honest, as far as I know it was all hush, hush."

Mary studied him a bit longer than necessary, he was hiding something still, she could tell, he was twitching. Standing to his feet Sean kissed the top of his mother's head. He was back in the circle of trust now and felt calmer now he'd told her. "Right, let me bang the kettle on. A nice cup of tea each is what we need, what do you think, mother? I'll cut us a nice slice of that angel cake too, you like that don't you?" Mary nodded slowly as she watched him from the corner of her eye. Sean was up to something and she knew he was covering up the truth. Considering everything that had happened he was just too cool, he was taking all this in his stride and this was so out of character for him.

Sean returned to the front room holding two cups looped on his fingers. "Don't just stand there looking at me… grab one from me then, it's burning my finger."

Mary sprang to her feet and helped get the cups from his fingers. They both stopped dead in their tracks when they heard someone coming down the stairs. The living room door opened and Paul clocked the brew on the table. "I'll have a brew Sean. Put me an extra sugar in it too." Sean asked no questions and plodded back into the kitchen. Paul's face looked a lot cleaner now all the blood had been cleaned off, but you could tell by his creased cheeks that he was still in pain. He held an old tea towel up to his head and he was still applying pressure to the wound.

Mary sat forward in her seat and spoke to him directly. "I'm getting off to bed. Paul are you sure you're going to be alright. If you want, I can phone an ambulance?"

Paul sighed as if the sound of her voice irritated his ears. She was doing his head in. "Mam, I'm fine, just go to bed will you? I'm not a kid you know. I'm a grown man." Mary snarled and made her way to the door. Paul was such an arrogant bastard at times and she hated that he thought he was above her in some kind of way. He loved power and loved giving out orders to those he thought were beneath him. He was a tosser really, a proper arsehole. Mary left the room with her cup of tea held close to her chest.

Sean passed the mug of tea over to his brother; he seemed edgy as if he couldn't wait to leave the room. Paul watched him and snapped. "Why the fuck are you stood there like a prize prick. Sit the fuck down will you, you're making me jumpy." Sean reached for his cigarettes and popped one in the corner of his mouth. There was silence as they both sat deep in thought. Paul blew a laboured breath and held his head in his hands. "I bet it's something to do with the Morgan's all this. I mean, who the fuck knew we had this job boxed off? Somebody's been talking out of school and when I find out who it is who's blabbed I'm going to torture the bastard, cut their balls off and ram them down their throat."

Sean inhaled hard on his cigarette and blew a thick grey cloud of smoke out in front of him. He dropped his head low and sat with his hands on his knees. "I don't know Paul. But someone must have had said something otherwise how did they know we were there."

Paul gritted his teeth hard. "Like I just said to you, there must be a spy in the camp, someone close to us," Paul rubbed his hands together as a cold air passed over his body. "Our Jud is going to hit the roof when he finds out about this. I'll tell you now, shit's going to hit the fan. He's going to go mental."

Sean stretched his arms over his head and headed to the door. Jud this, Jud that, he was sick of hearing it. Who did Jud think he was anyway, God? "I'm off to bed. Let's sort this out in the morning when we have a clear head.

I can't stand any more stress today my head feels like it's going to pop." Paul slurped on his cup of tea, he was deep in thought. Sean left the room.

CHAPTER NINE

MICHELLE BUCKLEY WIPED Larry's head with small balls of fluffy cotton wool. He'd been awake now for over a week but his memory was still a blur. He kept having flashbacks but was unsure of who he was. Larry's eyes were vacant and he just didn't look right, something was missing. Michelle finished cleaning his cheeks and lifted his fingers up to her mouth; she kissed each digit slowly and smiled at him. "There you go my little prince, you're all clean now." The doctors had already told her that his memory could return at any time but she hated that her dream could soon be over. She would have loved for Larry to stay the way he was, oblivious to his true identity. Michelle loved living in the land of fairies and this was the happiest she'd been in a long time. So what if she was living a lie, she was savouring every moment of being with the man she loved. She loved her role as devoted girlfriend. Even if he was a cabbage for the rest of his life she didn't care, he was still hers. Michelle had been at Larry's side twenty-four-seven, she always made a fuss of him and sneaked the odd grope of his genitals when he was asleep, she was madly in love with him. A sick twisted woman she was, mentally unstable.

Mary walked into the room holding a bag of goodies in her hand; chocolate, crisps and drinks. She passed them to Michelle with a sour face. "I've made him some apple crumble and a dollop of custard. He loves it he does," she spoke directly to Larry now who seemed in a world of his own, nothing registering. "Don't you son, don't you love a bit of cake and custard?"

Larry smiled not knowing what they were talking about. I don't think he really understood what his mother was saying but he agreed with her anyway. Mary sat down and took her coat off. Michelle was watching her like a hawk, scared she might uncover her dark secret. "You go and have a fag love. I'll stay with our Larry for a bit. I bet you're dead on your feet. You need to have a break for a bit. Go on, I'll make sure he's alright"

Michelle agreed and pulled her coat from the back of the chair. She needed a cigarette anyway, her nerves were shattered. "I'll be back soon Mary. I'm just outside if you need anything. Larry, I'll be back soon my little treacle tart."

Mary watched her leave with cunning eyes. Once she was alone with her son she nodded her head at him slowly. "Oh, Larry how on earth have you ended up with that big fat heifer. She's been good to you I know, but fuck a duck, that woman is ugly, a bleeding disgrace, you've scraped the bottom of the barrel there son, I can tell you."

Larry stirred in his bed and he was confused as he replied. "How long have I been with her, she said we were going to get engaged?"

Mary swallowed hard and gripped his hand tightly. "Oh, for crying out loud, please don't be marrying her. Do you know how many people have asked if it's true that you two are together? I swear to you son, nobody can believe it. It's so out of character for you."

Mary started to talk about Dawn and Jud and everyday life. All of a sudden Larry gripped the edge of his blankets and his toes curled at the end of the bed. He grabbed his head and he was squeezing it with force. "I know Jud. Jud's my brother, it's him who's done this to me, isn't it?" Mary was alarmed and she was watching the door for help to come inside. Larry was hysterical and he was screaming at the top of his voice. "Jud, you bastard! I'll have you for this, just you wait and see." Michelle ran back into the room and Larry snarled at her, he was raging, eyes bulging out from his head. "Michelle Buckley, what the fuck are you doing here?"

Mary jumped in, "Larry, she's your girlfriend. Michelle's been here with you every hour since you've been in hospital, she's never left your side."

Larry flung the blankets from the bed and tried to get up. The doctors were now in the room trying to calm him down, injecting drugs into his arm, restraining him. Larry screamed at Michelle at the top of his voice. "She's no girlfriend of mine, she's a fucking stalker." Michelle went bright red and she was looking for some support from Mary or the doctors, anybody who would help her. It was her word against Larry's now. How the hell was she going to get out of this one? She was bright red and sweating, her mouth was dry and her palms were hot and sweaty. "Larry, we've been together for months, even when you were seeing Dawn you were still seeing me. Don't tell me you've forgotten about us?"

There it was again, that familiar name he knew. Closing his eyes he squeezed them hard. "Dawn Pritchard, "he whispered under his breath as he started to calm down.

He remembered it all now it was all coming back to him. "Mam, get me out of this place. And you Michelle, fuck right off out of my face! How dare you tell people we're together you fucking dreamer, do one. As if I would bang you, are you right in the head or what?"

The doctors calmed Larry down and Michelle left in floods of tears. Her world had fallen apart and the man she loved was drifting away. Mary was beside her son and everything he'd been through was coming back to him. His face was white and he was crying, sobbing like a small child. His body was in a state of shock. "Where's Jud now mam?"

Mary hung her head low and whispered so nobody could hear her. The doctors were still in the room and she didn't want her dirty washing airing in public. "He's in the nick love, the big house. As soon as this happened to you he was arrested and he's been on remand ever since."

Larry chewed on his lip and his nostrils flared. "And, Dawn, where's she?"

Mary picked her coat up from the side; she wasn't looking at her son. "You just keep away from that dirty trollop, she's nothing but a scrubber. The trouble she's caused in this family is unforgiveable, she's better off dead. Larry, stay well away from her. I'm telling you now, stay well away."

The doctors were still dealing with Larry when Mary left the room, he was fighting the drugs but his eyes were closing slowly. As Mary came out of the hospital doors Michelle was stood waiting for her, she was in a state, sobbing her heart out, devastated. "How can he not remember me Mary? He's my life! What am I going to do without him? Why can't he remember the love we shared? Surely, he can't have forgotten about us."

Mary screwed her face up, Michelle was going over the top. Yeah, her son might have slipped her one, but there was no way in this world she could ever believe they were a true couple. Mary tried to console her. "He's been through a lot love. I think he's still in shock, that's all, maybe when he's calmed down and he's had time to think he might feel differently." Mary was lying through her teeth. Larry would never have this woman by his side again, she was a minger, a walking disgrace.

Michelle huddled closer to Mary and sank her head into her shoulders, she was blubbering. Snot dribbled from her nose as she spoke. "If he thinks I'm waiting about for him while he runs back to Dawn he's got another think coming. I'm not playing second fiddle anymore to anyone, it's me or her. He's breaking my heart Mary, honest, he's killing me." Mary carried on walking and shook her head. Her family was a mess and now that Larry was out of danger she feared for the safety of her other family members. It was war.

Sally walked into Maureen's house and collapsed onto the sofa covering her face with her hands. Dawn was watching the TV and tried not to look at her, she was aware she was there but pretended she'd not missed her. Sally reached for the remote and turned the volume down on the TV. She wanted Dawn's full attention. "Oh my god, I've just had to do the walk of shame home, I feel a right slapper. People were looking at me all the time. I know what they were thinking too. But ay, does this face look like it gives a fuck? I had the time of my life." Sally chuckled.

Maureen rubbed her hands together, she'd just got up out of bed and her hair was stuck up all over the place. "Come on then fill us in. Is it love or what? Dawn, look at her face, she's smitten already. Come on then, dish the dirt. I want to know all the gritty details. Don't be leaving anything out, especially the sex bits. Oooohh, I love a bit of porn."

Sally shot a look at Dawn and she could see she was green with envy, she wasn't one bit interested in her story. She sat up tall and made sure she rubbed salt in her wounds. "Stick this in your pipe and smoke it Dawn Pritchard," she mumbled under her breath. "Maureen, you're such a pervert. Anyway, he was so nice to me. I think he's the one you know. I was pissed out of my head and even when I was spewing my guts up, he still treated me like a lady. A real princess."

Dawn reached for her cigarettes and giggled sarcastically. "So I take it, he banged you then? What happened to playing hard to get?"

Sally screwed her face up, she'd heard enough of Dawn's sly digs. She defended herself and upped her game. "Fuck me Dawn, why are you so nasty to me? So what if I slept with him on the first night, you didn't hear me going on when you was shagging Larry on the first night did you? Remember, people who live in glass houses shouldn't throw stones."

Maureen loved that Dawn had been put in her place for a change; she didn't even reply to Sally, she just sat smoking her cigarette staring at the TV pretending she didn't hear her. Maureen continued probing Sally; she wanted to know the ins and outs of a cat's arsehole. "So, are you meeting him again? He seems a lovely man and he's got a few bob Danny Morgan too hasn't he?"

Here it was, Sally was in her element and she knew Dawn was still listening. She was going to wipe that cocky smile right off her face once and for all. "He liked me a lot for your information Maureen. In fact, he's even asked me to be his girlfriend. He's given me some money to get a new dress for tonight too. I'm buzzing you know. Since when has any man treated me like this before? I'm usually lucky if a man buys me a drink, never mind anything else." Sally fanned the money out in front of her and smirked. She pulled a twenty pound note out of the readies and passed it to Maureen. "Here you go Mo. Go and treat yourself, my money is your money and plus, you've always looked after me in the past, so it's about time I returned the favour."

Maureen didn't have to be asked twice. She snatched the cash out of her hand and rammed it down the front of her top and straight into her baggy grey bra. "Sally, that's so nice that is, thanks a lot love. It's a shame other people in this house don't share your morals where money is concerned."

Dawn stubbed her cigarette out and sighed. She knew her mother was having a pop at her you didn't have to be a scientist to work that out. "Mam, fuck off will you. I'm in no mood today to be arguing with you. Just piss off."

This was strange, Dawn never missed a chance of upsetting her mother, something was wrong. Maureen got up from her chair and pecked Sally on the side of her cheek. "I can go down to the bingo hall later on now. I might even have a little tipple when I get there too, just a top-up. The world's my oyster." Maureen left the room with a spring in her step, she was buzzing. Once she was gone Dawn turned to face Sally, she had a face like thunder. "You better get that dress dry-cleaned then hadn't you? I suppose it's all full of spunk now isn't it?"

Sally lay flat on the sofa and looped her arms above her head. "No, it isn't, that's where you're wrong. I was stripped naked when we had sex, so wind your neck in. Fuck me Dawn, I'll tell you something for nothing, you're turning into a right grumpy bitch these days, what the hell is going on with you?"

Dawn made sure Maureen wasn't listening; she leant forward and kept her voice low. "Jud rang me last night, he wants me to come and see him to sort things out."

Sally was horrified and brought her knees up to her chest. "Don't tell me you're going to go. He will have something planned for you. If I was you, I'd take it on the chin and let sleeping dogs lie. If you go there to see him, you'll be lucky to get out alive."

Dawn chewed on her thumb. "He seemed calm when I spoke to him. I could just say it was a mistake and I only slept with Larry once, I mean, Larry's not going to say any different is he? Plus, if he did tell him the truth, I can still say he's lying. It wouldn't be the first time he's lied would it."

Sally turned on her side and played with her hair. "You're dicing with death if you ask me. It's your choice, but if it was me, I would stay well away. The man's a fucking lunatic."

The door opened and in walked Spencer, Dawn's brother. He looked rough and hung over. "Move up Sally, I need to lie down. I swear the night I've had has been nonstop. I never knew I could still dance." He opened his hands and held a flat palm out to them both. "I'll tell you what though; these pills make you go all night long."

Sally looked closer at the pile of blue pills Spencer held in his hands, they were ecstasy tablets, a lethal drug. "Since when have you been into these Spencer, fucking hell, you're lucky you're still alive. It's been on the news about them, loads of people have died after taking them, you need to be careful," Sally stressed. Spencer flopped down on the sofa and he was still humming a tune. "Who did you get them from?" Sally inquired.

Spencer yawned and folded a pillow under his head. "Sean Watson, he was handing them out last night. I swear everyone in the pub was on them, even some of the old guys who play cards."

Dawn was interested now and delved deeper. "What Sean had them? What's that nob doing with stuff like that? I bet Jud doesn't know what he's up to?"

Spencer giggled and it was plain to see he was still high as a kite. He held his head back and smirked. "What's Jud going to do about it when he's banged up? Sean is just having a bit of fun that's all. Anyway, why are you so concerned? You're not part of the Watson family anymore anyway. Are you forgetting you shagged both of the brothers or what?"

Dawn was outraged and she threw her shoe over at her brother just missing his head. "Don't be smart Spencer, we all know what I've done. It's yesterday's news that. Anyway, Jud wants me to go and see him in prison, so I think we'll be back together before you know it."

Spencer's jaw was swinging low as he shot a look over at Sally. "Well, that' a turn up for the books. I wish you well Dawn, but you know Jud of old, he'll never let you get away with this, he'll have something under his belt for you. So mark my words, be careful, in fact, be very careful."

Dawn rolled her eyes at her brother. "Jud loves me, I know he will forgive me once I've spoken to him. So button it you two, you think you know it all, but you know fuck all."

Spencer was rambling and he was poking his fingers in Sally's waist, he was flirting with her. "Come and lie down here next to me Sally. I could show you a good time if you're up for a bit of fun."

Dawn left the room in a huff. "Oh, get a room you two and have done with it."

Spencer giggled and tried to pull Sally down to where his head was lay. Sally stopped him dead in his tracks. "Will you leave me alone? I'm spoken for now. I have a boyfriend you know?"

Spencer looked at her in more detail. "Stop lying and get them gums around my plums."

Sally was serious as she fought him off. "I'm with Danny Morgan you muppet, so keep your hands to yourself. In fact, I'm fed up not hard up, so jog on you no hoper."

Sally sat like a proud peacock with her latest update, she watched Spencer wriggling about trying to digest the information she'd just given him. "No way, are you serious with Danny? I've just left him a few minutes ago; he was in the pub sat with Sean Watson."

Sally held her head to the side. "Bleeding hell, that was quick, I've only just left his side. I wonder what his business is with Sean? I thought the Morgan's and the Watsons were at war?"

Spencer's eyes were closing slowly. "So did I," he whispered as he drifted off to sleep.

Sally looked at Spencer and smiled. He made her laugh, she loved having a bit of banter with him. Sally went to find Dawn, she made her way up the stairs and it seemed every step she took was a struggle, she had the hangover from hell.

Dawn was getting ready, she was in the mirror applying her black mascara, her mouth was open slightly, her head tilted back. "Have you chilled out now or what?" Sally asked.

Dawn carried on with her make-up and replied to her. "I am chilled Sally. It's you who's up your own arse, not me. Every other word, it's Danny this and Danny that. You need to play a bit harder to get instead of putting it on a plate for him. Men like Danny like a challenge, not some woman who's needy all the time, trust me, I know about men."

Sally held her hands on her hips. "Listen, let's agree to disagree shall we. Let me do my shit and you do yours, that way there will be no arguing."

"Fine by me," Dawn snapped, she'd seen her arse. A mobile phone was ringing and Dawn was looking everywhere to find it. "Quick Sally, look under them clothes there, it could be Jud." The phone was found and

Dawn answered the call. Sally watched as Dawn paced the floor listening to the voice on the other end of the line. "When did he get out of hospital? Are you sure Melanie that you've not got it wrong?" Sally was alert and she was trying to listen to the conversation. The call ended and Dawn plonked down on the side of the bed with her head held in her hands. "That's all I need. Fuck me, when it rains in this house it bleeding pours. Larry is out of hospital. Melanie Bishop from down the other estate has just seen him going into the pub."

Sally patted her shoulder and tried to comfort her. Dawn was actually crying, real tears too. "Come on, stop getting upset. Larry is history, he'll know it's over between you two surely. Just carry on like you were doing. Go and see Jud and try and salvage what's left of your relationship. Just leave Larry to his own devices and stay well away."

Dawn snivelled and wiped her nose on the sleeve of her jumper. "You and I both know Larry won't leave me alone. As soon as he can, he'll be in touch, trust me. He'll be out for revenge, I know him."

CHAPTER TEN

LARRY WALKED INTO The Foresters, he was unsteady on his feet and Sean was holding him up by his arm. He wasn't really strong enough to be out but he insisted that he went to the pub. Larry nodded his head at the lads already sat there and that was enough to let them know he was back on the scene. A few of them got out of their seats to shake his hand, the others just sat sneering at him. He was a like a soldier returning home from war. Larry was all skin and bone and his hair seemed to have turned grey and thinned overnight. Jud was lying heavily on his mind and something told him his brother had something up his sleeve. He had a gut feeling he was a dead man walking. Paul walked behind Larry, he was a broken man and his pride was hurt. After Jud found out about them being hijacked he went mental at him and told him he'd better sort it out as soon as possible. Paul was at a dead end though, nobody knew shit about the heist or, if they did, they were keeping it to themselves. Paul was in a deep dark hole of depression and every day he was falling deeper into it, his head was gone. He wasn't the big man he first thought, he was nothing without his brother backing him up, he was weak and vulnerable. Sean sat Larry down and brought him a brandy over to the table. Sean was watching every move his brother made and he was aware he was gunning for somebody. Larry was getting stronger each day and sooner or later he would be the main man in Manchester, or so he thought.

Michelle Buckley was in tonight and she was watching Larry from the shadows. She sat sipping her drink and tried to mingle in with the other punters in the pub trying to be discreet. Since Larry had been discharged from the hospital she hadn't seen or heard anything from him. She'd phoned Mary a few times but the reaction she got from her was to keep well away from her son and leave him be. Her heart was broken into a thousand pieces and somehow some way she was plotting to get Larry back by her side.

Larry gathered the men together. They were unsure of his leadership at first, but after a few harsh words he put them all back in their place. Sean sat next to his brother and every now and then he piped into the conversation. No one gave a shit what he was saying, but all the same, they had to listen to him anyway. Larry banged his flat palm on the table making it shake. "I want to know who had us over. Somebody knows out there, and it's our job to find out who it is. Who the fuck do these muppets think they are messing with, we're no pricks, so let's sort it out. Has anyone got any ideas?"

There was a silence and Paul spoke as he tapped his fingers on the table. "Jud seemed to think it was the Morgan's. He's heard pure shit about Danny in jail and he said this has got his stamp all over it. He's a proper dodgy fucker"

Sean was edgy and pulled at his jacket as he spoke. "Jud's fucking paranoid. He's always been the same about the Morgan's I think he's barking up the wrong tree with this. I just think it's some small time crew who saw a quick earner... opportunists. It's obvious they didn't do their homework otherwise they would have known it was our graft, come on Larry, think about it. It doesn't add up."

Larry cracked his knuckles, and bit hard onto his lips. "I don't want you to speak Jud's name again in my company, the guy's a twat. This is my shout now and what I say goes, do you get me or what?"

The team nodded and Sean plonked back into his seat, he was deflated. No one was listening to a word he said. Just at that moment Danny Morgan and his crew walked in and you could have heard a pin drop. "Get that prick over here to see me Paul, do it now, go on let's see what he has to say for himself. Drag the cunt over by his balls if he says no."

Paul stormed off and headed towards Danny like a charging bull. Larry could see Sally walking in behind him. Sitting up straight in his seat he stretched his neck to see. Where was Dawn, they were always together? Larry looked gutted as he saw Sally was alone. Sean got up from his seat and headed towards the bar. He was out to get pissed and he was knocking back the brandy like it was nobody's business. "Do you want another scoop or what Larry?" Sean asked. Larry declined and prepared himself to meet his opponent. He sat rubbing his hands together. Danny Morgan looked a lot bigger than he remembered him, more toned, firmer in the chest. The two men had been friends once, but that was then and this was now. Things had changed. Now it was Larry calling the shots and he wasn't allowing anyone to get close to him again, ever. This was business and he knew any friendship they once shared had gone right out of the window.

Danny sat opposite Larry; he was confident and offered his hand out to shake. "What's up mate," Danny asked as he clocked the other men around him closing in. Larry was just staring at him at first, looking for any signs of fear, any sign of guilt. There was none, not an ounce. This guy had more front than Blackpool.

Larry leaned forward and his warm breath tickled the end of Danny's nose. "What do you know about the lorry of electrical going missing?"

Danny leaned forward and held his chin tightly, pressing his fingers deep into it. "I know fuck all about it. Why, what's up?"

Larry didn't answer straight away. He could see Sally heading towards them and he needed a second to catch his breath, his heart was pounding inside his chest. Larry continued as Sally sat down next to Danny. He nodded his head slightly at her as their eyes met. "Some cunt has had us over that's why I'm asking. And," he paused, "the word on the street is that you know something about it?"

Danny chuckled and shook his head. He was cool as a cucumber, fearless. "Listen Larry, we all have our own earners, you know how we roll and we don't step on each other's turf. It's the law of the land isn't it?"

Larry knew he would have to up his game, this guy thought he was untouchable, above his station. He gave the signal to his men who were stood behind Danny ready to ambush him. All of a sudden they had him gripped and he was unable to move, he was head-locked.

Sally was raging trying to set him free, dragging at the

men's clothes with gritted teeth. "Get the fuck off him!" she yelled.

Larry was in Danny's face. He was nose to nose with him, eyes bulging. "If I hear one word, you're anything to do with this Danny, I'll cut your dick off and shove it up your arse. Do you hear me?"

Danny wriggled free; he was strong and ready to attack Larry, he bit one of the men's hand who was holding him, sank his teeth right in drawing bright red blood.

Sally stood up in front of them both; guarding Danny. She rammed her finger deep into Larry's chest. She wasn't scared of him and she was willing to put her neck on the line for the love of her life. "Listen Larry, Danny is not like that, why would he have you over? You've got your facts wrong. I suggest you go and find out the truth before you start kicking off with him."

Danny's men were around him in seconds and it looked like a war was about to break out. Danny stood tall and he made sure everyone there heard what he had to say. "Listen you fucking bunch of fairies, it's not my style to rip people off. Larry, if you ever try and pin something on me again, watch this space mate, because you'll be lay on the floor with a fucking chalk mark around you before you know what fucking day it is. Are you listening to me you daft prick?"

Larry knew he wasn't strong enough yet to fight this man, but sliding his hand into his pocket he pulled out a silver pistol. He pointed it at Danny and chuckled. "Oh, do you think so wank stain?" Danny dipped his head low and he scrambled to safety. The gun was enough to let the gang know that he was willing to pop a cap in them at the drop of a hat. His eyes were menacing and even after they left he was still sat there holding the gun in his hand, debating his next move.

Sean covered the weapon with shaking hands, he was frantic. Scared someone would see it. "Will you put that away in here, fuck me Larry, it only takes one plain clothes dibble in here and you'll be in the nick on a fire-arms charge. Put the fucking gun away you bell end." Larry let out an evil laugh. He could see Danny Morgan and his men running through the door. Larry Watson was back in business and now he was on the mend, no man was safe.

CHAPTER ELEVEN

DAWN PRITCHARD PULLED UP outside Strangeways prison in Manchester. It was pissing down and the heavens had just opened. The rain pounded against the pavement and bounced from the ground up against her legs. Strangeways prison was daunting, it sent a shiver down her spine, her hairs standing on end. The tall tower in the prison grounds looked like it held so many stories; scary, haunting tales that would make your toes curl. A lot of the local lads served their time here and they were like one big happy family once they were locked up behind bars. Hotel Manchester the inmates nicknamed it, it was a doddle to serve time there to some of the more hardened criminals who lived behinds its walls.

Dawn walked inside the visitors centre and told the officers who she had come to see. She was told to sit down and wait until her name was called. Dawn was dressed to impress. Wow, this girl was hot, she looked like she'd just walked off a catwalk. She had to be top notch to make an impression. Jud had to see her in her full glory and see what he was missing. He needed to want her again. Dawn's skinny jeans fitted her like a glove and her heels made her legs look long and slender. Maureen had got a glimpse of Dawn before she left to go to the prison and told her straight that she looked like a prostitute, the cheek of the woman, Dawn looked good, but that was just how Maureen was, upfront and personal. She always dug deep and said what she thought. Dawn ignored her anyway, what did her mother know about fashion? She was always wearing the same old clothes day in day out. She had no style, no desire to change her look. Maureen didn't have a clue about dress sense. She was a bag of rags most of the time.

Dawn turned her head slowly and looked at the other visitors in the centre. What a depressing place this was. There were a few scattered toys on the floor and the odd picture on the wall that the inmates had created during their sentence. This place was filled with misery and poverty. Kids screaming in the distance, mothers at their wits end as their children ran around the centre shouting and annoying everyone in there. Screwing her face up she pulled her black leather jacket tighter and tried not to make eye contact with any of the other people in the centre. She thought she was above them and there was no way she was ever being put in the same circle as these social rejects, she was classy, she had standards. This lot looked like they needed sheep-dipping. Scruffs they were who stank of sweat and stale tobacco. Sat to the right of Dawn was a young woman, she must have only been about eighteen years of age. As she smiled, Dawn could see her teeth were brown stumpy pegs, black in parts. She was in desperate need of a visit to the dentist, gummy she was. Sat with her was a small toddler, his nose was running with green slimy snot and the nappy he was wearing was nearly touching the floor. What a bloody shame. The woman was obviously looking for some company and she edged closer to Dawn's side.

Dawn inhaled and her expression changed. This woman stank of cat piss and she was just about to tell her to move out of her personal space when she said, "It's shit having to come here all the time isn't it?" Dawn checked over her shoulder first to make sure the woman was actually talking to her. Surely this tramp wasn't trying to make conversation with her; she didn't even know her and she wanted to keep it like that. Dawn smirked at the woman, hoping she would leave her the hell alone. She had enough on her plate without this clown adding to it. This woman was rough as a bear's arse, in fact she was putrid. Dawn kept her eyes low hoping she would leave her alone, but she didn't, she was begging for a friend. The woman started to speak to Dawn as if they were old friends reuniting after years apart. She tapped her on the arms softly and smirked. "My name's Gemma, my mates call me Gem though, you can call me Gem too if you want," the girl smiled and her full set of stumpy teeth were revealed. Her teeth were a dentists' worst nightmare. "Who are you here to see, your fella?"

Dawn checked her wristwatch and knew this woman was not giving up lightly. Checking the area she answered her quietly hoping she would leave her alone and piss off back under the rock where she'd just crawled out from. "Yeah, I could find better things to do with my time than sit in this shit-hole all day. It's not a nice place to be for someone like me" Dawn hissed.

That was it, Gemma moved her chair closer to Dawn and she was ready for a good old chin-wag. "It does my head in too. Plus, I've got that crying cunt with me today, he never shuts up either. Twenty-four hours a day he's crying, it's a wonder he's even quiet now. He's a right Gazza." Dawn smiled at the child who was now under the table playing with her shoes with his grubby little hands. Dawn gave her foot a small flick and moved him away. So what, she kicked him but he was touching her expensive shoes, he should have known better. The child got back up from the floor and continued playing with it. His hands were sticky and marks were appearing on Dawn's new suede shoes. She opened her eyes wide and shot them at the child. This time she kicked him away, he knew she meant business as she sucked hard on her gums and growled at him. "Are you bringing any shit in for your guy or what?" Gemma asked in a low voice.

Dawn was confused and hunched her shoulders. "Any shit like what?"

Gemma giggled. "Are you being serious or what, don't tell me you don't know the script for jail visits?" Gemma replied.

Dawn was getting annoyed and she gritted her teeth together tightly. She didn't have to listen to this shit and she was ready for carting her, slapping her if she needed to. "Listen love, just say what you have to say and leave me alone. I'm new to all this prison stuff. I don't have a clue what you're waffling on about. And," she snapped, "get your kid from off my shoes, they cost me over a hundred pound. Look at him, he's trying to suck on them now, for fucks sake sort him out."

Gemma bent down under the table and giggled at her son. "Ay you little bastard, leave this ladies shoes alone. There not like my cheap trainers, you can't just do that to people's shoes. They cost a lot of money. Come on, get from underneath there where I can see you. Suck on my trainers if you want, but make sure there's no dog shit on them. I'm sure I stood in some before."

The kid moved away from her grip and lay flat on the floor kicking his legs, there was no way she was moving him, he was stuck to the floor like glue. Gemma let out a laboured breath and brought her head back up to the table, she quickly scanned the area for any signs of danger and she just ignored the child under the table and sat back down. Honest to God, she just blanked the kid as if he wasn't there and carried on talking. "I bring parcels in for the inmates. I get a ton every visit I do. It's only a bit of brown and white though. I don't bring mobile phones in. I don't like bringing them in they're too big and bulky, they're on top. Plus, they hurt my snatch when I'm plugging them."

Dawn studied Gemma's face and she was frustrated because she didn't have a clue what she was going on about. "What planet are you on love? What the hell are parcels, and what the hell is brown and white?"

Gemma made sure no one was listening and covered her mouth as she spoke. "Heroin and cocaine. Parcels are what you call them, well, that's what the lads call them in the slammer. I've already plugged the drugs until we get over to the prison. I'm on the ball I am when it comes to earning a few quid." Gemma giggled and knew she would have to explain further, she placed her grubby hand on Dawn. "Plugged, means I've shoved it up my arse. You know, the old rusty bullet hole."

This woman was vile, hanging, she had no self-respect. Dawn was horrified, she rubbed at her arm and was seriously thinking of telling this woman to go and sit somewhere else. She was making her stomach churn. How on earth could she shove something up her arse, she was disgusting! This woman was off her rocker. She was still waffling and eager to make a few quid. "I can do a few drops for you if you want? I only charge one hundred quid for each parcel. I've done loads of them and I've never been caught up to now, so just say the word and job's a good 'un."

Dawn chewed on her bottom lip, she was interested now and this woman could be just what she needed to get Jud back on side again. Smiling at the drug addict she patted the middle of her arm with her fingertips, careful that she wasn't touching any of her flesh. There was no way she was having any contact with her properly because she might have caught something. "I could be interested in that Gemma, after the visit wait around for me and we can talk business. Sorry for being a bit moody with you just now, but I'm so stressed at the moment, you know how it is don't you?"

Dawn rolled her eyes to the back of her head, watching the woman with cunning eyes. Gemma agreed as she tickled the end of her chin. "Tell me about it love, that lucky fucker's in here, he has three meals a day, no bills to pay and he thinks he's got it hard. I've got it all to do. Trust me, I work my flaps off just so we can eat every day. I shoplift and I even sell my body sometimes just to earn a few extra quid. I used to get good money back in the day but once you've been on the scene for a while you get the slops. The punters say my fanny has been hammered now and it's like throwing a sausage up an entry, so I just get the horrible old perverts, you know, the ones who want all that kinky shit, anal sex, Bombay rolls and all that." Gemma bit hard on her lip and pulled her sleeve up slightly revealing the purple track marks on her arm. They looked bruised and sore. "The smack costs me seventy quid a day. I'm trying to sort my habit out but I just seem to get deeper into the shit each day. I mean, look at him there," she held her arms wide open to her son who was still rolling about on the floor nearby playing with some chewing gum that was stuck to the floor. "What chance has he got with a mother like me? I'll be in the nick soon, or dead won't I? And what then ay?" Her eyes clouded over and she swallowed hard. "He's fucked because he'll just end up in care. Just another case number he'll be, with nobody to love him. Sad really isn't it?"

Dawn actually looked upset, she was holding back the tears back. She never really realised that some people lived like this in the real world. Dawn had always been so involved in her own life that she'd never given a second thought to anyone else and their problems. This was a real eye-opener to her. Dawn gripped Gemma's arm and helped pull her sleeve back down. The bruises were knocking her sick. As she looked into her eyes she noticed that Gemma's eyes were pinned, she'd definitely had some drugs today, her mouth was open and she was ready for falling to sleep. Dawn checked the clock on the wall and they still had fifteen minutes to go before the visit. Dawn struggled with her conscience and she tried to listen to the woman's problems without judging her but she was struggling to hear the reality of Gemma's life, it was hard to bear. Gemma was slurring her words and every now and then she broke out into fits of laughter for no reason, she was off her head, high as a kite. She had bouts of sleep too. Her head just fell down onto her chest and she was out for the count.

Dawn bought the woman a cup of coffee and got the child some crisps and chocolate. She went over the top knowing that this could be the last meal the two of them would eat today. The kid had a lovely face too, well, when all the dirt was wiped away from his mouth and nose. He had lovely blue eyes but as she looked closer they held so much sadness. Dawn wanted children in the future and always thought she would make a good mother. Life was tough for this child and her heart twitched inside as she thought about the life he led with a drug addict mother and a father who was in prison. Did Gemma ever read him a bedtime story? Did she even cuddle the child, tell him she loved him? Dawn knew more than anyone how much a child needed love when they were growing up, she'd never had any love either. She was just left to grow up on her own; no love, no nothing. Perhaps, that's why she was so hard inside. Life had made her this way and circumstances had stolen the chance for her to ever wear her heart on her sleeve. She could never be weak, she could never let her defences down, not now, not ever.

The child touched her face with his little chunky fingers. Dawn never moved a muscle, she smiled at him and stroked her finger slowly over his blotchy cheek. This was a special moment and one Dawn had never experienced before. A loud-mouthed screw was calling out the names now for the visit. He was a right arsehole and he made everyone feel like they were criminals too. Gemma sprang to her feet and scooped her son up from the floor like he was a bag of shopping. "Right, here goes," she whispered. She walked past the prison guard and smiled at him. "Alright there boss. I hope you've been looking after my man for me while he's been in here?" Of course she never got a reply, she was riffraff compared to the officer and there was no way he would have given her the time of day. He knew her sort and he'd met plenty of them in the past. He looked her up and down and held a sour look on his face. Scum she was, nothing but a dirty low-life. Gemma had a spring in her step and she was eager to get over to the jail.

A crowd of around six people marched over to the main prison in a line. They were like ducklings waddling to the pond. Once they got over to the prison they were handed a basket to put their shoes and coat in and any other belongings they had. Dawn was watching the people in front of her closely and she was copying them. She handed in her visiting order and the woman asked to see all her identification. Once this was completed she had to walk through a security system to see if she had any forbidden items on her body. You would be amazed at what some people thought they could take into the jail. Knives, mobile phones, cigarettes and lots of other banned items. This jail was on lock down and eyes were watching from every nook and cranny in the hope they would catch a parcel landing. Dawn was asked to take her shoes off. Watching Gemma being searched in front of her, her heart was beating ten to the dozen. This woman was really going through with it, she looked normal, no sweat, no palpitations, nothing. Cool as anything she was, she never flinched. With her shoes off she stepped onto a box and was frisked by the officer. The female guard told Dawn to hold her arms out to the side of her, this was so degrading. What was the need for all this security, she was only going to see her boyfriend, not the bleeding queen of England. "Open your mouth and stick your tongue out," the screw said in a demanding voice. Dawn was ready for snapping and it was only Gemma shouting from in front of her that made her be quiet.

"Don't worry love, you'll get used to all this shit after you've been here a few times like me. Won't she love?" The screw just smirked at Gemma, she'd met her type a million times before and never replied. Dawn grabbed her shoes from the floor and sat on a small box to put them back on her feet. Once she had them on she went through some electronic doors and stood waiting for the other side to open. Gemma was with her and she was white now, nervous. She was constantly licking her lips and fidgeting, the nerves were kicking in. She had some balls this woman did, risking her freedom for a poxy one hundred quid. Gemma covered her mouth and whispered through her fingers. "I hate this bit. I hope that fucking mutt isn't here today. It makes my arse twitch something rotten. I swear, if it comes near me today it will get a kick right up its arse. I'll toe peck the fucker trust me."

Dawn could hear a dog barking as they walked up the flight of stairs. Groups of people were now being lined up and told to stand still while the sniffer dog walked past them. Gemma held the middle of her stomach and she looked like she was going to keel over. Taking a deep breath they both lined up ready for the inspection. The springer spaniel wagged its tail rapidly as it walked past Dawn, sniffing, panting. At one point it was nearly jumping up on to her but the officer pulled it away with a quick jerk of its lead. Dawn turned her head slightly now and watched as the dog approached Gemma and her son. Small beads of sweat were dripping down Gemma's brow and her hands were clenched into two tight balls at the side of her legs. She was praying under her breath. Dawn was holding her breath too, she closed her eyes, she couldn't look. That was close, amazingly the dog walked past Gemma and her son and never smelt a thing. The visitors were free to go into the prison. What a result this was, she was home and dry.

Gemma gave a cheeky wink as she left Dawn's side. She nudged her scrawny fingers into Dawn's waist as she left her. "Top one, see you after the visit. Just this last bit to go now and I'm on easy street, wish me luck." Dawn was gobsmacked. This woman was as bold as brass, she didn't seem to have an ounce of fear. She marched into the visitors centre with a spring in her step and walked to the table where her partner was waiting for her.

Dawn quickly looked for Jud, she took a few moments before she could find him among the prisoners sat at the tables. This seemed like the walk of death for her, every step she took she seemed to be thinking about her next step forward. This was D-Day. Her heart was banging hard inside her ribcage, she was hot and flustered and gagging for a drink. Her lips were dry and she was constantly licking at them. There he was, sat right in front of her - Jud. Her legs buckled from under her and she had to steady herself before she sat down to face him. They both sat staring at each other and neither of them spoke. You could have cut the atmosphere with a knife. Dawn licked her lips slowly and she refrained from any eye contact. She was shaking inside preparing herself for what was about to come. Jud broke the silence, why should he keep quiet, it was her in the wrong and not him. He was calmer than she thought he would have been, relaxed even. What the hell was he up to? The crafty bastard was having her over for sure, stitching her up, getting ready to strike.

Jud blew a laboured breath and dipped his head across the table. He could taste her fear. "So, let's hear it then Dawn, but do yourself a favour, don't try and fill my head with any bullshit because it won't wash with me anymore. I want you to tell me the truth, no cock and bull story, just the fucking truth. Are you listening to me or what?" Dawn inhaled deeply, this was it, she had to think on her feet. She had to make him believe her. She had to come up trumps and plead her innocence. Dawn reached over to touch his hand but he pulled away from her and sat back in his seat. What the hell did she expect, a bunch of flowers? "Just tell me the fucking truth," he snapped.

"Jud, I'm so sorry. It was just the once. I swear to you now, Larry was blackmailing me and he said if I didn't sleep with him again he was going to tell you. I swear, it was just the once. I hated lying to you but what else could I do when he had me over a barrel?"

Jud cracked his knuckles and held his head back. His eyes were closed, deep rage building inside him ready for exploding. "Nar, Dawn there is more to this than meets the eyes. When did this happen? Where did you have sex with him, come on, fucking tell me before I jump over this table and fucking destroy you. And..." he paused, "you know I will. I'll rip you in two you cheap fucking tart."

Dawn's heart was leaping about inside her chest, her jaw dropped. Jud was just staring at her, watching her like a hawk waiting for her to speak. "Jud, on my life, that's how it happened. I hate myself for what I've done to you. You were my life, my rock and everything I needed. I can't sleep without you. I can't do anything. My head's in bits. I just want us back together again. Just like we used to be." Wow, she couldn't half spin a tale. Thumbs up to her too if she could get away with it, why not try it. She was a right storyteller. How the hell could she just sit there and blatantly lie to him? Surely he was never going to fall for this one.

Jud banged his fist on the table and he looked directly into her eyes. "Do you think I could take you back after my brother has had his cock shoved up you?" he dipped his head into hers. "Nar, you're soiled goods now Dawn. Imagine what people are saying about me out there. I bet I'm a right laughing stock. They must think I'm a right dick-head. How could I have not seen what was right under my nose?"

This had all backfired on her now, she had to up her game. Dawn broke down in tears. This usually worked when she wasn't getting her own way. The tears streamed down her cheeks and she was sobbing her heart out. Jud watched the crocodile tears fall and sat with his arms folded. His eyes looked menacing and the tips of his ears were turning red, twitching slightly. What the hell was he up to? "So, was he better in bed than me?" he asked. "I bet you two were like fucking rabbits weren't you? How big is his cock, is it bigger than mine?" Jud was sick in the head. What kind of questions were these to ask? He was perverted. Dawn was shocked and she retaliated. How dare he speak to her like this, he was supposed to love her?

"Oh, fuck off Jud, that's just sick that is. For your information I was too drunk to remember it. So there you go, it wasn't a big session like you're making it out to be. It was just a shag that meant nothing. A quick wham bam thank you mam. There you go, I've said it now. Is that what you wanted to hear?"

This girl was pushing her luck for sure, did she not know who she was messing with, he could have stopped her breathing with one swift movement, killed her even. Jud grabbed her by the scruff of the neck and his nose was touching hers. His teeth clenched tightly together as he growled at her. "Yeah, it is sick, just like you shagging the brains out of my brother is sick. Did you think I would just take you back as if nothing had ever happened? For fuck's sake, get it into your thick head you're a dirty slut. My brother was having an affair with you. What do you think I should do? Should I just ignore it like it never happened? Get a grip you daft slag."

Dawn broke free, she was trying to stand up but he was pulling her back down. She was stressed out and ready to leave. "I don't have to listen to this Jud. I come here today to try and sort things out but it's obvious we're beyond that now so I may as well just go home. I've wasted my time I should have known better."

Dawn had called his bluff and she could see the panic in his eyes. He still loved her, there was no denying that, but to play the games, to make her pay, he didn't have time for that. He was locked up and needed it sorting out as soon as possible. "Just go and get me something to eat from the canteen" he said at last, "I just need to calm down. Go on, fuck off and let me sort my head out."

Dawn picked a ten pound note up from the table and marched to the canteen behind her. As she got there she joined the queue and waited to be served. Gemma was behind her in the queue and she could smell her before she could see her. She smelt awful. She was poking Dawn in the waist. Her voice was low. "It's all going smooth. I got the shit in just like I said I would."

Dawn was in a panic, there was no way she wanted to be associated with this junkie in public. "Okay, just speak to me later, fuck me, you're so on top. Piss off and leave me alone." Dawn moved forward to the serving hatch and placed her order. She got a cheese roll with a couple of bars of chocolate and two cups of coffee.

As she sat back down at the table Jud was back on her case. "Who the fuck is that bag-head you were just talking to?"

Dawn sat down and held a cunning smile. "That smack head is going to make you a rich man whilst you're in this shit-hole Jud." Dawn made sure the screws were nowhere near her table and chuckled. "She does drops, she charges one hundred pound a time. The dirty bitch shoves it up her arse to get it in here. She's brought drugs in today too."

Jud's head was all over the show. If a parcel was landing

in the jail he wanted to know everything about it. Dawn pointed the inmate out who Gemma was visiting today and informed him of the drugs he was concealing. Dawn smiled as Jud touched the top of her hand, he was smiling too now, he'd calmed down. She had a second go at winning him back.

"Jud, can we just put this behind us and move on. Larry meant nothing to me. You're the one I love. We can move away together. A fresh start, just me and you?"

Jud was thinking, he slurped on his hot coffee and looked directly at Dawn. "I want us to be together too. I don't trust anyone anymore and I know that Danny Morgan is the one having us over. I want you to run things for me as from now. Don't worry, it will be our little secret, nobody will ever know."

Dawn's face was beetroot, she was flustered. "Jud, I can't be involved in all that shit. I don't know anything about what goes on out there. I'd be hopeless and plus you've got your brothers to do all that anyway."

"I just want you to help me bring Danny Morgan down. I need you to be my eyes and ears out there. Anyway, I thought your mate Sally was hooked up with him. So it should be child's play to keep a close eye on him. Sally will fill you in anyway, she's alright like that Sally is, she's a nice girl."

Dawn twiddled the piece of hair dangling near her cheek bone. Sally and Danny were always together now and she knew she could easily inform Jud about his movements, she nodded her head slowly. "Okay, I'll do it, but Sally's a bit of a dark horse lately and she doesn't tell me everything, she hides shit from me."

Jud tapped his fingers on the table slowly and looked at her, the corners of his mouth started to rise. "Right, you better kiss me then. I swear to you now Dawn, if you ever do anything like this again, I'll personally put you six foot under. Do you hear me?" Dawn was smiling, she'd won him over. This was easier than she first thought. They shared a kiss. As Jud snuggled up to her across the table he was watching the inmates near him with a close eye. Jud was such a needy person. Any other man would have carted her and had nothing more to do with her, he was weak and vulnerable, a desperate prick with no pride. Love makes people do silly things, real silly things which they later regret. Dawn and Jud were back together.

A little later, Gemma stood outside the prison waiting for Dawn. She was bouncing about on the spot trying to keep warm, rubbing at her scrawny arms. The weather was still bad and the wind was picking up. Gemma's son was in his trolley and a ripped plastic sheet was all that was protecting him from the rain outside. He looked cold, the poor bugger. He was shivering. No hat, no gloves just a small grey cotton jacket to keep him warm. His lips were purple. Dawn walked out of the prison doors and Gemma whistled her from the other side of the road. She was stood under a small shelter outside an old shop in the distance. Dawn quickly scouted around the area and made her way towards her. Gemma was buzzing about like a bumble bee. "I told you it was easy didn't I? Right, what do you want taking in and when?"

Dawn had her instructions from Jud. There was no way he was taking a chance getting the drugs inside the prison himself, he was sending one of his wingmen out for them. "Give me your phone number and I'll sort it out with you. I'm not sure yet which day the visit is on but I know there is plenty of work for you."

Gemma was made up, she bent down and shook her son's leg that was sticking out of the pram. It was soaking wet. "Did you hear that kid, your mam's got a job? You can have that train set you've been going on about now," Gemma dropped her eyes low. "Ay, I know this might seem a bit cheeky, but," she paused and took a deep breath. "Can I have a sub off you until I do the first drop? I'm on my arse. I swear to you now, I won't let you down. I just need some money to get me and him something to eat tonight, he's starving." Gemma made sure Dawn could see her son's face in the pram. She'd been begging before in the past and knew what pulled at people's heart strings. She was doing a great job.

Dawn opened her handbag and searched for her purse. Gemma was at her side and she licked her lips slowly as she watched the woman peel off a twenty pound note from the bundle of cash she had inside her purse. "You better not be having me over Gemma, because," she snarled. "I might look like a nobhead who knows fuck all, but trust me I'm on the ball when it comes down to people having me over."

Gemma held the side of the twenty pound note and giggled. "Nar, I'm not like that. I'll tell you what, let me write my address on that piece of paper too, then it will give you peace of mind." Dawn made sure Gemma gave her the details she needed. She'd met her sort before and knew she would sell her own child when she was roasting for some drugs. Dawn said goodbye and watched her new friend walk off in the distance. She screwed her face up as she clocked the back of Gemma's tracksuit bottoms, they were heavily stained and she looked like she'd shit her knickers. That poor kid though, what a life he must be living, such a shame. Dawn watched them leave him sitting in the pram and her heart melted for him. Life had not been kind to him.

Dawn walked slowly away from the prison and she seemed to be relaxing. Jud had passed the buck to her now and it was up to her to bring his empire back up to where it was before. It was going to be hard but she knew she had to do it. Jud wanted Danny Morgan bringing down too, she could do that with her eyes closed. This was going to be like taking candy from a baby. Dawn chewed on her lips as she flagged a taxi down on the main road, her mind was doing overtime. Not only was she going to bring Danny down, she was going to bring Sally down too. She was sick to the back teeth of hearing about her new special boyfriend and how well he treated her. Dawn didn't believe this for one minute. The guy was a player, a womaniser. Dawn inhaled deeply and stood tall. She was back on the scene now, back inside the circle of trust. This was her time now. Heads were going to roll.

CHAPTER TWELVE

DAWN CHECKED HER WATCH again. Sally should have been here over half an hour ago. She was late, what the hell was she playing at? She knew Dawn hated waiting about for her, she must have been doing it on purpose to wind her up. Stepping to the front door Dawn opened it and stretched her neck out along the street. There was still no sign of her. Walking down the garden path she scanned the area, she could see a silver car pulling up near to where she was stood. The music was pumping from inside the car, a deep bass booming from inside. Dawn dropped her head and she could see it was Sally.

Opening the garden gate she made sure her low-cut lacy red top was in place. You could see the top of her breasts, just enough to give Danny an eye full, to tease him. Dawn was a flirt at the best of times and she didn't even care this was her best friend's man, he was fair game. Sally was still talking to Danny as Dawn opened the passenger door. Sally was surprised to see her and she seemed eager to get out of the car. Dawn was blocking her exit. She made conversation straight away. There were no flies on her, she knew what she had to do and wasted no time in doing it. Dawn fluttered her eyelashes and licked her lips slowly. "Hi Danny, I hope you're taking good care of my friend here?"

Danny was gobsmacked, Dawn very rarely spoke

to him and he was on his guard with her. She was after something for sure, she didn't chit chat with anyone unless she wanted something. He replied to her cautiously. This woman was dangerous, very dangerous. With his hands still on the steering wheel he chuckled. "I always look after my women Dawn, you know that, especially the good-looking ones anyway."

Sally nudged Danny in the waist and raised a smile. She was watching Dawn's every move. "It's all good then is it?" Dawn replied. Sally got out of the car; she was eager to leave. She knew Dawn was flirting with her man and she was ready to put a stop to it before it got any further. Sally had to make light of the matter, not to show how insecure she was.

Sally giggled as she spoke to her but there was many a true word said in jest, she was warning her away. "Ay, he's my man Dawn so step away from him and find one of your own, this one's taken." Sally reached back into the car and kissed Danny on his cheek. He kept one eye on Dawn as he kissed Sally, he was definitely interested, he couldn't take his eyes off her. This would be the icing on his cake for him, to steal Jud's empire and take his woman too. This would be the dog's bollocks, a good old kick in the teeth for Jud Watson.

Sally closed the car door and waited until Danny turned the engine over. Once he pulled away she poked her finger towards Dawn's face, she was making sure she knew exactly what she was saying. There was no going around the houses here, she was telling her straight. "Ay, don't you be starting making moves on my man. He's mine do you hear me, mine?" Dawn started to walk back her into the house and didn't reply. Oh, she was a cocky cow but she knew if she put her mind to it she could have any man she wanted, even Danny Morgan. Sally was in a mood, scared to death that her happy ending could be snatched away from her at any time.

They entered the house together. The living room was a shit tip as usual. Housework was a foreign word to Dawn's mother, she very rarely cleaned up. Of course she tickled round the place but it never looked clean, it was just shit piled on top of shit. Maureen was lay on the sofa and she was still in her nightie, curled up in a ball. She didn't look too well. Her eyes were heavy and her chest was rattling as she breathed. "Dawn, will you do me a Lemsip or something love. I'm dying here. I've got the lurgy."

Dawn plonked down on the sofa and sighed. "Well, you didn't have the lurgy last night when you had that guy back in your bedroom. And don't think I didn't hear you either. Screaming at the top of her voice she was Sally, like a dirty slut."

Sally was giggling. Maureen was in a class of her own, she never answered to anyone. Life was for living and she was certainly making the most of it. "I'll do you a drink Mo, you just lie down there and rest. I know what it feels like when you've had a great night of sex, you just need some rest." Sally sniggered, aware that Dawn was listening.

Mo was coughing and spluttering, she was trying to get her words out. "Oh Sally, my legs haven't been bent up like that for years. He was a wonderful leg-over, he made me melt at the knees. Ay, it was someone you know too, Dawn. They all want a piece of me these young ones do."

"Mother, you're a dirt bag," Dawn hissed. "Just turn it in will you. You're disgusting you are, a bleeding disgrace. Sally doesn't want to know anything about your seedy sex life so keep it shut. I'm sick to death of you."

Maureen rolled on her side and waved her hand in the air. "Oh, live a little, you miserable cow. What's so wrong with someone shaking my bones every now and then? I still have needs you know, I'm a passionate woman."

Dawn growled at her and sat back on the chair. She was pissing in the wind with her, she just never listened. Sally returned with a hot drink for Maureen. "Here, you filthy minx, get that down your neck, it should sort you out. I can do you a warm whiskey later on too, that always helps. It will sweat that cold out of you."

Sally sat down next to Mo and pulled the cushion on top of her lap. It gave her some comfort as she sat twisting the corner of it. Sally was agitated and she couldn't wait to air her views. Why should she hold it in and stew on it when it was doing her head in? Taking a deep breath she sat up straight. "Dawn, why are you interested in Danny Morgan all of a sudden. It doesn't make any sense? For months I've been with him and you've never once even attempted to make conversation with him or anything. Come on, what you playing at. I know you of old and I know you're up to something?"

Dawn played it cool, she popped a cigarette out of her packet and placed it into her mouth. She knew what she was doing and loved that Sally's back was up. This was just a taste of things to come. She sat twisting her hair looking at the TV. "I'm not interested in him, Sally.

I just thought it was time I met him properly. Don't tell me you're getting all paranoid about him? For crying out loud. I'd never touch your man. We're friends aren't we?"

Sally looked at Dawn and hesitated; she was going to say something but stopped at the last minute. Maureen chirped into the conversation. She wiped her nose on the corner of her sleeve and rolled on her side to get a better view. "I know you're my daughter, but come on Dawn, even I wouldn't trust you as far as I could throw you. In fact, Sally, what was that boy called at high school, the one you fancied for years and our Dawn ended up nicking him off you? You remember, the one you cried about for months."

Dawn snapped, Maureen was always against her, she never had her back. She always stuck up for her opponent? "Kevin Jacobs fancied me not Sally mother, so go on, what do you have to say about that? He was never her boyfriend in the first place."

Maureen rolled her eyes and blew a laboured breath. "Oh, come on Dawn, you knew Sally was smitten for him, you wasn't interested in him until you found out his dad owned a gym. I mean, she cried for months about him, didn't you Sally, wasn't you heartbroken?"

Sally was holding her own and she wasn't afraid to voice her opinion. Maureen was right though. She did love Kevin and Dawn had nicked him from right underneath her nose. "Yeah Dawn, your mam is bleeding right. You knew I liked him. It's like Mo just said, you thought he had a few quid and you was all over him like a rash thinking you could get some money from him," she snarled over at her and looked over at Maureen for her support. "Some thing's never change do they?"

Dawn chuckled and held her head back. There was no way she was biting, she was as cool as a cucumber and got ready to bring her friend back down a peg or two. "Listen Sally, was I or was I not the prettiest girl in the school? All the lads wanted a piece of me. Why would Kevin have picked you over me? Come on, think about it. You was just an average looking girl, he wanted a good-looker, that's why he picked me." Wow, what a low blow this was. Dawn wasn't arsed one little bit about hurting anyone's feelings. These girls were supposed to be best friends.

Sally clenched her teeth tightly, there was no way she was backing down. Who did this tart think she was anyway? Sally sat forward in her seat, she was ready to pounce, she'd scratch her eyeballs out if she needed to. "You were just an easy ride love. If we're airing our dirty washing here in front of your mam, then let's tell it how it really was," she opened her eyes wide and continued. "I'm sorry Mo, but she's winding me up and I'm not having it anymore. Dawn, you'd get your knickers off for anyone who had a few quid. Whereas I was a good girl, and valued my body."

Maureen sat up and shot a look at her daughter. She knew when she was younger she was having a lot of boyfriends but she never thought for one minute she was dropping her drawers for them all. Dawn blew thick grey smoke from the corner of her mouth and kicked her feet out in front of her. "Kevin made a play for me, it wasn't the other way around and as for having sex with him," she giggled and looked at her mother. "He didn't have it in him. Don't get me wrong, we did try, but he just couldn't get it up. You know what that's like don't you mother? Surely, most of the men you sleep with have had the same problem?"

Maureen was furious, she picked her cup up and she was going to launch it across the room at her. Dawn made her blood boil and she was ready to snap. "Well, you cheeky cow. As a matter of fact it's never happened to me. The men I sleep with never get brewer's droop. I'm a sexy woman, ask anyone of them. I'm a good bleeding lover. I'm like a porn star when I get in that bedroom. Anything goes, I'm not like you, misery guts."

The gloves were off and Dawn was on the wind-up, she was watching Sally from the corner of her eye. "So Sally, just say it how it is, am I not allowed to talk to Danny anymore because you're jealous of me?"

Sally was thinking, there was no way she wanted to admit that she was envious of her friend. If Danny ever thought for one minute that she was a green-eyed monster he would have kicked her to the kerb. He'd told her in the past that he hated jealous women, there was no way she was being branded one of them. Sally hunched her shoulders and folded her arms tightly in front of her. "No, you can talk to him whenever you want. It's no skin off my nose, but, remember, he's my man, not yours. Just remember the rules and we'll be okay."

Maureen was still annoyed and she wanted to get her own back. No one was talking to her like that, nobody, not even her daughter. "Rules Sally," she sighed and pointed her finger over at Dawn. "This is the woman who's just been caught sleeping with her boyfriend's brother;

she's not to be trusted. Dawn," she paused and swigged a mouthful of her drink. "I know I gave birth to you and you're my daughter but as far as men are concerned, you're ruthless. Sally, you just keep a close eye on her. I wouldn't trust her as far as I could throw her. Snidey she is, a fucking dark horse."

Dawn held a cocky look on her face. She'd won the argument today with her mother and that was enough for her, she ignored her last comment and carried on talking to Sally. "I will stick with the rules Sally don't you worry about that. So, let's go out for a meal or something then. If Danny's here for the long haul I should be getting to know him better. We can be mates can't we?"

Sally cracked her knuckles, she'd been backed into a corner and she had to agree. Dawn was a cunning cow and always had an answer for everything, a smart-arse she was. "Yeah, I'll sort it out, but, what about Jud. I thought he hated Danny?"

"You just leave Jud to me. I'll have a word with him," Dawn chuckled.

Maureen was confused. "So, I take it Jud's had you back then? Fuck me, has that man got no shame? He must be tapped in the bleeding head if he ever thinks you'll change. You've had more nob-ends than weekends. In fact, you've had more pricks than a second-hand dart board."

Dawn flicked her hair over her shoulder, she was used to her mother's snide remarks and just brushed her last comment off. "Mother, do me a favour ay and fuck off. You're bugging me now."

Maureen rolled back onto the sofa and pulled her legs

up to her chest, she was shivering and you could see she wasn't well. There were small droplets of sweat forming on her forehead and her nose was dribbling constantly. It never stopped Maureen talking though; she was a right gasbag.

Dawn tried to make light of the matter. She was sick of arguing now, she just wanted a bit of peace and quiet. "Come on then Sally, let's go out for a few drinks down to the pub, it's been ages since we've been out together. You know you love me really."

Sally was hesitant; she knew Danny would be in there now and she hated that her best friend would be all over him. How was she going to stop her? What chance did she stand against someone like Dawn? Maureen was coughing. When she finally got her breath back she looked at them both before they left. "Tell the neighbours to start doing a collection for the flowers for my funeral. I swear to you, I'm going to kick the bucket. It's touch and go if I make it through the night. Death is not far from me I can tell you."

Dawn closed the living room door behind her as she left. She shouted back at her mother in a sarcastic voice. "I'm sure you'll survive mother. You're a tough old cookie and I don't even think God is ready for you yet." Maureen was left groaning on the sofa. She was alone.

★

Mary Watson was sat at the kitchen table when she heard the letterbox rapping at speed. Whoever it was, they were eager for her to answer. Standing to her feet she headed to the hallway in a rush. There was a shadow at the door and it looked like a woman, she could see her face squashed up against the glass panel. Mary stood with one hand on the doorframe as she opened the front door and stared at Michelle Buckley. This woman had been hounding her for weeks now trying to get to see Larry. She was a stalker and never got the message that her son wanted nothing to do with her, she actually knocked him sick. Mary shook her head and sighed. This wasn't going to be easy, Michelle just wasn't getting the message, she was thick as two short planks. Mary treated her with kid gloves trying not to hurt her feelings. "Michelle, it's a waste of time coming around here love. I've spoken with Larry and he won't even speak to you. In fact, he said you're a head the ball who needs locking up behind bars."

Mary sucked hard on her gums, there was no other way to do this, she had to tell her like it was. Michelle looked different today, thinner in the face, fresh looking, glowing even. She was dressed smartly and she'd changed her hair style. Touching the side of Larry's mothers arm she spoke in a timid voice. "Mary, I just want a quick word with him, it won't take long. Once I've spoken to him, I'll leave him be. I swear to you. I'll never come here again."

Mary was alone in the house and if the truth was known she could have done with some company, even if it was from Michelle Buckley. She brought her inside the house for a chinwag. Mary had just got back from shopping and she had to tell someone her news. It was two for one on packets of bacon at the supermarket and she just had to tell someone about her bargain. "Right, you can come in for a bit and wait for him, but you know what our Larry is like. He'll just see his arse when he sees you and kick you right out, you've been warned." Mary was regretting letting her inside now and made sure she knew her son wanted nothing to do with her. "He won't listen to you Michelle, you're pissing in the wind if you ask me. Whatever you've done to him in the past, he's not happy with." Michelle rubbed at her arms, she couldn't look Mary in the eye and she followed her into the front room. "I was just going to put the kettle on if you fancy a brew love?"

Michelle nodded her head slowly. "Please Mary if you can. Can you put me an extra sugar in it too I'm feeling quite weak today for some reason."

Mary flicked the switch for the kettle and came back into the front room. She plonked down on the chair next to Michelle. She was a weird looking woman and Mary was finding it hard to believe that her son had ever loved this fat lump. "Has Larry mentioned me?" Michelle asked. Surely he must have been missing her like she was missing him.

Mary was trying to hold a straight face, of course her son had mentioned her but not in the way Michelle was thinking. He'd called her a 'fat psycho bitch who needed sectioning', but Mary kept that to herself. There was no way she could tell her that, no way in this world, she lied. "No love, to tell you the truth he's had a lot on his plate lately. After getting out of the hospital he's had a lot to deal with. I mean, our Jud is still locked up in jail and God only knows what he's planning when he gets out. It's far from over this trouble; it will be World War Three when our Jud gets out of prison. I'm thinking of running away, my heart can't deal with all the stress. I swear to you, I'm getting palpations just thinking about it."

Michelle played with the cuff of her jumper. "Does he know who grassed him up yet?"

Mary folded her arms out in front of her and snarled. "No, but when he does, God help them. I mean, people should keep their noses out of other people's business. This was a family matter that should have been dealt with behind closed doors not in bleeding public for everyone to see. Nosey bastards they are, just damn right nosey. And, when I find out who it is, God bleeding help them."

At that moment the door swung open and in walked Sean. This man was definitely gay, even the way he was dressed suggested he was batting for the other side. He was dressed in a tight lemon top and a pair of white chinos. Michelle noticed that he was covering something up on his arm too, it looked like a tattoo. Michelle stood up and grabbed at his arm. "Orr, have you had a tattoo done? Let's have a look then. I've always wanted one but I'm too scared. I would probably faint as soon as I saw the needle."

Sean pushed her out of the way, you could see he was distressed. What a big mouth she had, he was trying to keep this a secret. Mary was on it now and she was eager to see it too. She gripped his arm sinking her fingers deep into his flesh. "It's just a tattoo mother, nothing special, just fuck off will you and leave me alone."

Sean was edgy and grabbed his jumper from the side. He had to change the subject and fast. "Why's she here anyway mother, you know how Larry feels about her. He'll go sick if she's here when he gets home."

Michelle snarled at him, how dare he speak about her as if she wasn't there, the little rat. She stood up and reminded him with her eyes who he was actually speaking to. Michelle's brothers were well-known in the area and the Watson family often put business their way. In her own right this woman was part of the crime scene in the area. She never told anyone about it though, she was cunning and kept a low profile at all times. Michelle nodded her head at him slowly, he was getting told now. "We all know how Larry feels about me Sean, so just keep your opinion to yourself. Are you forgetting the nights I sat around his bedside nursing him back to health? I can't remember you being sat there, can you Sean?"

She'd shut him right up; he was lost for words. She was right though, he was nowhere to be seen when Larry was on his death bed. He couldn't look at her now. Grabbing a sports bag from the corner of the room his words were few. "Mam, I've got to go and drop this money off at the pub. I should have done it last night but it slipped my mind. If anyone asks you, say I went last night." He was pacing around the kitchen with haste. "I'll be back in an hour or so, so put me some tea out Mam. Are we having steak tonight?"

Mary stood proud and shook her head. "No we're on bacon and eggs for tea. It's back bacon too, bloody lovely it is. It was two for one at the superstore."

Sean raised his eyes, she was so easily pleased and she definitely needed to get a life. Michelle watched Sean with cunning eyes. She grabbed her coat from the back of the chair and stood with her arms folded tightly in front of her. Something was wrong with her, she was edgy. "Mary, I'm going to get going too. Sean's right, if Larry wants me, he knows where I am. I'm just banging my head against a brick wall trying to talk to him aren't I?" Mary didn't answer, she wanted a quiet life and she wasn't fuelling any further conversation. Sean came to his mother's side and pecked her on the cheek. "I won't be long mam, see you soon. Put me an extra egg on my tea. I'm starving." Sean was gone.

Michelle stood looking at Mary waiting for some kind of answer, some kind of help but it never came. Mary led her to the front door with speed. She was making her feel uneasy and something about her sent a chill up her spine. "Hopefully, me and Larry can work things out Mary. I love him with all my heart. If you can, will you have a quiet word with him and try and make him see we're meant to be together, he's my soul mate."

Mary patted her shoulder and watched her walk down the garden path, she let out a laboured breath. "Bloody lunatic! A couple of butties short of a picnic that one is," she whispered under her breath. There was no way she wanted her son anywhere near this woman. She was a crank. Love was a crazy thing and it made people act in some weird ways. Thank God Mary had no man in her life, love hurt too much.

Sean walked up the back alleyway of the pub; he'd parked his car at the end of the street. It was getting dark now and the wind was picking up. Whistling a tune he plodded towards it with a spring in his step. Life was good for him at the moment and he loved that he had no stress like his brothers did. Suddenly Sean froze on the spot, he turned his head quickly. Someone was following him. He could hear gravel crunching behind him. His head turned with speed over his shoulder, he searched the area. Sean couldn't see anyone and thought his mind was playing tricks on him. "Hello, is anyone there," he whispered into the night air. He carried on walking, his steps became slower and you could see fear in his eyes as he took another step forward. A chill passed through his body and the small hairs on the back of his neck stood on end. Sean carried on walking but he never stood a chance, his attacker hit him over the head with a forceful blow from behind and his body crumbled to the floor. Eyes rolling, gasping for breath, he tried to call out for help. "Help me, somebody help me," he muttered with his final breath. The grip around the sports bag was loosened and his attacker peeled his fingers from the bag.

"I think this belongs to me," they said in cold chilling words. The attacker was dressed in black and their identity was hidden. Sean lay staring into space, thick red blood dribbled down the side of his head and his body was shaking, he was in shock and he didn't look like he had long left. Sean tried to get his mobile phone from his pocket, but he was too weak. With one last desperate breath he stopped moving. His eyes were wide open but his body was lifeless. Footsteps running off in the distance could be heard, branches crunching, rapid breathing. The attacker was quickly off on their toes.

★

Dawn and Sally walked into the pub. All eyes were on Dawn, nobody had seen her since her affair had been uncovered. And so what, she didn't have to answer to any of these people. This was her business and nobody else's. Dawn held her head high; she wasn't bothered what anybody thought about her, she could handle anything they had to say. So what if people sneered at her, she was big enough to take it.

Larry was in tonight and as soon as he saw Dawn his heart was in his mouth. This was his woman, his heart's desire. He never wasted a second. He jumped to his feet. He was as cocky as ever and ready to put his stamp on her. How could she refuse him? He knew she still wanted him; she could never resist his charms. Larry went straight up to her and pinched her arse cheeks from behind. He had no shame, none whatsoever. A few of the men stood watching him and you could see them shaking their heads in the background. Did this man ever learn? Larry bent his mouth low and whispered into her ear. His hot breath tickling her earlobe. "Well, hello there sexy. I bet you never thought you'd see me again did you?"

Dawn was suffocating, she went white in the face and she was struggling to talk, she licked her lips rapidly. This was a nightmare and she wasn't prepared for it, he'd taken her by surprise. Sally smirked; this was going to be fun to watch. She stood back and enjoyed every minute of it. "Larry, I thought you were still in hospital."

Larry stopped her dead in her tracks. He placed a single finger on her wet lips. "You thought wrong then didn't you? I've told you before that Jud doesn't scare me. And what," he chuckled, "he put me in hospital for a few weeks. I'm still standing aren't I and when he's out of nick we can sort this out properly can't we. You know, man to man. A one on one." Larry was full of himself trying to make out he wasn't afraid of anything. Jud was going to rip his head off and he knew it. What the hell was he playing at thinking he could tackle Jud, he needed to give his head a shake? He flicked Dawn's hair from her shoulder and sank his warm lips into the nape of her neck, she moved away quickly.

People were watching and she was scared it would get back to Jud. His kiss was warm and her heart was pounding, she'd missed him, she'd missed his firm hands caressing her body. What the hell was she going to do now, her head was in bits. Just the thought of him inside her made her lose all control of her body, she had to calm down. She needed to clear her head. "Just fuck off Larry. You nearly ruined my life once. Why the hell you felt the need to fuck my wedding day up is beyond me. I'm done with you; now, get out of my face. I'm having nothing to do with you."

She pushed him away knowing all eyes were on her. Larry sniggered and went nose to nose with her inhaling her feminine fragrance, sweet fresh aromas. He wanted her, he needed her. "Come on Dawn, you know you can't resist me. I'm like a drug and you're addicted. Go on admit it, you've missed me, just like I've missed you."

Dawn smiled and tried to keep her cool but her heart was in her mouth. People were listening now and she had to make sure she gave him the message. Jud's spies were out in full and one wrong move would put her in danger. "Just leave me alone Larry, you're more trouble than your worth, plus, from what I've heard you and Michelle Buckley have been carrying on for months. So, sling your hook and go back to her. The cheek of you thinking you can come crawling back to me after having it stuck up her."

Larry clenched his teeth tightly together. He pulled her closer and snarled. "I don't know why she's even saying stuff like that, she's a crank and if she carries on chatting shit about me she's going to be dealt with. I mean it Dawn, me with Michelle Buckley, give me a break, ay. She's a minger, a rotten arse."

From the shadows Michelle heard every word. Her lips trembled and she held back against the wall. What a shame it was for her, her heart was ripped apart, she was gutted. A single tear rolled down her cheek and landed on her lip. She was snivelling. "I'll show you Larry Watson, you bastard. Just you wait and see. I give you my heart and this is the way you think you can treat me. I'll show you, I'll show you all," she growled. Michelle looked lovely too, she'd really made the effort tonight in the hope that Larry would see her and fall head over heels in love with her. Necking the last bit of her wine she left the pub.

Larry stood at the bar and whispered something into Dawn's ear. He smiled at her and left the pub too. Sally nudged Dawn in the waist and grabbed her closer by the arm. "Don't tell me you're even thinking about going near that prick again. I can see it in your eyes Dawn; don't be fooled by him, just stay well away. He's big trouble. Dawn, are you listening to me or what?"

Danny Morgan came over to meet the girls, he looked flustered. "Did you miss me?" he sniggered to Sally as he pecked her on the cheek. His eyes shot to Dawn and he looked at her a bit longer than necessary. "Great to see you back on the scene, Dawn. No point in hiding away is there. What's done is done. How's Jud anyway?"

Dawn was flirting and she wasn't hiding the fact either. Her eyelashes fluttered and she was constantly licking at her lips. "He's doing well Danny. He's up for bail next week so hopefully he can get back on his feet when he's home and sort this load of shit out. It's just a witness the police have got that's keeping him in there; some bastard has grassed him up. Without that statement he would still be on the streets."

Sally hugged Danny and made sure she had his full attention, she was out to prove he was her man and if this woman was trying to step on her toes, she would have to fight her first. Danny led the girls to a table not far from the entrance, he liked sitting there, he wanted to see everyone who came and went. He was always prepared for any trouble coming his way. Spencer walked inside the pub. He nodded his head at his sister and shot Sally a quick look, he smirked at her and headed to the bar. Police sirens could be heard outside and after a few seconds Danny went outside to see what was going on for himself. People were running in and out of the pub in a state, something was definitely going down. Danny walked outside and scanned the area. It was probably a fight taking place. Probably two women who'd had too much to drink. The dibble were all over the show. They were holding the crowd of people back and talking to some members of the public. Paul Watson was running about like a headless chicken and he was white. Danny edged closer to the crowd that had formed and he listened closely to them speaking.

A woman in her mid- thirties was distraught and her

heart was in her mouth as she spoke to the police officer. She was pissed and her words were slurred. "I was just having a piss over there officer," her finger pointed to the corner at the back of the pub. "I was stood waiting for a taxi and I was bursting for a wee. I've done it before and lots of us have a quick piss outside when we're drunk don't we girls?"

The officer was serious and he was urging her to continue. He wasn't interested in her fouling the streets, he wanted to know more about what she'd seen. "So what happened next," he asked in a stern tone.

The woman held her head in her hands and she was weeping. "Well, my knickers were around my ankles and I just saw him from the corner of my eye. At first I thought I was just imagining it. I've drank about eight straight Vodkas so I ignored it at first and plus the lighting wasn't that good. I was unsure of what I thought I saw at first."

The woman's friend could see she was on the verge of collapsing and she came to her side offering her some support. "Come on love, just take your time."

The witness started blubbering and she held her hands tightly on her knees, knuckles turning white. She looked up at her friend and shook her head slowly. "Mags, on my life, his head was mashed in and his face was covered in blood. I thought it was a mannequin at first but as I came closer to it I knew it was a man's body. I nearly shit my knickers I can tell you. My fella won't believe this when I tell him I was the one who found the body. Is the man dead, officer?" The policeman finished writing her statement down and asked the woman for her contact details. She repeated her question. "Is he dead or what?"

"I don't know anything yet Miss, but it's not looking good."

Paul Watson ran outside, he was retching at the side of the parked cars. "It's our Sean," he screamed at the top of his voice. "Some bastard has done my brother in. They've found his car at the back of the pub."

Danny Morgan zipped his coat back up and went back inside the pub. This was some heavy shit that he wanted no part of. As he walked back inside the pub he could see Larry sprinting outside followed closely by some of the other men. It was true, Sean Watson had been murdered.

Mary Watson sucked hard on her cigarette. She was grey and tears were rolling down her cheeks. "Why Sean? He's harmless, he never hurt anyone in his life, such a caring man he was. He would never have hurt a fly. How can I go on living without him?" Mary was out of her mind, she kept sobbing and shouting trying to find out the answers, she needed to calm her tormented mind. "I want Jud home, get on to the bleeding prison and tell them he has to come home. He'll sort this mess out, he'll find out who murdered his brother."

Larry poured another glass of whisky and slowly rubbed the edge of his finger around the top of the glass. "There's something bad going on here mother. Someone's out to ruin this family and once I find out who it is then I won't be held responsible for my actions."

Mary snapped and sprang to her feet. "It's your bleeding fault this is. If you wouldn't have been shagging that tart Dawn, our Jud would have been here with me and none of this would ever have happened. It's your fault. I'll never forgive you for this Larry, ever." Mary held her body tightly. "My son, my poor son. Sean, I want my son back," she screamed. Larry kept his head low; he knew his mother was right. He was speechless. Slurping at his drink he watched. Paul sat down near him. The family was devastated and he knew they needed to do something about it and fast. "It must be the Morgan's. I think it's time to pay them a visit. I mean a proper visit this time, not just a chat if you get my meaning?

Larry raised his eyebrows high and shot a look over to his brother. "Paul, get the lads together as soon as possible. Let's show these cunts what we're really about."

Mary was howling in pain, her heart was smashed into a thousand pieces. She ragged her fingers through her hair. "Oh, and you think that will bring your brother back, do you, you daft bastards. My son's dead and all you want is revenge. I want my Sean back, that's all I want. Bring him back please; tell me this is not happening. God, bring my boy back," she pleaded.

Paul helped his mother up from her knees; she was a dead weight, her body was folded in two. She was in a bad way. "Mam, come on, take a few tablets and go for a sleep. We've got to do what we need to do. I'll go and get Elsie from next door to sit with you. I don't want to leave you on your own when you're like this."

Mary retaliated and grabbed her son back by his hair, she dug her fingers deep into his neck. "I don't need anyone to bleeding sit with me, I'm not ill. I'm heartbroken here. Nobody is ever going to take this pain away from me. Larry, you need to sort this out, it's your mess, so you go and find them bastards and avenge my son's death." Mary spoke some strong words; she meant every one of them. She was so mixed up. One minute she wanted peace in her family and the next she wanted the world to pay for her youngest son's death. She sat at the table and watched as her boys got ready to leave.

Before they left Paul came to his mother's side and placed his hand on the top of her head. "Mam, it will be sorted, don't worry. The bastards are going down. Every fucking single one of them."

Larry bent down to kiss his mother too but she turned her head away from him and muttered under her breath. "Fuck off away from me, it's you who's done this, you and that slut Dawn."

Larry growled and left the room in a hurry. There was a cold chill in the air and it passed straight through Mary's body. She looked up to the ceiling and her face drained of any colour her voice was low. She whispered as she clutched the tea towel in her hands. "Sean, is that you son, have you come to see me? Sean is that you? Please speak to me, please tell me you're alright?" Mary kept her eyes up towards the ceiling, no one answered her, no one ever would. Sean Watson was dead.

★

Danny Morgan lay in the bed next to Sally. He was wide awake and hadn't slept a wink all night, tossing and turning, he had hot sweats, he was troubled. Dawn and Sally had argued last night and whatever went on between them, Sally was still upset about it. Danny rolled on his side and kissed Sally on the back of her neck. She shivered and sank her head deep into the pillow. Danny whispered into her ear. "Do you fancy a quick leg-over before I have to go out? I'm meeting the lads in an hour so it would only be a jerk and a squirt?"

Sally turned over to face him, she looked so in love. "Oh, what's happened to making love to me ay, that's soon gone out of the window hasn't it. What happened to lovemaking?"

Danny chuckled and pulled her closer to his chest. "You know what I mean, stop being a smacked arse. I make love to you all the time. Sometimes it's nice to just have a quick bang."

Sally stroked her finger across his bottom lip and smirked. "I love a good old bang too, but promise me we can make love later tonight?"

Danny dived on her and pinned her down holding her arms above her head, he was nibbling at her breast and you could see by her erect nipples that she was already aroused. Danny was inside her and by his movements you could see he wasn't going to be long, his thrusts were hard and fast, like a fiddler's elbow. Sally was groaning underneath him, lost in the moment. Danny ejaculated quickly and he fell onto the side of the bed with a smile on his face. He was right, it was quick. What a let-down this was. "That was just what the doctor ordered that was, cheers Sally."

She was trying to regain her breath, she was upset at the way he was talking to her, you could tell by her sour expression. Danny jumped up out of the bed and started to get ready. There was no kiss, nothing. He just disregarded her like a toy that he no longer wanted to play with. Sally lay on her front gawping at him, trying to work out why he'd changed, was he losing interest in her already? His body was fit, every inch of him was muscle, lean and firm. She watched him pampering himself in the mirror and commented on how many products he used on his face, he really did care about his appearance. He had every face cream under the sun. "Danny, you're so feminine you are, look at all the lotions and potions you're putting on your face, even I don't use that much."

Danny was blushing; he dipped his finger in the thick white cream and dabbed it to his cheeks. "Ay, there is nothing wrong with looking after yourself. Loads of men do it. What's wrong with caring about the way you look?" Danny paused and he stared at himself in the mirror for longer than necessary. He stood thinking and shook his head slowly. "Poor Sean Watson. I wonder what callous bastard done that to him, the guy was harmless. He just kept himself to himself and never bothered anyone did he?"

Sally sat up in the bed and tucked the duvet under her chin. "It's scary isn't it? I mean, a murderer is walking about out there. Probably looking for their next victim. I hope the police catch the bastard and bang them away in jail for life."

Danny zipped his jeans up and pulled his black t-shirt over his head. Once his trainers were on he grabbed his car keys from the side of the bedside cabinet. "Right, lock up when you're leaving and I'll see you later." Sally kissed Danny and tried to pull him back on the bed, but he wasn't having any of it. "See you later babes," he shouted as he left. Sally was alone and bored, stretching over the side of the bed she opened one of the drawers. Her eyes dipped low as she examined things further. The drawer was filled with old letters and other oddments. A silver ring caught her eye, it looked expensive. As she examined, she tried to read the words engraved on it. "Me and you forever, love S".

Sally dropped the ring back inside the drawer as if it carried some kind of disease. She lay back on the bed staring into space. Surely it was from an old girlfriend or something; she was just being paranoid, and insecure. He wouldn't cheat on her would he? No way, he loved her and she believed him. Lying alone in the bed her mind was doing overtime, something just didn't feel right, a gut instinct, call it. Sally looked at her mobile phone at the side of the bed. She was in two minds if she was going to make a call to Dawn and mend their friendship. Picking her mobile phone up she found her number in the contact list and just stared at the name. Dawn had been a right cow last night and Sally told her straight that she was a self-centred bitch who was lucky to have any friends at all. Sean Watson was dead and all she cared about was how she was getting home. Harsh words had been spoken between them and now that the dust had settled Sally was regretting what she'd said. She sat tapping her fingers on her front teeth and finally decided to make the first move. She wasn't stubborn and she hated falling out with people. "Hello Dawn, it's me Sally, where are you? I think we both need to apologise for last night. We were pissed and both of us were out of order, what do you think?"

Sally listened closely, she could hear a man laughing

in the background, she gritted her teeth together and shouted down the phone. "Dawn, are you listening to me or what? Dawn," she screamed. Eventually Dawn answered her. Sally was chomping at the bit and you could see her knuckles turning white as she grabbed her phone tighter. The two girls arranged to meet for lunch at a cafe in the town centre. Once the call was over Sally was white with temper, goose pimples appeared all over her arms and she was rubbing at them with speed. Pacing around the bedroom she bit down hard on her bottom lip. "I bet Danny's with her, yeah that's it. Dawn you slut, let me find out you've been near my Danny and I'll make sure you pay for it. I'll rip your fucking head off." Sally rang Danny's mobile phone, her head was spinning. She just needed peace of mind. The phone rang and rang but there was no answer. Where the hell was he? He always had his phone nearby. Grabbing her clothes from the end of the bed she got ready as fast as she could. She could smell a rat and wanted to see with her own two eyes where her boyfriend really was. She was nobody's fool and she was on a mission.

Danny sat in the old lock- up with his boys stood around him waiting on his orders. The shutter was down and they were all stood talking. Boxes were piled high all over the place and nearly touching the ceiling. This was like an Aladdin's cave. Danny rubbed his hands together and addressed his men. "Top job guys, this lot is going to sort us all out for sure. It's just what we need to get where we want to be. Tony, you need to be careful who we flog this lot to. I want it all to go together in one hit, not dribbs and drabs we're not a fucking catalogue. I don't want people paying us ten pound here and five pound there. It has to go altogether."

Tony sniggered and agreed. "Don't worry boss I'm on it. This lot will be sold as one big parcel. I know just the man for it too."

Danny paced the floor and tickled the end of his chin with his fingers. "If the Watson's find out it's us who had them over it will be war. Blood will be spilled. We need to be ready for them. Tony, get some shooters from Stiggy down the boozer and make sure we're all carrying one at all times."

Steve who was Danny's wing man let out a laboured breath. He'd been grafting with the lads for some time now and didn't really like their work ethic. Yeah, by all means go and earn a crust but pissing on your own doorstep was something he wasn't happy with. He was an old-timer and in his day you would never double-cross any other grafters in the same area. The saying was true, there was no honour amongst thieves. It was a dog eat dog world and only the brave survived. Jud Watson was a man he'd dealt with in the past and Danny Morgan was underestimating him. He'd seen Jud in action and this man didn't take any prisoners, he was a hard cunt, a ruthless bastard who tortured his victims and he made sure they never messed with him again. Steve chewed on his fingernails and looked at the others; he had to make sure they were all singing from the same hymn sheet. "So, what if Jud gets wind of this, what then, who's going to take the rap for it. You know I wasn't happy having Jud and his boys over. So, it's you Danny who needs to sort it out. We're just the donkeys here, remember that when the time comes."

Danny made a nice neat line of cocaine and snorted it hard up his nostril. Taking a few seconds to feel the rush from the drug he sat with his jaw swinging low. "You just leave that arsehole to me. I can take anything he's got to give me, the fucking old-timer. I'm the new kid on the block and he knows it."

Steve shook his head. This man was talking out of his arse. Yeah, Jud was older than Danny but he was also a lot wiser and he'd shit bigger than Danny Morgan in the past. If it hadn't have been for the money Steve would have walked away from this graft, done one and never got involved. Christmas was just around the corner though and everyone around him was skint, they were all living from hand to mouth, he had no other option than to be involved in this heist. His kids needed presents and by hook or by crook he was going to provide for them. There was no way they were going without, no way in this world. Steve had quietened down over the years and the time he'd spent in the nick had mellowed him. Prison was a thinking place and every hour that passed inmates were planning their life without crime on the outside. It never lasted long though, times were hard on the outside and before long every convict was back to square one. The sniff was passed around by Danny. He loved that he was strong, he felt like a man of steel. He loved that he thought he was untouchable.

Jack Preston rubbed at his arms and looked Danny directly into his eyes. "Fuck me, its shit about Sean Watson isn't it? I wonder who done him in?"

Danny snarled and gripped his knees tightly, his

knuckles turning white. "That bent bastard deserved everything he got. It was only a matter of time before somebody wiped him out anyway. He was a dirty little rat. Did you know he was giving drugs to the young lads in the pub? Yeah, spiking them and taking them home and shoving his dick up their arses? I bet it was one of his victims who did it. You can't blame them really can you?"

Jack sat thinking. What was the big change with Danny all of a sudden? He was good friends with Sean at one time and they were always in some corner whispering to each other. Something wasn't right. Danny searched his pockets as his mobile phone started ringing. It was Sally's name on the screen. Sneering at his phone he displayed the caller's identity to his boys. "See what I mean lads, they get a little piece of me and they're hooked. Fuck off, Sally you stalker," he chuckled as he rammed his phone back into his pocket. The lads ignored him and started to count all the electrical goods they had. You name it they had it; microwaves, flat screen TVs the fucking lot. There was a butty to be made here for sure. A good crust for all those concerned. Steve made a few calls and everything was going to plan, they had a buyer for the lot. The lad's spirits were high and each of them had a smile on their face knowing that they were on a good wedge for this lot.

Just then Ged, Danny's younger brother, came inside the lock- up and he was frantic. He ran straight to Danny's side. "Jud's up for bail tomorrow. I've just seen Simon in the shop down the road and I heard him telling someone. Fuck, fuck, fuck."

Danny held his head high and slowly turned his head. With a clip around the ear he sniggered. "Just chill your beans and stop flapping. This lot is going soon and nobody will be any the wiser. Stick with me Ged and you'll be wearing diamonds. Relax, everything is sorted." Ged rubbed the side of his head. Danny was a right dick-head and sometimes he wished somebody would come along and knock him down a peg or two, he was a right smart-arse and he was getting too big for his boots.

CHAPTER THIRTEEN

JUD WALKED OUT of the courtroom with a big smile fixed firmly on his face, chuffed as fuck he was, what a great result. His solicitor had done well and got him out on bail. Of course this came at a price but sometimes in life you had to pay for what you got. "Well done our kid," Paul said as he shook his brother's hand. "Glad to have you back home." The solicitor walked over to Jud and he let out a laboured breath. He was dressed smart in a grey suit and a white crisp shirt. "You swam the channel there mate. I thought Judge Monley was going to reject your application for bail. He can be a right cunt sometimes."

Jud chuckled and patted the top of his shoulder with a firm hand. "You never let me down do you. Money always talks in places like this doesn't it?"

The solicitor was going beetroot; he licked his lips and rubbed his hot sweaty palms together. He knew he was a bent bastard and hated that he had to do things underhand to make sure he had a better life. He was just the same as everyone else really. He'd do anything to keep his head above water. Jud was right everything did come at a cost. The solicitor kept his voice low and spoke clearly. "Just make sure you stay at your bail address, Jud. You know what these bastards are like if you break your bail conditions, they'll have you back in the slammer before you know what day it is. Just make sure you don't rub the old bill up the wrong way and try and keep a low profile until all this is over. If you go within one step of your brother they'll have you hung drawn and quartered. You know that don't you?"

Jud nodded and Paul was hanging on his every word waiting for him to agree to his bail conditions. "I can't promise that can I, Malc?"

Paul dropped his head; this wasn't what he was wanted to hear. The shit was going to hit the fan and he knew before the week was out Larry would be lying in a ditch somewhere. There was no way Jud would ever let this go. The solicitor said his goodbyes and rushing off to his next court case. His job had been so much easier since the witness had withdrawn their statement. Luck, had been on Jud's side today and someone out there had his back. Jud sniggered, "Malc, keep your mobile near you at all times just in case the rozzers try any funny stuff. You know what they're like, they'll try stitching me up given half the chance."

Malc nodded his head as he started to walk off. "No worries Jud. I'm here if you need me."

Paul and Jud stood alone outside the courtroom. The rest of the firm had wanted to come to court too but Jud told them to stay away. If the judge would have clocked them all sat in the courtroom he would have dismissed his application for bail for sure. Jud's men all looked dodgy as fuck, especially Simon, he was weird looking, with scars all over his head. Jud took a deep breath and headed outside.

Dawn was stood waiting for Jud, she smiled as she saw him, free at last. Paul's face creased and he grabbed his brother back by the arm before he walked any further. "Tell me you're having a laugh? What the fuck is that tramp doing here?"

Jud quickly pushed Paul away and shot him a look. "Just keep your beak out of my business. I know what I'm doing. If you know what's good for you, you'll keep your mouth shut won't you." This was a direct threat; Jud was waiting on an answer. Paul sank his head low and didn't reply. Paul was puzzled. Dawn had slept with his brother and yet he was still with her, was he right in the head or what? He was going soft.

Dawn walked up the few steps to meet Jud, her heels clipped softly along the ground. You would have thought nothing had gone on between them, she was acting like everything was normal. She'd done as he'd asked and made sure the parcels landed for him in the jail, keeping him a happy man. Gemma the drugs mule was another story though; she was becoming a nightmare for Dawn. She was glad Jud was out now so she didn't have to keep seeing her. The girl had no shame; she was constantly dropping her son off at the house for Dawn to babysit him whilst she went out shoplifting. That was all going to stop now, it had to. Jud was home now anyway and she had no further use of her. Gemma was getting told straight. Their friendship was over. Jud kissed the top of Dawn's head as she wrapped her arms tightly around his body. He'd lost weight and he seemed quieter than usual. Here it was, the quiet before the storm.

Jud placed his arm around Paul shoulders. "I want you to get all the team together tonight. Danny Morgan is the first on my to do list. Do you hear me?" Paul stood kicking his foot against the floor, he couldn't look up he was fuming inside and hated the thought of Dawn still being in the picture. "I want to go to the cemetery before I go home too. Did our Sean have a good send off or what?" Jud sighed and his eyes clouded over. The prison wouldn't let him go to his own brother's funeral. They thought it was a plan for an escape and did everything in their power to make sure his application for compassionate leave was denied.

Paul had to speak now and his voice was low as the memory of his brother strangled his heart. "Yeah, loads turned out for it. You would have been proud of us all. He had a great send off." Jud took a deep breath and swallowed hard. Dawn was holding his hand and ready to leave. Paul was unsettling her and she didn't feel safe around him. This guy was gunning for her and she was trying to keep a low profile. As they headed to the car park Michelle Buckley stuck her head out from behind a brick wall close by, she smirked and headed off in the opposite direction.

The heavens opened as Jud walked up to his brother's grave. A blackbird was nearby and it was hopping across the headstones, jumping, chirping. It seemed to be watching Jud as he bent down on one knee at his brother's resting place. Jud was taken aback with emotion, he was alone and he'd told the others to wait in the car. This was his moment with his brother and he wanted to say goodbye his way. The rain fell heavily onto Jud and the flowers at the graveside seemed to be falling apart in front of his eyes. Reading some of the cards attached to the flowers he let out a roar from the pit of his stomach, a deep, loud painful cry, like an injured animal. His hands gripped some earth near him and he squeezed at it with all his might. "Some bastard will pay for this, Sean. You know I will avenge your death, it's just a matter of time." Standing to his feet he looked around the area and he could see a few other people at the graves nearby. Death was so final, so heartbreaking. To know you will never see your loved ones again, to feel that emptiness inside was heartbreaking.

Paul sat in the front seat of the car watching his brother in the distance. He turned his head slightly and spoke to Dawn who was sat in the back. "So you think you've had our Jud over again do you? Trust me you dirty slapper I'm on to you and it's only a matter of time before I uncover you as the dirty slut that you really are. You might have fooled Jud, but there is no way you're having me over."

Dawn sat forward in her seat; confident now knowing Jud would protect her if he tried to lay one finger on her. She gripped the side of his seat and spoke in a cocky tone. "Listen nobhead. Don't you dare speak to me as if I'm just a bit of shit on the bottom of your shoe? I've said I'm sorry to Jud so what the hell has it got to do with you if he's forgiven me or not. We all have secrets don't we Paul?" She held a look at him and licked her lips slowly. "It's such a shame I'm not as quick on dishing the dirt on you isn't it?" Paul grabbed her fingers from the chair and squeezed at them hard. She dragged them away with speed as Jud got back into the car. There was a strained silence.

★

Mary sat at the kitchen table with her arms folded in front of her. She looked like she had the cares of the world on her shoulders. Jud wasn't allowed near her house due to his bail conditions and he'd told her she would have to come to Dawn's house to see him. Oh, she'd kicked off royal, telling her son she would never sit in the same room as that slapper Dawn again but after some serious thought she'd come around to his way of thinking. What other choice did she have? How could Jud come back to her house when Larry would be here like a sitting duck, he would be like a lamb to the slaughter if his brother got his hands on him? Larry walked back into the kitchen and Mary sneered at him, he was worried and he had every reason to be. "You know he's out now don't you?"

Larry turned his head slowly and brushed her comment off. He was playing the big man but you could see the fear in his eyes. "I'm not arsed mother; let him do what he's got to do. If it's a fight to the death he wants then so be it. I'm not bothered anymore. He's a prick and when I see him I'll tell him that to his face."

Mary bolted up from her seat as if boiling water had been poured all over her legs, her face was bright red and she was screaming at the top of her voice. "Now you turn it in, you trouble causing bastard. This stops here, do you hear me? I'm going to speak to Jud soon and hopefully this mess can be sorted out once and for all. For crying out loud you're brothers, bleeding flesh and blood."

Larry froze, he swallowed hard. "He's no brother of mine. Are you forgetting he tried to kill me, what kind of a brother is that ay?"

Mary bit hard on her bottom lip and went nose to nose with him. "The same kind that sticks his dick up his brother's girlfriend," she snarled. Mary was holding nothing back, he was getting told. Larry moved out of her way, he was aware that she could lash out at any moment. She was sneaky like that, she often belted her sons from behind when they least expected it. One minute you could be talking to her and the next she would strike a blow without any warning, she was crafty.

Larry was feeling sorry for himself. "Oh, so it's me who's getting the blame for this then is it? It doesn't matter that the tosser put me in intensive care, does it?"

Mary felt her heart sink low, she loved her sons so much and knew they were both to blame somewhere along the line. Two wrongs don't make a right do they? Sitting back down in her seat she played with her fingers. Since Sean's death her life was empty, she had nothing to live for anymore, she wanted to die. Sean was her only companion and he was the only one of her sons who spent any time with her. They watched TV together, they even baked together, she missed him so much. Her voice was low, desperate, she didn't know what else to do. "Will you please sort this mess out Larry; it's killing me this is. I swear, if this goes on any longer I'll have a bleeding heart attack. The doctor has told me I'm living on borrowed time. My blood pressure is through the roof."

Larry could see how distressed she was and placed a comforting hand on her shoulder, his eyes clouded over. There was no way he was backing down. There was too much at stake. His face creased at the sides as he spoke to his mother. "Mam, we're both grown men, we can sort this out between ourselves. I know I was to blame for sleeping with Dawn, but think about it, I've done him a favour really. He could have married her and then found out what she was like, imagine what would have happened then, at least he never put a ring on her finger did he?"

Mary looked up at him, she just couldn't hold her tongue. "Oh, and I suppose you want to put a ring on her finger do you?"

Larry was taken back and didn't know what to say. He liked having sex with Dawn yeah, but as for wife material he wasn't sure. Mary calmed down and sat eating a chocolate biscuit, she was comfort eating, she always did this when she was upset and recently she had been devouring pallet loads of cakes, crisps, biscuits and anything else that she could get her hands on to ease her aching heart. "I saw Michelle yesterday Larry and she was asking about you."

Larry lifted his head up from the newspaper and his jaw dropped. "Why the fuck is she still on the scene. Mam, I wish you wouldn't talk to her, she's not right in the head and if she carries on hounding me I'll start opening my mouth about how sick and twisted she really is. I mean, come on mam, she told everyone she was my fucking girlfriend when I was at death's door. Imagine if I would have snuffed it, everyone would have thought she was my woman."

Mary gasped her breath, her heart was low and she was sick to death of all the arguing. "She just loves you Larry. Love is a strange thing and its makes people do crazy things, she needs to be treated with kid gloves and let down slowly."

"Mam, she's a nutter. When I was in the hospital she was touching me you know, yeah hands down my pants, messing about with me. I remember everything. She even had sex with me."

Mary covered her mouth with her hand and her eyes were wide open. "Stop lying, that's disturbed that is. No, don't you be saying that about her. Nobody is that sick."

"On my life mam, the dirty cow was messing with me. That's why I snapped at her when it all came back to me." Mary rubbed slowly at her arms, this made her stomach turn over, she felt sick inside. Larry flung his newspaper on the table and grabbed his coat from the side of the chair. "Right, I'm off out. I'll see you later on."

Mary was going to say something but stopped at the last minute. Why waste her breath anyway, nobody listened to her. She missed her husband at times like this; she missed the loving touch of a man. These were her golden years and she should have been relaxed, taking things easy, enjoying the finer things in life, chance would have been a fine thing. Checking the clock on the wall, she shook her head. It was time to go and see Jud. Mary wasn't looking forward to this one little bit and she knew she had to be on her best behaviour once she set foot inside Dawn's house. She wanted to swing for Dawn and scratch her eyeballs out, this was all her fault, and she was going to make sure the hussy got everything that was coming to her. This was her family and she was taking control of it once and for all.

★

Dawn sat next to Jud on the sofa. She dropped her head onto his chest and she was searching for some kind of affection, forgiveness. Jud was distant from her and she knew she had some sucking up to do. Yeah, he'd told her it was all forgotten about but the look in his eyes told her he was lying. Maureen walked into the room and as per usual she was half-cut, she ran at Jud with open arms, she was so over the top. Arse-licking as always. "Son, I'm so glad you're home. I've told Dawn how lucky she is that you've forgiven her and I know she is going to mend her ways. You've been through a lot and I'm just glad it's all over."

Maureen bent over and kissed him on the lips, perhaps a bit longer than she needed to. Dawn gritted her teeth tightly as she watched her. For crying out loud here she was trying her best to forget about everything that had happened and mouth almighty here was bringing it all back up, she was a right shit-stirrer. Jud hugged Maureen. God, this woman stank of ale, her breath was hanging too, death breath. Maureen plonked down on the sofa and she wasn't moving, even though she knew the couple may have wanted a bit of time alone together. "My mam should be here shortly Maureen. I've told her to come here to see me, is that okay with you?"

"Yeah, that's fine. I've not seen Mary for a while we can have a chinwag and a catch up."

Dawn was white, she didn't know about this. "Why is she coming here Jud, you know she will only start on me. I wish you would have told me, at least then I would have been prepared or something."

Maureen pointed her finger at Dawn. She was loving every minute of this. "You have to take it on the chin, Dawn. If it was me and you'd done this to my son I would have kicked you right up the arse and carted you as far as the wind could carry you."

Jud smirked, he loved Maureen's sense of humour. And, for once she was right. Dawn had to eat humble pie no matter how she looked at it. Her face was sour as she pulled away from Jud. This had put a dampener on her day. Jud sat tall and reached over for his cigarettes, he'd been blazing at least twenty a day now to ease his stress levels. Sally came into the room and she almost collapsed when she saw Jud for the first time, her jaw was swinging, she was blushing and trying to straighten her hair. Jud knew where her loyalties lay, he smirked at her. Maureen was after bumming a cigarette from Jud and she kept staring at him as he sucked hard on the nicotine. This was Maureen all over, she was always after something from him and he knew she was licking arse to get herself back in the circle of trust. "Here you go Mo, get a fag if you want one," Jud sighed.

Maureen stood up and helped herself to his cigarettes. Jud's eyes were still on Sally, studying her. He sat forward and cupped his hands around his knees. "So, I hear you're messing with the big boys now then Sally, is that right?" Her face was beetroot and her mouth was dry, she swallowed hard and looked him in the eye. What did she have to be scared of? Danny was her protector now and there was no way Jud was doming her and making her feel uncomfortable. "Yeah, you've heard right then Jud.

Not that it's any of your business though. I think it's best if we don't discuss Danny as I can't see what it's got to do with you anyway. It's best left alone."

Dawn sat up and leant forward. These two had only just made friends and here she was again being a gobshite with her man. Sally had changed and Dawn hated that she no longer had any control over her. Sally sat down and twiddled her hair, nervously waiting for Jud to kick off. Maureen broke the silence and started to talk to her, she could see she was crumbling and wanted to end the silence. "Ay, Jud's mother is coming over here soon. I wouldn't like to be in our Dawn's boots when she comes, would you?"

This woman just wouldn't shut up. Sally smirked and licked her lips slowly, it was time for a bit of shit -stirring too. "I'm sure Mary will forgive you Dawn. It's all in the past isn't it?"

Jud's phone started ringing and as he looked at the screen his jaw dropped. He walked into the hallway and closed the door behind, he was edgy and eager to get out of the room. The light was low as he sat on the stairs and answered the call. "What the fuck do you want? Do you know what I'm going to do to you when I get my fucking hands on you?" The veins in the side of his neck were pumping with rage, his knuckles turning white. "Let's do it then. Me and you, a full on straighter." Jud ended the call and stood thinking for a few seconds. This must be a set-up. There was no way Larry would have attempted to contact him without any back up. He didn't have the balls. He knew he would rip him to shreds given half the chance. Something wasn't right, he was up to something. Larry was a cunning bastard and Jud knew somewhere along the line he was hatching a plan to bring him down. Somebody started to knock on the front door. Jud could see their shadow through the pane of glass. He approached it with caution aware that he could have been attacked at any second. Opening the door with his fingers gripped tightly to the wooden doorframe he was ready for action. Jud gasped for breath and smiled as he met the eyes of his mother.

She looked old today, sadness in her eyes. The death of her youngest son had definitely taken it out of her. Her eyes clouded over as she pulled him closer. "Come here you and give me a hug. Oh Jud, I've missed you so much. I'm so glad you're home." Mary's cold hands cupped around her son's face as she kissed his cheeks. Jud invited her inside the house and at one point he nearly broke down crying too. He hadn't had any real time to grieve for his brother properly yet and now he was out of jail the floodgates of emotion were opening. Anger stirred in the pit of his stomach, he wanted revenge, he wanted to make his brother's murderer suffer just like he had. People were taking the piss out of his family and now it was time to set the record straight. Now it was time to avenge his brother's death. Mary inhaled deeply and her expression changed, her voice was low. "It stinks of wet dog in here, phew, they need some bleeding air fresheners," she walked a few steps further down the hallway and grabbed Jud back by his arm. "Bleeding hell, the dirty bleeders, look at the colour of the walls. I said to myself when I was walking up the garden path that this house was minging and I'm right. Jud, just take a look at the net curtains on the front of the house, they're grey."

Jud shook his head as he led her in to meet the others. Mary had always been so house-proud and having crisp white net curtains up at her windows were a must in her eyes. That's just the way she'd been brought up. A clean home was a happy home she was always led to believe and she agreed with it, nobody should live in a shit- tip. Mary walked in behind Jud and she was horrified as she saw the state of the place. How could this woman invite guests around to her home when her abode looked like this, it was an utter disgrace. "Bang the kettle on for Mary, Sally," Maureen commanded, "do you want a cup of tea love? I hope so because we've got no coffee in."

Mary sat down and flicked the invisible dust from her coat. There was no way she was taking it off, she could be bitten by fleas or any other bug that was lurking in her chair. Mary started to itch at the thought of fleas. Her fingernails scratched the top of her head slowly as her face creased. Dawn sat up straight and kept her head low, she hated feeling like this, she hated not being in control. If Jud wouldn't have been here she would have told the old cow straight to keep her nose out of her business, but Jud was here, she had to show her some respect and keep her trap shut. Jud sat down next to his mother and she patted the top of his knee. "I'm so glad you're home son. Now, let's call a truce so you and our Larry can sort this mess out. You're brothers, blood remember."

Jud knew this was coming and tried to keep calm. She didn't have to know what was going on, she didn't need the stress. He smirked and told her what she wanted to hear "Anything for you mother. I'll meet up with Larry soon and sort this mess out. You're right, it's gone on long enough."

Mary gulped hard. She looked at him closer. Was he taking the piss out of her or what? This was so easy, no, this couldn't be right. She asked him again to make sure she'd heard him right. "Jud, swear on my life you mean what you've just said. I don't want you lying to me."

Jud sat back and looped his arms over his head. He looked over at Dawn and smirked. "What is done is done isn't it. I've forgiven Dawn and as far I'm concerned it's water under the bridge. It was a mistake on both parts and I want to put it behind us."

Dawn didn't know where to look. This was all going so well. Well, until Maureen started with her mouth. "I've already told Dawn Mary how lucky she is to have your Jud back. He's such a good man to forgive her. I think she's learned her lesson here Mary, she won't drop her knickers again in a hurry will you Dawn?"

Well, what a thing to say. Here was Dawn keeping a low profile and Maureen just couldn't keep her big mouth shut. I'm sure she was doing it on purpose. This was it, Mary shot a look at Dawn and their eyes met for the first time. Mary was breathing heavily and her nostrils were flaring at the sides. She didn't trust her as far as she could throw her. Women like her were all the same, they could never be trusted. Jud watched his mother and he was on standby just in case she leapt over him and started to strangle Dawn. Sally came into the room holding a mug of tea, she passed it over to Jud's mother. Spencer was here now too and he sat down next to Sally. They were both watching Dawn and Spencer kept sniggering into Sally's ear. Something had amused them both. Mary dropped her eyes down to the white cup, dark brown rings were visible inside it. There was no way she was drinking anything in the house, the place was riddled with germs and other bacteria.

Jud sat back and chuckled. "So is Larry still engaged to Michelle Buckley then or what? Our Paul told me they're an item now." Jud held the bottom of his stomach and shook his head. "That woman is a crank, why the hell is he going near her. He knows her of old, she's nothing but trouble."

Mary rubbed at her arms and there was definitely a chill coming over her body. She wet her lips slowly with the top of her tongue and held her body tightly. "Larry told me she was touching him when he was in a coma. You know, touching his private parts. She's a bleeding lunatic." Dawn reached for her cigarettes from the edge of the table, this was knocking her sick. She knew Michelle was not right in the head but this was in a league of its own. Mary continued and everyone was hanging on her every word. "Larry said she'd done it a few times too, not just the once. I mean, what must be going on in her head, she's sick and twisted. She should be in a hospital getting some help. Fancy molesting Larry when he was ill, that's shocking that is."

Sally couldn't help but find it all amusing. Maureen nearly choked on her cup of tea and burst out laughing. This was amusing her too and she sniggered. "Well, the saucy cow. I bet she had sex with him too. Let's face it, if she overstepped the mark of touching his dick, who's to say she never had it off with him? She has to get it while she can. Come on, let's face it, the girl's ugly as fuck. No one would touch her with a bargepole."

Dawn was horrified and sucked hard on her cigarette. Jud was watching her from the corner of his eye. He changed the subject quickly. "My solicitor said I should get a walkout in court if Larry denies everything. I'll probably get a few months community service or something but I'm not arsed over that. I'll do that on my head. It's better than being locked up in the slammer for years isn't it?" Jud checked his wristwatch and jumped to his feet. "Mam, I've just got to nip out. You can stay for tea if you want. I'll get us all a takeaway if you're staying?"

Mary was on the spot. There was no way she wanted to go home to an empty house, no way. What, to stare at four walls all night again. Even though Mary was sitting in a shit-tip with Dawn and her mother, anything was better than going home to an empty house. Mary was lonely, empty inside. Sick of talking to herself. She answered him before he changed his mind. "Alright then I'll stay. I've got nothing better to do have I?"

Dawn couldn't hide her disappointment. She tried to raise a smile but everyone there knew she was struggling. She knew the moment Jud left her side she would be like a lamb to the slaughter. Sally watched Jud leave and she was edgy. He was up to something and she needed to let Danny know to watch his back. This man was dangerous and she knew without any shadow of doubt that he was on the hunt for her man. Jud was too confident as he left the room. He walked out as if he knew something was going down. Sally secretly pushed her mobile phone into her back pocket and headed to the toilet. Maureen stretched her hands above her head and yawned. "We can go for a game of bingo down at the legion if you want Mary. It's happy hour if you fancy a quick tipple?"

Mary smiled, it had been years since she'd had a social life. She was always going out when her husband was alive, but now she was like a hermit. There was no dancing for her anymore, no singing as she walked home from the pub, no nothing. Her life was dull. Dawn was shocked and her mouth was wide open. "Mam, Mary isn't into the same kind of things that you are. She won't like it. Just leave her alone."

Maureen snarled at Dawn. "Mary has got a voice you know. Take your hand from up her arse and let her talk for herself."

Mary smiled and cleared her throat. "I'm fine Dawn, I can speak for myself. And, yes Maureen, I would like to come with you. You get no medals for staying at home do you?"

Dawn was distraught, Maureen was a lush and she knew she didn't have a penny to go out with. How embarrassing was this, Maureen was a sponger and she sat back as she waited for the question that usually came next. Maureen reached into her handbag and opened her purse. "Well fuck a duck, I thought I had a tenner left to go to bingo. Bloody hell, we'll have to go another time love."

Mary sat forward in her seat and Dawn knew what was coming next. She's watched Maureen do this hundreds of times before and it never failed to get her a free night out. What a crafty old cow she was. "I can sort you out Mo. It will be my treat. Don't worry, I'll pay for you."

Maureen sprang up from her seat and danced across the front room as Sally came back inside. There were no flies on her for sure. "Just let me get a quick wash and I'll be back with you in a flash. Ay Mary, you might even get a new feller if you play your cards right. They're some alright blokes who come into the bingo, you'd be surprised."

Dawn blushed, what on earth was Maureen saying. Mary was a respectable woman, a churchgoer, she just wasn't like that. Mary chuckled and rubbed her hands together. At last she had a friend, a social life. So what if it was Maureen, beggars can't be choosers. Sally sat down and she seemed edgy, she looked worried. She'd told Danny that Jud was out now and that he'd just left the house. Danny was going to have to be extra vigilant from now on, he had to be. Spencer stood up and left the room. The women were doing his head in, he was going for a lie down.

Maureen walked back into the front room dressed to the nines. Her hair was still stuck up but it didn't seem to bother her. She dragged Mary up from the sofa and she was eager to get her out. There was no way she wanted her to change her mind. This was a free night out and another chance to get pissed out of her head. "See you girls later. Don't worry Dawn, I'll look after Mary for you. What time do you want us back for something to eat?"

Dawn was relieved to see the back of them both if the truth be known, and she didn't give a flying fuck if either of them came home again. Maureen led Mary out of the room and you could hear them both laughing in the hallway. Sally turned to face Dawn. "Well who would have thought it ay, Mary and Mo out on the razzle together. I bet your mam gets her pissed out of her head."

Dawn seemed in a world of her own and something was lying heavy on her mind. "Did you hear what Mary said about Michelle Buckley touching Larry whilst he was in a coma, that's so sick. I'm going to see the dirty slapper and tell her straight. Fuck me, she's knocked me sick."

Sally blew a laboured breath. "And, why are you so bothered. Jud is home now so don't be fucking it all up again by getting involved with Larry."

Dawn shook her head, her heart was low and she was actually tearful. "Sally, I love them both but in different ways. I thought Jud was the one for me but as soon as Mary mentioned Larry with another woman I felt sick inside. If I didn't love him then why am I feeling like this? Jud is a good guy, he'll look after me yes, but is that enough? Money can't buy love Sally and I think I've made the biggest mistake of my life."

Sally was deflated. She just knew Dawn had been lying to her all along, she could see it in her eyes that she still loved Larry Watson. Sally loved all this drama, this meant that Dawn was no threat to her and her relationship with Danny. Her head had been in bits lately and now she knew she was just being paranoid she started to relax. This was hot gossip, what the hell was going to happen next? Was Dawn going to throw her hand in and tell Jud that she still loved his brother or was she going to continue living a lie?

Just then, Spencer walked into the front room, he just came from nowhere, out of the blue. He was supposed to be in bed having a lie down. He sneered at his sister but never said a word. He just picked his car keys up and left the room.

CHAPTER FOURTEEN

JUD PULLED UP at a car park at the back of the pub. It was dimly lit and his vision was poor. He'd needed glasses for ages now but just kept putting off a visit to the opticians. He tugged hard at the bulletproof vest hidden away under his coat. He never went to any sort of meeting without it. Jud knew he was a sitting duck and always made sure he protected himself the best he could. The trees were swaying about and there was an eerie silence looming. Jud was alone; he was waiting for his brother to turn up. He was ready for him and his adrenalin was pumping. Jud knew he was going to give Larry a belt no matter what. Come on, what did Larry expect? The guy had shoved his cock up his woman, there was no way of escaping that fact, he was getting mashed up, done in. Jud stood tall as the night air wrapped around his body, it was bitterly cold as the wind picked up speed. Jud dipped his head and zipped his jacket up fully.

This was the place his brother Sean had taken his last breath. Just near the bushes not far from where he stood he could see the flowers placed on the floor where mourners had left them to show their respect for his younger brother. Sean must have known his attacker. Surely, he knew them, recognised their face before it happened. Could it have just been a random killing like everyone was saying? Or did somebody have more to gain than they were letting on? The money that was taken from Sean was still missing, this could have been the reason for somebody ending his brother's life. People would do anything when they were desperate for cash and ten grand was a lot of money. But, was it enough to brutally kill somebody, to end another human being's life? Jud listened to the music playing from inside the pub, the bass was pumping through the walls. As he stood watching the area he could see a shadow approaching him in the distance. Jud took a deep breath and flexed his fingers, it was show time. This shit was going down.

As soon as he saw Larry for the first time he was getting a crack, just to let him know he meant business. Jud had lay awake in his cell nearly every night planning what he would do to his brother when he finally got his hands on him. Some sick shit had gone through his head. He'd planned to have his brother raped and bummed within an inch of his life, to burn his face off, to cut his dick off, the list was endless. Larry stood back in the shadows of the night, there was no way he was getting too near his brother. He knew more than anyone what he was capable of and kept his distance. Spotting him in the distance, Jud nodded his head slowly and spoke. "So, big man. Why are you hiding away? I thought you wanted a shot at the title. Let's see if you've got what it takes to put me on my arse," Jud took a breath before he continued. "See, that's your problem Larry, you've always been a coward, always hiding away in the shadows doing your snidey shit. Come on then, step forward and let's do this like men. We'll have a straightener. A one on one."

Larry stood frozen, he kept looking over his shoulder

and his heart was pounding inside his chest, he was stuttering. "You don't scare me Jud, you never have and, just for the record Dawn loved it, she enjoyed every minute of what we had together. You knew she wanted me, she's always wanted me."

Jud gritted his teeth, why wasn't he running at him and knocking ten tons of shit out of him? This was his woman he was talking about, his Dawn, his heart's desire. "You can have the shag-bag Larry. Do you think I would touch her after you've been near her? Come on lad, give me a bit of fucking credit. I've known for sometime that you two dirty bastards were at it. Like two fucking rabbits weren't you?"

Larry swallowed hard, he was bluffing for sure, this was just his plan so he'd let his guard down. "If you knew about us then why were you still marrying her? Come on, you're lying. You didn't know shit."

Jud's laughter echoed throughout the night air and it seemed to unnerve Larry. "So you don't mind if Dawn's with me then? I know she still wants me and it's just a matter of time before she comes back begging me to take her back."

Jud had heard enough, it was time for war. He wasn't fighting for the love of Dawn now though, no way, this was a battle of pride. His feet pounded along the gravel footpath and Larry never stood a chance. He fell to the floor like a lead weight. Jud sat on top of him and hesitated. Somebody was coming, he could hear their struggled breath running towards him. Larry was fighting for his life now and managed to break free.

A voice in the distance was screaming at him. "Jud,

don't do it. You'll go back to jail if you finish him off. He's not worth it, just walk away." Michelle Buckley walked towards Jud and gently touched the side of his arm.

Paul Watson now came running towards them both and he pushed Larry away from Jud. "Larry, fuck off home, why are you even here? For fucks sake just do one."

Jud looked puzzled, what the hell was Michelle doing here? How did she know they were meeting here and how did Paul know too. Jud paced the floor ragging his fingers through his hair. What the hell was happening? "Paul, how did you know I was here?"

Paul looked at Michelle and nodded his head. "She rang me and told me to get my arse down here as quick as I could."

Michelle watched Larry walking off in the distance and she started to follow him. Jud grabbed her back and his warm breath was blowing in her face. "Start talking now bitch, how did you know we were meeting here?"

Michelle was scared, her lips were quivering. "I saw Larry from the roadside heading behind the pub and I saw you waiting for him too. Jud, I was worried you would do something you would regret."

Jud smiled at Michelle, she was harmless really and he'd always had a lot of time for her in the past. She knew everything, she knew who was selling what and where their stashes were hid away. She was a good friend to have on side. Once he'd calmed down he headed towards the roadside. "Thanks for that Michelle, I'd have probably killed the cunt if I was alone with him any longer. Anyway, talk to me. I want to know who's selling electrical goods around here. You know my lads were had over don't you?"

Michelle was relieved, Jud was so unpredictable and she knew he could have ended her life at any time. She was ready to talk, but she held her cards close to her chest, she wanted something in return. Jud was a good person to have onside and she was going to make him work for anything she told him. Paul was at his brother's side and he whispered into his ear. "She's a lunatic Jud, you know what she'd done to our Larry don't you?" Jud chuckled and he told Michelle to go and wait inside the pub for him. He passed her a twenty pound note and asked her to get the beers in.

Michelle took the money from him without any further questions. This was a free night for her and if the truth was known she was glad she had somebody to talk to about her aching heart. She never had many friends, she trusted nobody. You could say she was a loner, but that was by choice, she preferred her own company. Paul watched her leave and patted the top of Jud's shoulder. "This is getting out of hand now Jud. Just let Larry get on with it. We've got business to take care of and you know if we drop our guard for one second Danny Morgan and his boys will be on us like a rash. I've got a meeting tomorrow with some guys from Cheetham Hill and they've got some good gear for us to have off. They're the main suppliers around that area and the word on the street is that they're packing. Smack, sniff, magic, ketamine, the fucking lot. They're only a couple of nobheads too, so it will be like taking candy from a baby." Jud sucked hard on his gums, he was interested. "Right, let me get a few scoops down my neck and we can talk some more. I just need to speak to Michelle first though. She knows more than she's letting on and I'm going to make sure she tells me everything."

They both walked to the entrance and as they walked into the boozer a few heads turned. Jud was a hard case and a lot of people would have liked to see him fall; he was cocky and full of himself.

Michelle walked over with two drinks in her hand. "Shall we sit down," she asked him.

Jud followed her to a seat and from the corner of his eye he spotted Spencer, Dawn's brother. He ignored him and carried on with his business. Michelle sat down and dropped her head into her hands, she was desperate. "Your Larry has fucked my head up big time Jud. I love him from the bottom of my heart and I'd do anything for him. He's my life, I've never loved anyone like I've loved him." Jud smirked, was this woman for real or what? He knew he had to listen to her pouring her heart out and remained patient. "I'm pregnant with his child Jud," she whispered under her breath.

Jud swallowed hard and nearly choked on his drink. "Are you being serious or what," he asked. Michelle lifted her jumper up and there it was growing inside her stomach. He looked closer, he wasn't sure if it was just her blubber or she was really with child. "Have you told him about the kid?"

She snivelled and wiped a tear rolling down her cheek. "He won't even speak to me Jud, he's said some nasty things to me and he said he wishes I was dead."

Jud had to up his game, he had to get her to trust him. A text alert came to his phone and he smiled as he read it. "Love you, not long now," the message read. The number wasn't Dawn's either. Jud tucked his phone away in his jacket pocket and continued listening to Michelle. He'd calmed her down now and promised her he would help get Larry back in her life. He was a lying bastard of course but he played the part well of a concerned friend. "Michelle, tell me who's had me over. Who had the electrical van off? I know you know something. You know everything that goes on around these parts."

Michelle sat chewing the side of her fingernails and she was ready to spill the beans. She bent over towards him and checked nobody was listening to her. "It was Danny Morgan and his lads. I know they've got a buyer for the lot too. The guy is picking the lot up on Thursday this week. It's stored in a lock-up in Miles Platting, full to the doors our kid said it was."

Jud's face creased at the sides. He rubbed his hands together and his nostrils flared. "I fucking knew it. I knew it was that cunt and his boys. Well, watch this space now, I'll show them pricks what I'm all about. This shit is going down."

Michelle wasn't sure if she'd done the right thing or not. This meant war and she'd started it for sure. Jud gulped his drink down and watched people on the dance floor. His mind was ticking over and he was ready to strike. Seeing Paul at the other side of the room he sat staring for a few seconds. "Right Michelle, thanks for that and I'll do my best with Larry. I don't know why you're even arsed about him anyway, he's a waste of space."

She dipped her head and placed her hand on her stomach. "I need him for this child Jud, he's your nephew." Her stomach didn't look like that of a pregnant woman, where she placed her hand it sank in, it was hollow, surely there was nothing inside? Something wasn't right. Michelle smiled and watched Jud leave her side, she was a cunning cow. She was up to no good.

Jud marched across the pub and stood next to his brother. He nudged him in the arm causing him to wobble. "Right, get the lads together and get a van ready. It's going down let me tell you. Get the shooters ready too, I'm going to blow them cunts up." Paul wasn't really listening and he was chatting a woman up at the bar. An older woman she was. A pensioner. He was talking the usual bullshit, saying anything to get into her knickers. Jud gripped him by the throat and pulled him closer. He was fuming. "I said, get the fucking boys ready. Danny Morgan is the one who had us over and we're going to take back what's ours," he went nose to nose with him now. "So, dump the old tart and get on it, do you hear me? Move your arse!"

Paul swallowed hard and quickly swigged the remainder of his drink. "I'm on it now Jud, just chill will you?"

Jud stood tall and he was breathing heavily, chest rising with speed. As they walked from the pub, Paul was already on the blower rounding the boys up. "We're going in team handed Paul. We're going straight through the fucking doors, booming them in. And, if Morgan is there, God fucking help him. I'll cut his bollocks off and make a necklace out of them." Paul didn't say a word...

★

Maureen was as pissed as a fart and Mary wasn't far

behind her. Her cheeks were rosy red and she'd taken her coat off and slipped her shoes off under the table. "I'll tell you what Mary, you're a right dark horse you are. You've had a few gins and you're still standing, proper hard-core aren't you?"

Mary was sat back in her seat and from nowhere a wave of emotion took over her body. "I wish my life was as straight forward as yours, Mo. Look at you, you don't care what people have to say about you, you just do whatever you want. For years I've lived my life for my boys and look where it's got me. They don't care about me, they don't care if I'm lonely. It's all about them and what I'm doing for them. I cook, I clean, I iron for them and what thanks do I get? No Mo, as from now on I'm looking after number one. I need to start making the most of the years I've got left. I could be dead tomorrow and who would care?" She held her hands out in front of her and hunched her shoulders. The gin had got a grip of her and she was blubbering. "Nobody cares about me. Well, the boys would miss my cooking I suppose but there is no one on this earth who loves me for me. I don't share my life with anyone. I've become a misery, a bitter old woman. Go on Mo, shoot me now. I may as well be dead."

Mo smirked and covered her tobacco stained teeth with her hand, she'd always hated her teeth and wished she'd looked after them more when she was younger. She reached over and took Mary's hand in hers. "Mary, just fuck the lot of them. Fuck them all because that's what I do. Do you think our Dawn cares about me?" Her eyes were wide open now and she was getting her back up. "Because, let me tell you, she's one selfish bitch.

She doesn't do a tap for me and I could be lay dead in a gutter for all she cares. You're Jud's got his work cut out with her you know. She's such a self-centred bitch. Even from being a kid she always wanted more than I could give her. Take, take, take, she never gives anything back." Mary finished the last bit of her drink and slammed her glass down on the table."

"Mo, I know she's your daughter but she makes my blood boil. How can anyone sleep about with their fiancés brother?"

Maureen sniggered. She moved closer to her and slurred her words. "She probably gets that from me love. I know it's nothing to be proud of but I slept with my sister's fiancé too. I've slept with a lot of men that I shouldn't have if we're being totally honest here."

Mary nearly choked. She made the sign of the cross across her body. "God forgive you woman, how could you do that to your own flesh and blood? All that hurt and pain you caused."

Maureen pulled away from her and swayed about in her seat, at one point she looked like she was going to fall off her chair, her legs wide open, not a care in the world. All her dirty washing hanging out for the world to see. "She had it all Mary and I had nothing. Day after day I watched her dressing up in all her new clothes that he'd bought her and I wanted to be someone's special woman too. Plus, if he'd really loved her he would never have slept with me would he?"

Mary was gobsmacked. "That's terrible Mo, did your sister ever find out about it?"

Mary sniggered and raised her eyebrows. "No, she had

her suspicions but she never had any real evidence, she married him anyway."

Mary was distressed. Was this how it was in the real world? Was it every woman for herself? Was Mary that gullible that she trusted everyone? Mary had her back up and folded her arms tightly in front of her. "Well, if I was your sister I would have scratched your bleeding eyes out. Honest to God, you would have been six foot under."

Maureen blew a laboured breath, she had no shame over her past. She hadn't valued her body and she'd get her kit off for anyone buying her a drink, especially if it was gin. Mary chuckled loudly and undid the top button on her blouse. She was having a hot flush, sweating and bright red. "That's how I should have been I suppose. What thanks do I get for keeping my knickers on? None whatsoever! I was a good woman. I never cheated on my man. I never slept about and look at me now - an old woman with nothing worth living for. No list of lovers, no dirty weekends or one-night stands. I'm just a lonely old woman."

The booze was talking now and she was feeling sorry for herself. Maureen held her hand on her heart, she felt this woman's pain, she felt her heartache, her loneliness. Sat looking around the pub she spotted a couple of men sat in the corner. She licked her lips slowly and nudged Mary in the waist. It was time to liven things up, get the party started. "Shall we get into them two over there? I know one of them and he's up for a good laugh?"

Mary hesitated, her heart was pounding inside her chest and she looked horrified. "No love, look at the state of me. I'm not ready to meet anyone yet. I look like something the cat has dragged in. No, just let's stay here. You go over if you want?"

Maureen wet her fingers in her mouth and swooped her hair back from her face. "Watch and learn Mary Watson, watch and learn. I'll show you the ropes. Come on, follow my lead."

Maureen was waiting for nobody she was already walking across the room towards the men, she was strutting her stuff now, hips shaking, arse wiggling, lips puckered tightly together. This woman was going for gold. She stood looking at the men and placed one hand on the side of her hip. "Hello, do you mind if me and my friend Mary come and join you. I can't see the point of us all sitting apart when we could be having a chat and getting to know each other can you?"

Mary was by her side now and she was smiling at one of the men nervously. Mary didn't ask to sit at the table, she just pulled up a chair and sat down. Maureen smirked and sat down beside her. "So are you buying us two ladies a drink or what?" Mary Watson could have died and sank into the floor, this wasn't her style, no way, she would never ask a man to buy her a drink, she had pride, self-worth. Maureen was in a league of her own, she had no shame, just bare-faced cheek.

Mary had to speak up, there was no way she was being tarnished with the same brush as her. "Hold on Mo, I don't want another drink I'm fine. If I drink anymore I'll be on my back."

The man at the side of her chuckled and nudged his mate. "Bleeding hell get her a drink, I've not had a woman on her back for years."

Mary blushed bright red, she was beetroot. She'd forgotten what it was like to have any attention from a man. Maureen was wasting no time at all she knew the ropes and she knew what she wanted at the end of it. A leg-over and a few free beers were all she ever asked for. The man sat beside Maureen put his hand in his pocket and asked them both what they were drinking. Mary was panicking now as she looked at the time, they were only supposed to be going to bingo but Maureen had dragged her down to the boozer. "I think we need to go home Mo," she said in an anxious voice.

Maureen was having none of it. Chances like this didn't come along every day and there was no way she was walking away from a free drink, she might even get a quick shag at the end of the night too. There was no way she was going home, she was on a roll. "Oh Mary, come on, these nice gentlemen have offered to buy us a drink, the least we can do is have one with them."

Mary was on the spot and the guy she was sat with did seem friendly, he had a gentle smile. "Just a quick one then Mo, then we need to go home."

The man chuckled out loud again and he was in stitches laughing. "I'll give you a quick one love. I'll be in and out before you know it."

Mary sniggered, she liked this cheeky man, he reminded her of her husband when he was alive, quick-witted, a charmer. He now introduced himself as Stan Morgan. He was around the same age as Mary and had a pot belly. His nose was bright red at the end of it and he was definitely a lush, he was half-cut. "You just watch your tongue before I slap you one," Mary hissed. She was pissed yes, but she was wasn't having a man talking to her like this, she had morals, she wanted respect. Maureen was away with the fairies now, she was just sat looking around the pub as she waited for her man to return. She was a sure thing, she didn't care if she'd got a name for herself, she was a good time girl and she wanted to make every second on this earth count. She had no regrets, none whatsoever.

Jud stood outside the lock- up with his men. There were eight of them stood there with him. Tooled up and ready for action, ready to snap anyone's jaw who came near them. Big meaty blokes they were too, full of muscles. Jud got the crowbar from Paul and attacked the locks on the shutters, ripping them off. There was loud banging and shouting; they were nearly inside. Jud sparked a cigarette up and stood looking at all the boxes as the shutters lifted up fully. He held his back and sniggered as he rubbed his hands together. "We'll see who's laughing now, won't we smart-arse. Do you know what lads, we should wait here until they come back for it all and batter fuck out of them. Shanghai surprise them, take them clean out."

Paul looked flustered he just wanted in and out of the gaff, no messing about, he was edgy. "Jud, let's get this lot shifted first, then we can think about Danny Morgan. Let's get it all loaded up and get off from here before somebody clocks us. That's all we need the fucking dibble turning up isn't it?" Jud shot a look at his brother, he was losing his bottle for sure and usually he was up for anything but today his arse was twitching. The lads started to load the van up, there was some hard work here and it was going to take some time to get this lot shifted, it was packed out.

Jud watched his men and he was plotting something, his head nodded slowly as the last TV was loaded into the back of the van. "Right Paul, you take that lot up to our warehouse and the rest of you wait here with me. We're having these bastards tonight one way or the other. We'll wait here for them and as soon as they come through the door we'll wipe the fuckers out," his voice changed and he spoke in a low tone. "Leave Danny Morgan to me though, he's mine. I want to hurt that cunt, make him suffer."

Paul was relieved that he wouldn't be there when it all kicked off. He took another man with him and left his brother in the lock-up. "Jud, I'll be back as soon as I can. I'll give Jezza a ring and get a buyer for this lot as soon as I can. The sooner it's gone the better." Jud didn't reply, his mind was on the game and he was ready for war.

Maureen and Mary walked down the road together swaying about, singing inside an empty beer bottle. They'd had a great night and the two men they'd met had offered to take them both out the following night. Mary looked like a weight had been lifted off her shoulders. At last, a life of her own, the companion she'd always dreamt about. The intimate nights in front of the TV curled up on the sofa sipping wine and munching on peanuts. Maureen was steaming drunk and Mary had to help her stand up as they walked down the garden path. She'd wanted to stay with her new fella but Mary had put the block on it and brought her home. She was legless and in no fit state to entertain anyone. Maureen wobbled about and stood with one hand resting on the wall. "Let our Dawn say one word to me Mary and I'm going to swing for her. I'm sick of her dictating to me. I mean, Mary let's face it, she fucked up big time with your Jud didn't she?"

Mary seemed to have calmed down, she was on a high and nothing was going to ruin her moment. "We all make mistakes Maureen. Come on, you've even said yourself that you slept with your sister's husband to be, so who are you to judge?"

Maureen had seen her arse, where was the support? "Yeah, I get that Mary but she never admits when she is wrong. At least with me, you get what you see. I'd rather have ten of me than one of her, she's deep, so bleeding deep." Maureen slid her key into the lock and her face was serious as she made her way into the front room. Her shoulders were held high and she was ready for anything Dawn had to throw at her. She pushed the living room door open and met the eyes of her daughter. She held a single finger up in the air and waved it about in front of her. "Before you start with the moaning, me and Mary have had a few drinks that's all. We had a game of bingo and thought that we'd have a couple of drinks and a chat. So straighten your face before I straighten it for you."

Dawn sat up in her chair and she wasn't one bit bothered. If the truth was known she'd been glad of the peace and quiet whilst her mother had been out. The film she'd just been watching had just finished and she was ready for bed. Mary was loud, she was full of confidence and she seemed to be warming to Dawn. "Has our Jud still not been back I'm starving?"

Dawn played with her hair and answered her. "He phoned me about an hour ago and said something had turned up. He said to order without him." Dawn was hoping Mary was paying because she was skint. Jud hadn't left her a penny and she knew her mother was potless as always. "Oh, let's order something, I'm starving. I'll have something to eat and then I'll get a taxi home."

Maureen switched the TV off and turned the radio on. She was still in a party mood and she was dancing across the room. Her skirt was hitched up over her knobbly knees and she was hopping about dancing. "What do you two eat, shall we have a kebab from that place on Moston Lane. I've heard its lovely?"

Dawn nodded and grabbed her phone but never dialled the number. She dipped her head low and spoke. "Mary, Jud hasn't left me any money and I've not got any on me. I could go to the speed bank though if you wanted?"

Dawn watched Mary with cunning eyes waiting for her to reply. "No love, there is no need for that, this will be my treat. I've had a great night with your mother and it's the least I can do." Maureen told them what she wanted to eat and sat down and lit a cigarette. Once the order was made Mary sat next to Dawn and touched her hand. "Listen, I've been thinking about everything that's gone on and I'm ready to forgive you. I know what our Larry is like and okay you made a mistake, you're not the first person to make a mistake and you won't be the last. I just hope you've learned your lesson."

Dawn was glad of the forgiveness but something wasn't right with her. Larry had been lying heavy on her mind and no matter how much she tried she just couldn't stop herself thinking about him. Her heart was heavy and she had some big choices to make. If she left Jud again he would find her this time and kill her for sure. And, did Larry really love her like he said he did? There was only one way to find out and earlier she'd texted him telling him she wanted to meet him. Dawn was a double-crossing bitch for sure and she could never be trusted. Jud was her bread and butter though, he could give her all she wanted in life but could Larry do the same?

Danny Morgan sat talking on his mobile phone in his car. He was anxious and whoever he was talking to wasn't happy. "Listen, I've told you before, you do what you have to do. I'm not giving you a penny. Fuck off and don't ring me again. I'm not arsed anymore." Danny ended the call and launched his mobile phone on the seat next to him. He flicked the car's engine over and screeched away, he was fuming. Turning the radio up full blast he set off to meet the buyer at the lock-up. This was easy money for him, he'd hardly had to get his hands dirty. He was just there to collect the cash. The donkey work had already been done. Danny turned the engine off and locked his car. The street was quiet, it was dark and his vision was poor. As he walked to the lock-up he noticed a few cars parked along the roadside. This was strange because nobody ever came here through the night and usually the place was deserted except for the odd lovers hidden away in the shadows of the night. Slowly, he walked further up the street, his eyes creased as he noticed the shutter on the lock up had been damaged. With a spring in his step he sprinted up to it and lifted the shutter up fully, dragging at it with two hands. Danny didn't stand a chance.

As soon as he popped his head under the gap Jud gripped him and dragged him inside by the scruff of the neck. "Get here you dirty no good bastard. Did you think you could have me over and get away with it? Nar, you're going down you dick-head." Jud head-butted Danny and he sank to his knees. The others were stood over him and they kicked ten tons of shit out of him, really hammered him. Blood surged from the side of Danny's mouth and his eyes were swelling instantly. Jud made the men tie him up and they sat him on a wooden chair facing Jud. Danny was in a bad way, blood bubbles were coming out of his nose and one of his teeth at the front was missing. "Come on then Danny let's hear it. Let's hear what bullshit you have to say about this. You should never piss on your own doorstep lad, you must have known you'd be caught."

Danny was spitting blood, he wasn't a big hard man now. He was weak and ready to talk, to tell them anything they wanted to know. To beg for his life. "It is what it is Jud. I never knew this graft was yours honest. You know me Jud, I'm not no low-life. I stick to the rules."

Jud hurled a cup at him and watched as it crashed against his head. "You tell me what you know about my brother's death. Come on, I know you know something about it, don't fuck with me Danny because I'll hurt you bad." Danny was shaking, his whole body went into shock, eyes rolling about and he was starting to fit. The men stood around him and held no pity. Jud let out a menacing laugh and cracked his knuckles. "Look at the big fairy now lads. They're all the same these wankers. They talk the talk but when it's time to walk the walk they all fold in two. Get him up lads and go and dump him somewhere. Leave the cunt to die for all I care." Jud could have finished him off there and then but he didn't move a muscle. This was enough to let him know that he was the Lord of the manor now. Jud was back on the scene and nobody and he meant nobody would ever try and have him over again. The men dragged Danny Morgan's body to one of the cars nearby. They threw him in the back of it like a sack of spuds, his head smashing against the window. He wasn't dead yet but he was struggling to breath and every now and then his eyes rolled to the back of his head. He'd be lucky to survive the night.

Mary walked inside her house. As predicted she was alone again and the same pain in her heart took over her body, the same emptiness. Sitting at the kitchen table she looked around the room and smiled. Her hand touched the old pine table, her flat palm stroking across the grain. This table held so many good memories from when her boys were younger but now all that remained were the tears that had been shed over the years. Tapping her fingers slowly on the table Mary glanced over at the wall clock. The ticking from it was the only noise she could hear. Standing to her feet she made sure the back door was locked and headed off to bed. As from tomorrow she would live her life for herself and nobody else. She deserved a bit of happiness and the man she'd met tonight could give her all the things she'd been missing. So what if people thought she was an old fool? So what if they said she was too old to find love again? She was going to give it a go. What did she have to lose? Mary turned the lights off and hummed a tune as she went upstairs to bed. When she got to the top she did a little dance and clapped her hands above her head.

CHAPTER FIFTEEN

"COME ON JUD we have to make a move. These bastards won't wait around for us - no way, come on. Move your arse before you fuck it all up." Paul stood pacing the floor in Dawn's house, pulling at the waistband on his jeans. "Bleeding hell, hurry up," he moaned again. Today was the meeting Paul had set up with the drug dealers in Cheetham Hill and he didn't want to be late. Paul was a bit obsessive. He liked things to be neat and tidy and if he said he would be there at a certain time, then he would be there. He was punctual. Dawn walked into the room and shot a look at Paul. There was no way she was feeling out of place in her own home, he could take a running jump if he thought she was keeping quiet too, she held no shame.

Jud stood up and grabbed his keys from the table. "I'll be back later, we'll go out tonight to the pub if you want?" Dawn wasn't listening to him and her mind was somewhere else, she was edgy. Jud shouted at her again. "Oi, fucking deaf lugs, are you listening to me or what?"

"Yeah, I heard you the first time. I'll be ready, just give me a ring later. Fuck me, there's no need to shout." Jud nodded his head at Paul and that was enough to let him know he was ready to leave. A quick peck on Dawn's cheek and Jud left the room. Maureen walked into Paul as he was leaving the room and they both just stared at each other for much longer than was necessary. Maureen smirked at him and went to sit down. Once the front door banged shut Dawn ran to the window and made sure they'd gone, she watched them both getting into the car with eager eyes. Her head was in bits, speeding thoughts around her mind, decisions to make. Dawn was nervous and every time she heard a noise she nearly jumped out of her skin. Her eyes were glued to the kitchen window. The sound of someone coming into the room made her freeze, her eyes wide open.

Dawn hitched the curtain back a touch, she stretched her neck to get a better look. She smirked as she watched the silver Golf drive away. "Oi, fucking plant pot, get away from that bleeding window," Maureen shouted behind her. "What are you gawping at anyway?" Maureen chuckled and edged closer to her. "And, the way you call me for being nosey. You're just as bad as me. Let's have a butcher's then, come on what's so bleeding interesting?" Maureen squashed her nose up against the rain stained window and scanned the area. She could see the back of Jud's car driving off in the distance. Her instincts told her Dawn was up to something, she turned her head slowly and growled at her. "What are you up to lady? Don't you dare try and lie to me, because I know you inside and out. It's written all over your face, come on, what are you up to?"

Dawn hated that Maureen could see through her. She knew she was right and it pissed Dawn off that she couldn't get away with anything. "Mam, just fuck off and leave me alone. Why do you always think I'm up to something, ay? Just make a brew and leave me alone. I've got a lot on my plate at the moment."

Maureen poked her finger deep into Dawn's chest. "Because lady, nine times out ten you bleeding well are. You're a shady cow, always hiding something. Remember, if you mess with fire then you'll get burnt."

Dawn snarled and moved away from the window. "I was seeing who was in the car with Jud, that's all. I just like to know who he's grafting with. There's nothing wrong with that is there? Fucking hell, shoot me for even caring."

Maureen flicked the kettle on and rested her body on the side. "Orr Dawn, can you brew me a drink. I'm not feeling too good today. On my life, I feel like I'm on my last legs. I've had pains in my chest and everything."

Dawn chuckled and grabbed a cup from the sink. "You were fine last night mother. Life and soul of the party you were when Mary was here with you. Fancy taking her to the pub with you! She's a bible-basher mam, she's not like you. She's prim and proper."

Maureen had her back up. "I don't give a flying fuck if she goes to church or not. She's no different than me. She found a new man too. So put that in your pipe and smoke it."

Dawn's jaw dropped, she covered her mouth with her hand and her eyes were wide open. "Stop it mam, no she never. Stop pissing about!"

Maureen popped a cigarette out of her packet and slid it into the side of her mouth. "Yeah, that's shut you up hasn't it? I'll tell you what Dawn she can't half drink too. I was pissed as a fart and she was still standing. I thought you told me she didn't drink?"

Dawn poured the hot water into the cup and

sniggered. "Well, you dark horse Mary Watson. Fancy that ay. I didn't have you down as a drinker or a man-eater."

Maureen sat behind a cloud of thick grey smoke. She was coughing and spluttering and banging her clenched fist on her chest as she tried to get her words out. "She's on a date with him tonight too. Stan, I think he said his name is. You know me I don't listen properly when I'm pissed." Maureen crossed her legs and sucked hard on her fag. "Oh, I bet they'll be some cobwebs down them knickers of hers won't they Dawn? I mean, it must be years since anybody has shook her bones." They both sat giggling in the kitchen.

The back door opened and in walked Sally. She was a right moody cow these days and something was definitely going on with her. Her happy-go-lucky personality had gone and she seemed to always have something on her mind. Sally plonked down on the chair and sighed. "They done Danny in last night, he's in a bad way. You know it was Jud don't you?"

Dawn shook her head. "Sally, I don't get involved in Jud's business. If Danny has been taken down then all I can say is he must have deserved it."

Sally sucked hard on her gums, she wanted to defend Danny but she knew she would be fighting a losing battle. Maureen patted Sally's arm. "It's all just part and parcel of that world, love. If Danny has done something to Jud then he must have known he was a dead man walking. Jud never lets sleeping dogs lie, you should know that more than anyone."

Sally shot a look at Dawn and agreed. "Yeah, I know Jud is fair, but I was seeing Danny and we kind of had a good thing going on. Well, until now. He's told me it's over. He said I was a double agent and wants fuck all to do with me anymore. He said I stitched him up."

Maureen stubbed her cigarette out and sipped on her black coffee. "I thought you two were in love, you don't seem that bothered that he's carted you. I thought you'd have some tears at least."

Sally was nervous and fidgeted about. "I thought it was love, but I don't think he's for me. He's too high maintenance."

Dawn rested her head in her hands on the table and looked at Sally. "You're a right dark horse you are. Who is it you've got your eye on now? Come on, there's more to this than you're letting on. I know you, come on who is this new guy."

Sally held her head to the side and dipped her eyes low. "Danny was boring if I'm being honest with you, he was alright to start with but he wasn't for me. I think he was seeing someone else too. I'm pretty sure of it. Do you know when you just know their mind's not with it when they're with you, well, that's how he was with me. He was hiding something from me." Sally played with the cuff of her jumper and carried on speaking. "I've been to see him in the hospital and now I know he'll be okay I'll be taking a step back and see how thing turn out. If he wants me then he'll have to change won't he?"

"Correct Sally love, it's about time you stood up to these men, you should be nobody's fool," Maureen chirped in.

Dawn sighed and licked her lips slowly. "Oh, says you mother who's been a doormat for years. You need to practice what you preach! Look at me, I never take no shit from men. It's my way or the highway."

Maureen was on the defensive and she was taking no prisoners. "Well, we all know about how you handle men don't we! Hold on, was it only the other week you was crying your eyes out begging Jud to have you back. Begging him to give you another chance. So, stop talking out of your arse and tell it how it really is."

Sally smirked and kept her head low. "Fuck off mam. I don't put it on a plate for men like you do," Dawn replied.

"No, you make them pay for it, that's the only difference between me and you love."

Dawn stood up and flicked her hair over her shoulder. "Whatever mam, you know the truth and so do I."

Sally got a text alert and she quickly read her message. "Who's the text from," Dawn inquired.

"Oh, just my brother asking to lend some money. He's skint again and he's after a tenner."

Dawn studied her and continued to get ready. Maureen left the room with her brew, she snarled at Dawn as she went passed her. "Where you going all dolled up?" Sally asked.

Dawn had to tell someone, she had to let the cat out of the bag it was killing her. "I'm meeting Larry soon. Just for closure that's all. We parted on bad terms and I want to put it all to bed. You know, so me and Jud can move on."

Sally played with a small piece of paper on the table, ripping it slowly into tiny pieces. "Well, on your head be it. Only you know what you want in life don't you?"

Dawn was relieved, usually Sally gave her a hard time and made her question her judgement, not today though, she just left her to it. Dawn was singing as she brought her face up to the mirror to apply her mascara, her mouth was open wide as she tilted the small brush along her long eyelashes. Spencer popped his head in the room and winked at Sally, he was whistling a tune as he left. He never said a word.

Jud and Paul sat in the flat facing two other men in the room. Drugs were on the table and some white powder was there ready for sampling. "Let's see what you've got then," Jud sneered, still watching the men eagerly. Paul sat forward and rubbed his hands together as the Asian man called Chachy placed another bag of white powder on the table. Paul knew someone had to try the sniff to see if it was bang on. There was so much shit floating about these days and everyone was out to make a quick few quid by mixing the cocaine with other similar looking products like benzocaine and hay fever tablets. Everybody was at it and nobody actually ever got any raw sniff that hadn't been tampered with anymore. It was all about making as much money as you could. Nobody cared about other people's health, whether they lived or died, it was all about lining their pockets. Greedy fucker's the lot of them. Paul knew the cocaine had probably been bashed with a few other products but he was willing to take a chance and shove it up his nose. Jud also liked a few lines of sniff every now and then but he only took the drug when he was planning on a long night out. Just a line, nothing much. All the lads dabbled in it. It was a social drug and almost everyone on the scene was having a bump when they were out partying.

Chachy chopped a line of white powder. Eyes were on him now and he had to be the first to snort the drug. Once he'd finished he passed the rolled up twenty pound note to Paul. Jud was watching eagerly, the other man was straight headed as he was and every now and then they both held a look for longer than it was necessary at each other. Paul felt the rush from the drug and his jaw was swinging low, he was twisted and his voice was getting gradually louder and louder. "Top shit that is Jud, fuck me the rush from it was mega, fuck me I'm wired already."

Chachy was the same, he was full of life and stood up bouncing about the room. "So, are you lot on it or what then? We can do you a good deal."

Paul was about to answer when Jud stepped in. "How much have you got first? We're not buying it in dribs and drabs we want bulk, can you supply bulk or what?"

Chachy looked at the other man who was white and had dark tanned skin. He had amazing brown eyes too, like big chestnuts. Josh stood up now and slowly paced the floor in the room. "Listen, we can get whatever you want, just tell us where and when and how much you need and we'll sort the rest out."

Jud heard a noise behind him in the other room and shot his eyes to the door. "Who else is here with you," he quizzed.

Josh twisted his head and chuckled. "Just chill, that's my woman Olivia she's in bed waiting for me."

Paul smiled and licked his lips. The cocaine made him feel horny and given the chance he would have been in the bedroom with the woman banging her brains out.

He had no standards when he was like this, he'd shag anything with a hole, any age, any colour and sometimes any sex. Jud shook Chachy's hand and walked over to Josh. "We'll be in touch. Just let us get our ship in order and we'll be back to you to sort it out."

Josh was gutted and you could see he wanted to make a deal today. As they both left he kicked his foot into the bottom of the door and let out a laboured breath. "Fucking time wasters again. I'll tell you what Chachy, don't invite anyone else here. They do my head in, fucking tyre kickers they are."

The bedroom door opened slowly and Michelle Buckley walked into the front room. Walking straight over to the window she hid away from view. Josh was by her side. "Sorry love, we did our best with them. We could have earned a right butty off them. Never mind ay, next time we'll stitch them up good and proper." Michelle Buckley nodded her head slowly as she watched the car drive off from the roadside. "I'll get you bastards, somehow, someway, I'll get you."

Jud sat back in the car and gasped his breath. He gripped the side of his brother's arm causing the skin to turn white, pinching at it hard. "Nar, something's not right with them two geezers. They looked shifty as fuck. Are you sure there not fucking dibble, plain-clothes officers?"

"Stop being paranoid, Jud. Fuck me, if we get some gear from them two muppets, we'll smash it. I was thinking buy some first then watch them and see where they go for it and then take the main man down."

Jud rested his head on the window. "I'm not feeling this Paul, come on, do they look like they're in the know of the drugs world, the gaff was a shit-tip. They're just two low rank pricks out to make a quick earner for themselves. Let's hold back and keep a close eye on them for a few weeks."

Paul blew his breath and started the engine, he'd seen his arse and he was in a strop. "Yeah, whatever you say Jud," he moaned. Jud was always the same. If he hadn't organised the graft he was cautious to get involved. He liked to do his homework first and these two guys looked iffy as fuck. No, this job wasn't for him. He had ways and means to make big money and this wasn't one of them.

⋆

Dawn was dressed to kill wearing a short black skirt and a bright pink vest top. You could see the edge of her black lacy bra sticking out from underneath it. Despite what she was saying, she was on a mission, she knew what she wanted and she knew how to get it. Larry had told her to meet him at a flat where he was staying. He was watching his back and only a few people knew where he was living. Dawn walked up to the front door and casually flicked her hair back over her shoulder. She hitched her skirt up high and pressed her breasts out in front of her. Knocking quietly on the front door she stood back waiting for him to answer. Did she really want Larry or was it just the sex she wanted? By her own admittance Larry was a better lover than his brother, a stallion in the bedroom. He turned her on and knew what she liked. Sex with him was mind-blowing and no matter how much she tried to forget it, she could never say no to his love. Was it lust or was it love she was feeling? She didn't know. Her head was battered with it all.

The front door opened and Larry stood there in his tracksuit bottoms and a grey t-shirt. The stubble on his chin just made him look even sexier than usual. His dark hair was messed up and he looked like he'd been working out. Small beads of sweat dribbling slowly down his forehead. "Well, come on in then stranger. I'm just going to jump in the shower and I'll be with you. I've been busting a few weights and got a sweat on." Larry smiled at her and held his hand on the doorframe. "Unless, you want to join me and rub my back down."

Dawn blushed and walked inside. "Just do what you're doing Larry and then we can sort this mess out. Just hurry up and get a wash."

Larry grabbed a towel from the side and headed into the bathroom. "Go in the front room, I'll be with you soon. Make a drink if you want. I've got some wine in the fridge if you fancy a tipple."

Dawn didn't reply and headed to the kitchen, she was nervous and made her way to the fridge. A glass of wine was just what she needed to steady her nerves, a bottle in fact, she was shaking from head to toe. She sat down in the front room and she could hear Larry singing in the shower. He made her smile and a warmth rushed through her body. She stood up and looked out through the window. She had to make sure nobody had seen her come here, she had to make sure this secret remained between them both. Larry came out of the shower and stood in front of her with just his bath towel hanging around his waist. Small droplets of water glistened on his tanned body and Dawn had to look away from him. A feeling in her groin was stirring, a need, an overwhelming desire to touch his masculine body, to kiss him, to feel him inside her just one last time. Larry knew what he was doing and he could tell by her reaction that anytime soon he would be lying in bed with her pounding her brains out.

"So, come on then Dawn, why the big change of heart?"

She sat tapping her fingers on her front tooth, searching for the answer. "Larry, this is all one big mess and you've messed my life up. I was getting married and you fucked it all up. Why didn't you just let me go and then none of this would have happened?"

In her heart she was waiting for him to say the words, I love you, or even I couldn't live without you but Larry was playing it cool. "I said what I said Dawn because you would have been living a lie for the rest of your life. You tell me now it's Jud you love and I'll open that front door and let you walk away. I swear, I won't come near you again."

Dawn swallowed hard, he'd called her bluff. Her head was spinning and she didn't have a clue what she wanted, she loved them both. "Larry, we both had fun didn't we and you even said yourself that we were just fuck buddies, do you remember saying that?"

Larry sniggered and sat down on the sofa, his legs opened slightly, she could see his wedding tackle. "We were at first, Dawn but you know as well as I do that we had a connection. I'm not saying it was love because I don't know myself what it was, but all I can say is that it felt good."

Dawn's heart sank. So she was just a bang in other

words; a fuck buddy, a sack-emptier. Here she was ready to put her heart on the line and this prick was just after a quick leg-over. No, she was laying the law down now and saying it how it was. She had to tell him, have no regrets. "Larry, I've got feelings for you. I know I went running back to Jud when it all kicked off but I was mixed up and my head was done in." She was embarrassed and tried to pull back. "Anyway, you wasted no time moving on, you was shagging Michelle Buckley so what does that tell me?"

Larry smashed his clenched fist onto the table. "Listen, that woman is off her head. I'll tell you this once and once only, she was never my woman, she lied and told everyone we were together when I was nearly dead. The moment I came around and found out what she was saying I put her right in her place, she's a fucking crank. As if I would have that troll as my girlfriend. Come on Dawn, look at me towards her."

She glanced over at him and she knew he was right. He could have any woman he wanted and he was never short of any offers. "Right Larry, tell me now if you want me or not. I don't mean as a fuck buddy, I mean as a girlfriend. Me and you in a relationship, no more games?"

Larry dropped his head and he knew he'd have to answer her. But, what were the consequences? What about his brother Jud? If he said he wanted her then he knew the fight with his brother would be to the death. Was he strong enough to do this? Was he able to get rid of Jud once and for all? He never answered her, he stood up and walked over to her. Bending his legs slightly he sank his mouth into the nape of her neck. She was butter in his hands and nothing else seemed to matter at that moment. They were two adults craving each other's body. Larry led her to the bedroom and slowly he undressed her. This was no wham bam thank you mam this time, he was making love to her; real sensuous love. Dawn shivered as his hands caressed her body, goose bumps rising on her skin as his fingertips stroked against her smooth skin. "Oh, Larry," she moaned as his finger slid inside her. Her hands gripped his hair and with every movement inside her, she was in heaven. Their two bodies lay entwined together on the bed, lost in the moment, ravishing every second of each other's flesh. "Tell me you want me Larry, tell me you love me, "she whispered. Larry held her face in his hands and bit hard onto her bottom lip. Their eyes met and without him speaking she knew he wanted her, he loved her. Larry lay on top of her now and lifted her leg over his shoulder, he wanted to go deeper inside her, make her groan, fulfil her every sexual desire. The two of them were sweating, rolling about on the bed enjoying the secret they shared. Dawn was ready to orgasm, her toes curled and her long talons sank into his back as she screamed out with pleasure. "Fuck me Larry, fuck me," she screamed at the top of her voice. Larry's body was tense and as his back arched, his facial expression changed. He gritted his teeth tightly and closed his eyes. The sex between them was over.

Dawn lay down on the bed and she was still trying to catch her breath, her hand was on her breast as she looked over at Larry. "See what I mean about us two. How can we just give this up? Larry we need to get away. Start again and make a new life for us both." Larry reached for his cigarettes and passed one to Dawn. Her eyes clouded over as she realised then that she could never walk away from the man she loved.

Larry blew the smoke from the corner of his mouth as he stroked her hair as she lay on his chest. "I want you Dawn. I will do whatever it takes to make sure you are mine forever. Just bear with me for now. I'll sort it all out. I'll do whatever it takes."

Jud pulled up at the pub and sat thinking. War was about to be declared and he needed to be prepared for whatever the Morgan's had planned for him. And, there would be plans, they wanted his blood. Everybody was talking about it and he knew he'd have to end some fucker's life pretty soon. Paul was in a party mood, still high from the drugs he'd taken. "Are you coming in for a few beers or what then?" he asked.

Jud seemed in a world of his own and his mind was doing overtime. "No, you go inside, I'm going to take Dawn out, she'll be spitting feathers if I'm not home soon."

Paul screwed his face up. Just the sound of her name made his skin crawl, she was a wrong' un and the sooner he uncovered her for the dirty bitch she really was, the better. She was the one who'd caused the rift between his brothers and she was getting what was coming to her, the dirty slag. Jud sat staring at his phone. He was texting somebody. As he read the text he smiled and nodded his head slowly.

Dawn sneaked out of Larry's house and kept her head low. Quickly checking her wristwatch she ran down the street. Stood away out of sight Michelle Buckley cracked her knuckles. She was white and ready for snapping. She knew every move that Larry made and to find out where he was hiding was easy. Her brothers were good friends with him and she always listened through the walls to all that was going on in their lives. "Bastard," she sneered. "I'll show you now, Larry Watson. I'll show the lot of you." Michelle zipped her coat up and headed home. Her heart was low and somehow, someway she was going to put a stop to all the pain she was feeling. Dawn was living on borrowed time. She was going to hurt her, finish her, to make sure she never went near Larry Watson ever again.

The Morgan brothers sat around Danny's bed in the hospital. He was in a bad way and the last twenty four hours had been critical. Ged Morgan sat by his brother's bedside listening to the beat of his brother's heart. It was time, it was war and he was willing to do whatever it took to take the Watson brothers down. Mike Morgan was sat next to him and whispered, "They're going to pay Ged, they need to know we're not some two bit pricks who will take this sitting down. We need to hit them where it hurts, we need to rip out his lifeline, hit Jud where it hurts. We need to take something he really cares about, something that will let him know we mean business."

Ged nodded his head slowly. "Take his bird, take

Dawn. The guy is smitten with her and he'll do anything to get her back."

Mike chuckled and patted his hand against his brother's leg who was lay in the bed. "So, that's it then. We'll take the dirt bag and see if that rattles his cage. I want what he owes us too."

Ged stood up and walked about the room. "We'll take it all back, everything he owes us, is coming back. Our Danny will pull through soon and we'll be back to normal."

Mike touched the top of his brother's head with a flat palm. "Don't you worry lad. Jud Watson is going into a body bag and anyone else that gets in our way."

The brothers left the hospital and jumped into the cars. They had a lot of things to do and time wasn't on their side. The shit was about to hit the fan. Spencer Pritchard watched the Morgan brothers leave and he waited until the coast was clear. He flicked his cigarette butt onto the roadside and dipped his head low as he entered the hospital. What the hell was he doing here? Jud would have killed him stone dead if he knew he was visiting Danny Morgan.

Dawn straightened her hair and quickly changed her clothes. "Mam, has Jud been back yet?"

Maureen lifted her head up from the sofa and yawned. "No, well, saying that I've been asleep so I don't think so."

Dawn rushed about the front room and Maureen was watching her. "What are you up to snidey knickers. I've told you time and time again that you can't hide anything from me."

"Mam, piss off, just go back to sleep."

Maureen sat up and stretched her arms above her head. "Where you going anyway? I'll be on my own again. I'm not going out for ages yet, why don't you sit and talk to me for a bit. We can bond."

Dawn kept her back to her mother. "We're going out for something to eat mam. You can get a Pot Noodle out of the cupboard if you're hungry. I swear, don't be doing your puppy eyes to Jud when he gets here because you're not coming out with us. You're a right cling-on sometimes. Get a life of your own. You'd think Jud was your fella and not mine the way you go on."

Maureen switched her eyes to the clock on the wall. "Go on then, piss off. I'm used to being left on my own. You'll regret this when I'm dead."

Dawn heard her mobile ringing and rummaged into her handbag to locate her phone. Stood looking at it in her hands she took a deep breath. "I'm ready Jud, just give me two minutes to get my shoes on." The call ended and Dawn was running about the room like a blue-arsed fly. Grabbing her handbag from the side she clocked her mother's face. "Oh, cheer up mother it might never happen. You've got a date anyway so start getting ready instead of just lying there."

Maureen pulled the cushion closer to her and cuddled into it. "Yeah, I'll get a bath in a minute I just need to find a bit of bleeding energy first."

Dawn gave herself one last look in the mirror and left the room. Maureen sat alone. Closing her eyes she tried to catch forty winks before her date. It seemed just like seconds had passed and Maureen bolted up from her position on the sofa. Someone was banging at the front door and they were desperate to get inside. "Shut the fuck up banging like that will you," she screamed into the hallway. If this was Dawn she was going to give her a bollocking for forgetting her keys again. She was like that Dawn was, she never made sure she had her keys before she left the house. Maureen dragged the front door open. Her eyes were wide open and she was stuck for words. "What are you doing here? Dawn said if you set foot inside this house again she'll make sure everyone knows your secret."

Paul Watson was drunk and he was cocky as he pushed past her. "Mo, you know why I'm here and you want it as much as I do. You're my guilty pleasure and I can't help it if I'm addicted to an older woman. You're my Mrs Robinson. Come here you saucy old mare and give me a kiss."

Maureen clicked the catch on the front door and led her toy boy into the bedroom. They were laughing and joking and eager to get to bed. Paul had been sleeping with Maureen for years. It all just sort of happened. It was Dawn's birthday party and they'd all come back to her house for a few extra drinks after the pub. Paul was sat there and before she knew it he was making advances towards her. Of course she was flattered, he'd swept her off her feet with his compliments, he was a right charmer. Nobody had ever spoken to her like that before. The two of them sat up all night talking and before they knew it they were in bed together. Paul had tried to sneak out of Maureen's bedroom in the early hours of the morning but it was too late, Dawn had clocked him. The funny thing was, she never said a word to him, she just shook her head and smirked. He knew she had this over him and she was always threatening to reveal his secret whenever he got above his station. Dawn had confronted Maureen about it too but she never got any sense out of her. Her mother just chuckled and told her she was living her life. So what if Paul was the same age as her own son? If she could still pull a man that young, then it was all gravy in her world. She was a "MILF" and proud of it. A dirty cougar who'd pulled a young stud. Paul's eyes were rolling, he was off his head. He'd always hunt Maureen down when he was like this. His twisted mind craved the body of an older woman. Maureen found the energy she was looking for and took control in the bedroom. She was the leader, there was no way she was letting any young stud rule the roost on her watch. This woman was filthy and the things she was willing to do to please her man was sickening. Paul groaned as she sank her lips around his penis. He pressed her head down further and closed his eyes. He was in heaven, she was just what the doctor ordered.

CHAPTER SIXTEEN

DANNY MORGAN COUGHED and spluttered as he tried to regain his breath. It had been days now since he'd been admitted into hospital and he was just about on the mend. This guy had severe injuries, wounds that would be with him until his dying breath, a reminder that Jud Watson would always stand in his way in his quest to take over the Manchester Crime scene. Spencer Pritchard reached over and touched the side of Danny's cheek, his finger slowly stroking him, carefully looking into his eyes. "We need to end this once and for all Danny. Someone is going to end up dead. Can't you sort this shit out and walk away. I love you and I don't want you in the firing line anymore. I've showed you what I would do, to prove my love for you Danny. I've betrayed my own family and everyone else I love. Now, you need to do the same for me and show me you care."

Danny rolled on his side and ragged his hands though his hair. "Ssssshh, will you. You never know who's listening. The walls have ears." Danny was an undercover gay and he hated that people would judge him if they found out his secret. Danny had been bi-sexual for as long as he could remember and he'd met Spencer a few years before. The only reason Danny slept with women was to keep his secret safe, he preferred men. Danny sat up and looked directly into Spencer's eyes. "I know you love me. Fuck me you've told me enough times. Sean Watson didn't have to die though," he rolled his eyes and let out a laboured breath as he continued talking. "He was never a threat to you. I told you that. He was just a bit of fun that's all, someone to pass the time with. He never deserved to die. I know he said he was going to uncover me as a gay but death, Spencer, there was no need for that. I could have silenced him in some other way."

Spencer turned his head away and looked out of the window, his eyes clouded over and the reality of what he'd done for the man he loved hit home. "You were always flirting with him, Danny. I just lost the plot. I never meant to kill him. I was just going to warn him off. You know how jealous I get. I swear to you, I just pulled in the car park and spotted him. I was only going to chat to him but before I knew it the guy had snuffed it."

Danny could tell he was lying and sat back in his bed. "Spencer, don't think I'm fucking green. You knew what you were doing the minute you saw him going to the pub. You wanted Sean out of the picture from the moment you'd seen the ring he bought me. It was a present, a gift, nothing more, nothing less, just a gift."

Spencer was agitated, his mouth was dry and he was panicking. "No, it wasn't like that Danny, I just flipped. I swear down, I never meant for him to die."

Danny shook his head and closed his eyes slowly as the vision of Sean Watson's face filled his mind. "You killed him so he could never be with me again. Plus, the ten grand you took from him was a bonus too. I suppose it's all fair in love and war isn't it, but come on Spencer, killing somebody out of jealousy is pretty fucked up. I don't know how you sleep at night."

Spencer snapped, he loved Danny or so he said he did, but he wasn't listening to this. This guy had double standards. "Danny, you've killed a man before for less, so that makes us two of a kind in my eyes! That runt was slipping drugs into the young guy's drinks. He was abusing them, you know that. I told him straight that I was on to him and he didn't listen to a word I said. So it's hard fucking luck, isn't it, he paid the price. The fucking dirty pervert."

Danny sniggered. He was right, Sean Watson was into some seriously sick shit. Danny had a fling with him in the past and he thought he could have made a life with him but once the sick shit started he wanted out of the relationship as soon as he could. Sean was into young boys, bondage and shit like that. Spencer had done him a favour if the truth was known but he would never tell him that. Sean was threatening to tell Jud about Danny and that wasn't good. Danny's family were as anti-gay as any other around there and he always hid away behind his masculine imagine. His brothers would have disowned him if they ever got a whiff of his sexuality. Especially Mike, he hated the thought of two men sharing a bed together, he hated gays full-stop.

Spencer moved closer on the bed. "I've still got the money I took from Sean. Let's run away together, live a life without all this shit. There is nothing keeping us here is there? We can have a stress free life, be together, no more lies. Give me the key to the safe and I'll get the money we need to book our tickets."

Danny stroked the end of his chin, playing with the

sprinkle of dark hairs that had grown there. "Are you having a laugh Spencer? What fucking planet are you on? Jud Watson has to pay for what he's done to me first. I can't just run away from this, imagine what people will say. No, this cunt is getting weighed in before I go anywhere. He's getting wasted, trust me. Spencer, look at my face, look at what that twat has done to me. I'm scarred for life now."

Spencer snivelled, he was a right soft get and had the emotions of a woman. "Jud will get what's coming to him Danny. Our Dawn will see to that. She was going to see Larry today. I heard her talking about it to Sally."

Danny folded the pillow behind his head. "Fuck off, stop lying. Wow, your sister doesn't give a flying fuck does she? Ruthless she is. I thought she loved Jud. Sally told me she was making a go of it with him."

Spencer raised his eyes. He hated that the man he loved was seeing another woman to hide his guilty pleasure. And just the sound of Sally's name on his lips made him cringe. "Our Dawn is a slut you know that. I love her but don't like the way she behaves, she's got no shame. It breaks my heart really because imagine if she really does love Larry, it's a hard one to call. Jud will destroy her if she does this to him again. He's forgiven her once, he'll never do it again. Perhaps, she needs to leave Manchester too. It's the only way forward if you ask me."

Danny agreed, and even though he didn't like siding with Jud, he thought he'd be within his rights to stop her breathing. The girl had made a laughing stock of him, embarrassed him big time. Spencer closed the curtains around the bed and slid his hand underneath the blanket, rummaging about. Slowly, you could see his hand moving about, jerking to and fro. Danny closed his eyes and dragged Spencer's head under the covers. Groans could be heard. Spencer dug his hand in the drawer and you could see him stealing the key for the safe.

Dawn sat eating her meal with Jud. She was in a world of her own and wasn't concentrating, away with the fairies. The pair of them seemed edgy, distant towards each other, hardly talking. What if she just blurted it out? What if she just come clean and told him she loved Larry, would it be that bad? Surely, he would understand that she couldn't help it. Sipping on her glass of red wine she touched the top of her glass with her finger. She was watching Jud texting on his phone. Okay, she wasn't in love with him anymore but how dare he be so ignorant while he was in her company. She coughed to get his attention. "Who's on the phone?" she asked.

She leaned forward trying to get a quick look at his phone screen. Jud snatched his phone back and shoved it in his shirt pocket. "Nobody that concerns you, my love," he was smirking at her, hiding something, sneering. Jud was in a funny mood tonight and he was so snappy, he couldn't be arsed with all her drama. "Have you finished with your food yet, or what? I'm knackered and I want to go home." Dawn picked at her food playing with the pieces of meat on her plate. Jud was on one, growling at her. "Fuck me, you've hardly touched it anyway, wasteful you are. It's the last time I'm bringing you out for something to eat, you're a waste of fucking time you are."

Dawn looked at the food on her plate, he was right.

She'd hardly touched it, she had no appetite whatsoever and every mouthful she took was making her feel sick. "I wonder how your mother is doing on her date," Dawn said in a cocky tone, looking straight at him. Jud sat forward and she realised he didn't know a thing about it. Something tells me that she did know what she was doing though and any chance she got she would have a dig at his family members. "Oh sorry, didn't you know?" she chuckled. "Me and my big mouth, ay. Oh well, what's the harm in you knowing. She's a grown woman. She's entitled to go out on a date isn't she?"

Jud gulped the rest of his drink down his neck and banged the empty glass on the table. "Is she fuck allowed out on a date. She's my mother. I don't want her getting a name for herself like your mother has."

Dawn growled at him and she was looking for an excuse to cause an argument anyway. Yes, he was right. Maureen was a slapper but there was no way in this world she was letting him talk about her like that. Maureen was a woman with needs just like Jud's mother was. "What do you mean by that, Jud? Go on, say what you have to say about my mother? Go on! I dare you."

Jud had just about had enough of this smacked-arse, she was doing his head in. He was sick to death of treating her with kid gloves. Every day it was the same, nothing ever changed. It was too much hard work and he'd had enough of it. The pair of them locked horns and neither of them were backing down. This was a slanging match. "It would do your mother a world of good to get a good shag anyway, she might straighten her miserable face then. At least, my mam knows how to have a good time, she's lived, unlike your sour- faced mother."

Jud sat back in his chair, the gloves were off. If she wanted a slanging match then she was getting one. He was ready for her, holding nothing back. "Your mam sleeps with anything, as long as she's getting a drink off them. My mother has class, she has standards. All of us Watsons have standards," he chuckled and looked Dawn up and down. "Well, I used to."

Dawn had seen her arse now and she was out to hurt him, dig the knife in and twist it deep. "Oh is that right you tosser. You'd be surprised at what you Watson brothers will sleep with. I'd stop it right there Jud, before I say something I might regret."

This was going off big time, other people in the restaurant were looking at them both now and you could see the waiters on standby ready to pounce. He went nose to nose with her, the vein at the side of his neck was pumping with rage. "Dawn, you're a slut and so is your mother. You're both alike. I don't even know why I ever had you back, second-hand goods you are, damaged. Go on, fuck off, get out of my sight before I slap you, you cheeky slut! Fuck off before I lose my rag!"

Dawn stood and grabbed her coat from the back of the chair. She was more annoyed at the way Jud was treating her than anything else and she hated that he'd lost any respect for her. But then again this was what she wanted wasn't it? A way out, to walk away and live her life with the man she loved. She stood tall with one hand placed firmly on her hip. "If I go now Jud, then that's me and you done with." She stood watching him waiting for some kind of reaction, there was none. He never flinched.

Dawn screamed at the top of her lungs, she wanted an answer. "I said if I go now, then we're done. So, what's it to be?"

Jud had heard what she said and he never moved a muscle. "Go on, fuck off. I won't be stopping you. Is that what you're waiting for, for me to stop you?"

Dawn looked at the others in the room and she knew she would have to walk away. Her pride was at stake and everyone was hanging on her every word. "So, we're done then?"

He smirked at her and sucked on his gums as if he hadn't a care in the world. "Go and live your daft selfish life with someone who will put up with you. Let's see how long they last ay," he ranted. Jud shouted over to the waiter to bring him another drink and completely ignored her.

The shit was going to hit the fan now, nobody ignored Dawn Pritchard, ever. "Do you want to know why you'll never be the man for me Jud, let me tell you, should I?" You could have heard a pin drop and the couple sat near their table, moved out of the way quickly. "You're shit in bed, there you go. I've said it. You don't tick any of my boxes in the bedroom department, you never have. Fucking boring you are, like shagging a pig in a fit."

Jud smirked and took his drink from the waiter. As he took a large mouthful from it he looked directly at her. "And, you think you tick all my boxes do you. Let me tell you some facts love, shall I? It's like shagging a wet lettuce shagging you."

Giggles could be heard from the corner of the room. A man covered his mouth with his hand and sniggered.

Jud was in full control of this situation and he'd not finished with her yet. He addressed the other diners in the room. "See this slut here, everyone," he pointed at Dawn waving his finger up and down. "This slapper thought she could have me over, when in fact it was the other way around. I've always known about her and Larry my brother and do you know why?" his voice was getting louder. Dawn hunched her shoulders and flicked her hair over her shoulder. She was waiting for him to continue, to say what he had to say then she was leaving. "Because, your own mother told me. Yep, your own flesh and blood grassed you up, you silly bitch."

Dawn wasn't having any of it he was bluffing for sure. "My mam would never say anything like that Jud, stop lying. As if she would tell you that!"

Here it was, the killer blow, the knockout punch. The moment he'd been waiting for. "Oh, she would when my cock was stuck inside her. Ask her Dawn, go on, ask her how she used to pay all her bills. You know more than me that she blows all her own money on the beer. She's in deep woman, you know that more than me. She's been sucking my cock for years, like mother, like daughter isn't it!" There was a collective gasp in the restaurant. This was unbelievable, real life drama.

Dawn reached over and grabbed his drink off the table. Jerking it back she flung it all over him. This was a show not to be missed and people were moving forward to get a better look of the action. Jud licked his lips as the cold lager dribbled down his face. He'd not finished with her yet either. "I'm in love with someone else too. So you go running back to Larry and see if he wants you now.

Don't ever think you can have me over."

For once in her life Dawn was speechless, her mouth was moving but not a single word was coming out. She looked at him closely, was he just saying this to hurt her? She wasn't sure. Bending down she grabbed her bag and barged passed the people at the side of her. "Drop dead Jud Watson, drop fucking down dead." Dawn stormed out of the restaurant, she was a woman on a mission. She wanted answers from her mother, there must have been some truth in what he'd just said, otherwise why had he said it in the first place? Surely, Jud was lying, even Maureen would never stoop that low would she?

Dawn stood at the bus top on the main road. She'd been there about ten minutes and there still wasn't a sign of a bus anywhere. Her purse was empty and all the change she had was just enough to pay her fare home. The roads were quiet tonight and not a single person was about. A cat crawled from the bushes behind her and when she first spotted it her heart nearly stopped, she nearly shit her knickers. Dawn was fuming, she kept walking up and down and stamping her feet on the ground. Bashing her head against the bus shelter, kicking at it, banging her head on it. "Cheeky hard-faced bastard, how dare he speak to me like that? And, you mother, oh you're going to get it too. Just you wait until I get home you dirty no good slapper. I'll fucking sort you out once and for all." Dawn turned her head quickly as a hand pressed firmly over her mouth. She was being dragged kicking and screaming into the bushes and it was there she met her attackers' for the first time. Mike and Ged Morgan tied her up and dragged her to the boot of the awaiting car on the other side of the road. Her mouth was taped up and every now and then her body folded as a fist from one of the brothers pounded into her body.

Mary Watson sat in The Foresters drinking her brandy with her date Stan. He was an absolute gentleman and all night he'd been treating her like a princess, buying her drinks, pulling her chair out for her. Maureen hadn't turned up for her date and the guy she was meeting had left earlier. There was no way he was being a gooseberry. Mary had really made an effort tonight, she was glowing. Her hair was styled and she'd been to town and bought herself a new outfit. She had her glad rags on tonight and she was out to impress. Stan looked over at her and he smiled. "Do you know what Mary? I've had such a great evening with you tonight. It's just what I needed to take me away from my own life. You know, the usual problems and stress. My family worries would curl your toes. You don't know the half of it."

Mary sat back and rolled her eyes. She understood, she knew more than anyone how much your home life affected your everyday life. "Stan, you're talking to me now. I bet whatever your life consists of, mine is ten times worst." He smiled, did he want to burden her with his worries or just keep it to himself? He'd only just met her and he didn't want to put her off. Mary broke the silence, why should she hold it all in, a problem shared was a problem halved in her eyes. "My sons are driving me mad, Stan. They're into everything and some nights I don't sleep a wink. My son was murdered, my poor Sean.

He was my baby, gone, and for what, bleeding greed and gangland crime." Stan sat forward in his seat. This woman was on his wavelength and he held a look of relief on his face. Mary moved closer and started to pour her heart out. "I've got two sons half killing each other Stan and God knows how it will end up, one of them is going to end up dead, I'm sure of it." Mary held her head to the side and her bottom lip trembled. "Sometimes, I just want to pack my bags and run away from it all, just run as far away as possible and never come back, seriously. Our Jud is dangerous and I never know what is going on in that sick twisted head of his."

Stan stared at her and his face creased, his jaw swung low. He moved closer. "Mary, tell me your son isn't Jud Watson, the Jud Watson?"

She dipped her head and tapped her fingers on her knees. She was ashamed of her son's reputation and hated admitting to anyone he was a criminal. "Yes, Jud is my eldest son, why, do you know him?"

Stan picked his pint up and took a large mouthful, he swallowed hard. "Mary Watson, bleeding hell why didn't I click with your surname?"

Mary looked puzzled. "Is there something wrong, love?"

Stan ragged his fingers through his fine grey hair and pushed his glasses further up his nose. "Mary, I'm Danny Morgan's dad. Your Jud has kicked fuck out of my son and put him in hospital. Callous cunt he is, nothing else."

Mary swallowed hard, surely she'd heard him wrong. This couldn't be right. "Stan, you mean you're the father of them bastards who've been at my boys for months trying to hurt them?" Mary's back was up and she was in fighting mode now, shoulders back, fists curled ready to attack. Her boys were her world, yes, she could call them, but as far as she was concerned nobody else could damage their name. Maureen gritted her teeth tightly together. "Your Danny has been winding Jud up for months, he had him over and double-crossed him. He deserved everything he got in my eyes. You don't piss on your own doorstep."

Stan was bright red, steam was coming out of his ears. He knew how the world worked and knew given half the chance Jud would have done the same to his son. He was no fool. "Mary, Jud is an out and out bully. I know he's your boy but ask anyone who knows him, fucking liberty taker he is. The Watson brothers are well known for taking what they want, no matter what they have to do for it." Stan shook his head. This date was going pear-shaped now. A total flop. "I met your youngest son now come to think of it, he was always with our Danny a while back and he seemed sorted, not like the others. The best of the bunch if you ask me."

Mary bit hard on her bottom lip and started to get her stuff together. The night was over in her eyes. There was no way she was sitting around listening to him slate her boys. "Why would my Sean be with your Danny? No, I think you've got that wrong. Sean hated Danny just the same as his brothers did. Stan, don't you be bad mouthing my sons' name because I'll bleeding swing for you. I will you know, I've shit bigger than you. I'm not afraid of any man or woman, ask anyone who knows me."

Stan looked at her and was aware she was capable of

throwing a decent punch. Her hands were bigger than any woman's he'd seen before. "Turn it in ay Mary. Sit back down and let's talk this out. We're both innocent in this and as we said before we're both fed up with it. You said it yourself that you feel like running away. Well, me too." Mary froze, should she stay or should she go? She was hovering, unsure of her next move. Stan reached over and touched her arm softly. "Mary, please sit back down and let's talk about this like two grown adults. We're the innocent parties in all this. Why can't we just call a truce?" Mary dropped her handbag back down on the chair and sat down with her arms folded tightly across her chest. Her face was like thunder and if he even tried to put her sons down again he was getting a bunch of fives smashed right between his eyes. Oh, yes. She was having none of it. "My lads just got caught up in the world they knew nothing about Mary. I've had all the trouble like you've probably had. Police booming my door in every other night. Men threatening to kill me, cars being set on fire. It's been terrible if I'm being honest with you."

Mary was still in a strop, she was cooling down but her guard was still up. "Stan, my boys are just the same and we do what we do to protect them. I'm sorry to hear about Danny but, come on, it could have easily been my Jud lying there half dead."

Stan nodded his head. His eyes clouded over and his lip trembled. "It was all the stress that killed my Fiona off, she was my wife." Mary swallowed hard and touched the end of his fingers on the table. It was a crying shame for him and she knew exactly how it felt losing a partner. Stan continued as his eyes clouded over. "The lads knew she was ill and when the doctors told us she didn't have long left the family just went to pot. Our Danny was only sixteen when she left us. Cancer is a horrible thing to go through. A bleeding nightmare that I wouldn't wish on my worst enemy." Mary looked at her empty glass, she felt his pain, she understood his emotion. Stan clocked her glass and smiled. "Bloody hell, what am I like ay. I'll get you another drink."

Stan went to the bar and Mary was glad he'd given her some breathing space, a chance to clear her mind. What were the chances of this happening? It was spooky and Mary didn't know if she should grab her belongings and just flee into the night without saying goodbye. Jud would shit a brick if he knew she was seeing the father of his enemy. But, what about Mary? She deserved some happiness and for years she'd never met anyone she'd clicked with like she had with Stan. It was time to think about herself. She was doing what was right for her this time and nobody else. You only get one chance at life and she was taking it. Mary watched Stan standing at the bar and smiled. She folded her coat neatly at the side of her and placed her handbag back on the floor.

★

Dawn was tied to a chair. She was rocking about and nearly falling over. Mike Morgan was pacing around her and every now and then he kicked the leg of the chair she was sitting on. Mike went nose to nose with her and pulled the tape off her mouth with a swift movement. "Bastards," she screamed as soon as she could speak. "What the fuck are you doing this for? Let me go and I'll keep my mouth shut about it. I swear I won't say Jack shit."

Mike chuckled as he sat facing her. He popped a fag into the corner of his mouth and blew smoke out. "So, you're the tart who's been causing all the trouble in the Watson household?"

Dawn was wriggling about and the chair was wobbling. "I don't know what you've heard about me but just let me go. Fucking hell, what do you want with me anyway?"

Mike shot a look over at Ged and rubbed his hands together. "I'm not sure yet. Do you know what Jud did to my brother? Let me tell you shall I." He spat at her from where he was sat and his cheeks were bright red as he continued. "He half fucking killed him and now it's payback time. You're getting it too, now. I'm going to scar you for life, mess that pretty little face up."

Dawn had to think quick, show no fear, find her inner strength, her poker face. If she showed these men any fear whatsoever she would be making a rod for her own back. Taking a deep breath she raised a half-hearted smile. "So, Danny Morgan is your brother?"

Mike nodded. "Give the slut a round of applause, the penny has finally dropped. Quite clever really aren't you?"

Dawn sat thinking for a few seconds and she was aware she was in a dangerous situation. She had to buy some time. "And, what has this got to do with me?"

Mike ran at her and dragged her head back, this shit was going down, he meant business. His warm breath sprayed into her face and as he spoke her heart skipped a beat. "Listen, you cocky cow. Don't think anybody can save you here. This is our turf and I won't think twice about slicing you up. I'll scar you for life if you think you can chat shit to me." Mike pulled a small knife from his back pocket and forced it into the side of her cheek. The skin was turning white and any more pressure she would have been bleeding. She gasped for breath, panicking.

"I'm not with Jud anymore. I told him tonight it was over. He doesn't care if I'm dead or alive. I love Larry Watson. I want to be with Larry, nobody else."

Ged came over and pulled his brother away with force. Mike was a crank and he wouldn't have thought twice about slicing this gobby bitch into a thousand pieces. Ged took over now, "Well, we'll have to take your word on that won't we but I hope for your sake Jud loves you otherwise you'll be going into the canal with a concrete slab tied around your neck."

Mike sat back down and he was giving Dawn the evils. He was always like this when he had a beef with somebody. What was the point in talking when he could just kick the living daylights out of her? His own girlfriend knew when to stop and he always made sure he kept her in check. What right did a woman have to answer him back, none in his eyes, none whatsoever. He hated women who had too much to say for themselves and always made it clear that on his watch he wouldn't stand for any back chat. Mike watched the door open in the distance and smiled. Dawn couldn't see who came into the room and she closed her eyes expecting a belt from behind. The death blow. Ged sniggered as the woman walked past him, there was nothing better than watching two women fight to the death. Mike pulled a chair up for his guest and the scraping of legs along the floor could be heard.

Dawn slowly opened her eyes and she had to catch her breath when she saw who it was sat facing her. "What the fuck is that lunatic doing here?" Dawn hissed.

Mike held his head to the side and looked at Michelle for some answers. This was her call and he was sitting back watching the entertainment. "Oh, you didn't expect to see me here did you Dawn? Did you really think I would let you take Larry from me without a fight?"

Dawn's heart was pounding inside her ribcage. This shit had just got real. Michelle was a ticking bomb and she knew whatever happened here today she was not walking away without any injuries. What could she do now? She'd have to think of something and fast, her life was in jeopardy. "Michelle, what is your problem with me? I know Larry loves you and I've accepted that now. Okay, you've won, you can have him."

Michelle was listening and the corner of her mouth started to rise. This was a top plan that Dawn had come up with and it seemed to be working. Michelle was listening now. "What, Larry has told you he loves me?"

Mike and Ged looked at each other and there was no way they were keeping schtum, this woman was being had over. "Whoa, down there, Michelle. Dawn has just told us she loves Larry and she's getting off with him. She's having you over, don't listen to a word she's saying. Honest, don't be fooled by the conniving bitch, she's a lying cunt."

Dawn attacked back. Her eyes were wide open and she was constantly licking her dry cracked lips. "Ignore them Michelle. I just said that to shut them up. But, it's true what I just said. Me and Jud are over. I'm leaving

Manchester and I'm never coming back. What's left here for me anyway," she raised her eyes and forced some tears into them hoping to gain some sympathy. "I need a new life Michelle. Jud would never let me be free living around here would he? I've got to leave for my own peace of mind. As a woman you understand that don't you?"

Michelle was falling for this bullshit hook, line and sinker. She walked over to Dawn and started to untie her. Mike jumped in. "What the fuck are you doing? She's our way to Jud. Leave her there, fuck me Michelle, don't be fooled by her lies."

Michelle turned around and growled at him. "Listen you pricks. I told you I wanted Dawn here. Don't jump on the bandwagon now thinking you can take her from me. A deal is a deal. Remember, you scratch my back and I'll scratch yours."

Ged shook his head. She was right, Michelle had passed them so much information lately and it was only through her that they had the Watson's electrical shipment away. Of course she always got a bung from any jobs she'd helped create, but every now and then she called in her favours and today was one of them. Michelle had a stash of money saved up and over time she had her hands in some big ventures as the silent partner. Michelle was funding a lot of the crime in the area and a lot of men held the utmost respect for her. Of course she was a lunatic but money talked and nobody flinched when she funded their latest scheme, they all kept it shut.

Dawn was free, at last she could move her arms and legs. She went to stand up but Michelle gripped her by the throat, sinking her fingers deep into her jugular vein. "Not so fast my dear. Do you think it's going to be that easy to get away from me?" Dawn weighed up the situation and clocked the men still stood in the room. Yes, she could have had a go at Michelle, try and hurt her but she was outnumbered. She sat back down slowly and listened to what Michelle had to say. "I want you gone tonight. I'll take you wherever it is you want to go. But I want you gone from Manchester, gone from Larry's life for good."

Dawn saw a way of earning a few quid here and dropped her head low. "Michelle, I would leave tonight but I need to get some money together first. I need a place to stay, food. I can't just leave with nothing. I'll have to try and get some cash together, then I'll be out of your hair for good, I promise."

Michelle paced up and down the room. Up and down she walked, up and down. She was in deep thought as the others just looked at her. Could she chance Dawn still being around and seeing Larry? He might want her again and then what chance would she stand? Michelle weighed up the situation. He'd already told Dawn he loved her so what the hell was she waiting for, she had to get rid of her now while she still had the chance. "I'll give you some money to leave. Two grand should be enough to get you on your feet shouldn't it?"

Dawn gave a cunning smile, this was like taking candy from a baby. She had no intention of leaving but there was no way she was telling this crank that. Especially, if she was bunging her a few quid. Dawn spoke in a low voice. "Michelle that would help a lot. I realised now that I don't stand a chance against you. Larry told me straight that you're the woman for him and I'd never match up to you. He's besotted with you."

Dawn was that good, she was actually believing this bullshit herself. Michelle was actually buying this cock and bull story. Was she for real or what? The red glow on her cheeks was going brighter by the second. She was having it, she actually thought that Dawn was telling the truth. At last, Larry Watson loved her. The happy ending she'd always dreamed of. The man she loved in her arms forever. "I'll need a few hours before I leave though Michelle. I can't go until tomorrow night. I need to get my ship in order before I can go anywhere because I don't want to be having to come back do I?" This was unbelievable, Dawn had more front than Blackpool. Hats off to her though, she was getting away with it.

Ged and Mike shrugged their shoulders, this was her shout and she was the one calling all the shots. Michelle walked to the small window and inhaled the fresh air. "Right, fuck off from here and I'll be in touch with you." Walking back to Larry's other woman she went nose to nose with her. "Dawn, I swear if you think you can have me over then you can think again. I'll find you, and I'll kill you. Mark my words I'll do time for you."

The hairs on the back of Dawn's neck stood on end and a chill passed through her body. At this moment though she just wanted to get out of this place. It was the early hours in the morning and all she wanted to do was get back home safely, alive. Michelle raised her eyes to Ged who was stood by the door. He let out a laboured breath and shook his head as Dawn ran past him. She was free, the moment she got out of there she just kept running and running, never stopping for breath, her head twisting like an owl in a barn. Dawn didn't have a clue where she was. Her heart was beating like a speeding train and she was forever looking over her shoulder. Her feet pounded on the pavement, she wasn't stopping for love nor money.

Jud lay awake in bed and looked at the female body lying next to him. He had a lot on his mind and big decisions to make. If the truth was known he was sick to death of the life he was living. He hated that he could never rest, never sleep and never let his guard down. There was always someone out to end his life, take his empire away. Reaching over he stroked the side of the woman's face. "Oi, sleepy head. Come on, we have to leave soon. I've got a lot of sorting out to do and I want you out of the picture for a while until the dust settles. Danny Morgan will be out of hospital soon and heads are going to roll. It's war."

The woman raised her head from under the duvet. "Jud, are we ever going to be together. I mean, just me and you like you said it would be. Just tell me now - if we're not, I'll walk away."

Jud snuggled next to her and his hot breath made her shiver as he spoke to her. "Sally, you know I love you. You've been the only woman I've trusted in a long time. If it wasn't for you, I would have never found out about Larry and Dawn. Don't get me wrong I'd heard it before but you told me facts; times, dates. Sally, just sit tight for a little bit longer and I'll show you how much you mean to me."

Sally was fed up. "Jud, I don't want to live in her shadow for the rest of my life," she sighed, "even after I told you she was sleeping with Larry you was still prepared to marry her. I've done everything to make you happy. I slept with Danny Morgan for you, doesn't that show you that I'd do anything to be with you, even lie to my best friend." Sally curled up in a tiny ball and dragged the duvet over her shoulders. What a Judas she was, selling her best friend out like that. A grassing bitch. Sally spoke with her back to Jud. "I gave it all up for you Jud. I should never have done what I did with you and every day I hate myself for it but you can't stop love, can you?"

Jud lay on his back and looped his hands behind his head. "We've always had a connection Sally, right from day one. Yeah, I was with Dawn but come on, you saw the way she acted around men; she was a tart, a dirty flirt who was always wanted more than she could have. Whereas you Sally," he reached his hand over and started tickling her back. "You have always been happy with just me. I'm not going to lie to you, yeah, at first it was just a bang but as time went on I started to have feelings for you. Do you feel the same about me Sally?" There was a pause and Jud poked his finger deep into her waist. "Sally, how do you feel about me?"

She rolled over and sank her head deep into his chest. Playing with the dark sprinkle of hairs there she looked up into his eyes. "I love you Jud. I've tried to fight my feeling for ages but they just won't go away. I'm going to tell Dawn too. She has a right to know. I don't care what happens after that, I just need to get this off my chest and move on with my life."

These were strong words and Jud knew one way or the other Dawn would break her neck for betraying her. He shook his head and cupped her face in his hands. "I'll be the one to tell Dawn about us Sally. You just go to the house and get everything you need. Say your goodbyes too because as soon as this fight is over, we're getting off. I want us to start a new life in the sun, perhaps Spain, or Greece, what do you think?"

Sally smiled, Jud was her Prince Charming and she believed she was getting her happy ending after all. But there was something in her smile that just wasn't right, she was playing some kind of game with him. "I'll do anything to make you happy, Jud. I've waited this long for you so another few weeks isn't going to make any difference is it? Why don't I get all the money together and go and hide out until you're ready."

Jud chewed on his fingernail and shook his head. "No, you leave all that to me Sally. I'll sort everything out." The two of them shared a passionate kiss before they started to get ready to leave the hotel. Sally checked her mobile phone and there were twenty-one missed calls from Dawn in the last ten minutes. It was D day, time to come clean, time to confess all. This was her fight and not Jud's. She could do her own dirty work.

Dawn screamed around the house looking for Maureen. "Mam, where the hell are you? Come on you dirty trollop. I know you're in here somewhere."

Maureen must have been in the toilet because the

sound of the upstairs toilet flushing could be heard. Maureen walked out of the room with a fag hanging out of mouth and her hair stuck up all over. "Fuck me, who's died? What's all the shouting about?"

Dawn ran up the stairs and dragged her over-sized t-shirt over her head. "You're a disgrace you are. Did you think I wouldn't find out about your dirty, sleazy secret or what?"

Maureen pulled away from her daughter and headed down the stairs. "I don't know what the hell you're harping on about. Brew me a drink and then tell me again when I'm awake."

Dawn ran behind Mo and she nearly sent her flying down the stairs. She was trying to drag her back by her hair. "You've slept with my Jud, he's confessed everything to me. Go on, tell me it's not true."

Maureen fought her off and ran down the stairs, she barged into the kitchen and flicked the switch on. "Oh my God, he's winding you up. He's just saying that because you slept with Larry."

Dawn was behind her shouting down her neck. "No, stop fucking lying. He said it's been going on for years. Come on, tell me the truth, don't lie to me, mother."

Maureen snatched an old t-bag from the side and plonked it in a cup. There was no way she would turn around and face her daughter, she kept her back to her. "He's out to hurt you, bloody hell, think about it Dawn. I'm your mother for crying out loud. I'd never sink that low. I've got my own men. I don't need your cast-offs."

"He's been paying you he said, paying the loan men off for you. Go on tell me the truth you dirty prostitute.

Because, that's what you are mother, if he's been paying you for sex. I mean, what the fuck is he playing at, you're an old granny. Fuck me, you've only got two of your own teeth in your bleeding mouth. You're a gummy fucker."

Maureen had heard enough and turned round slowly and went nose to nose with Dawn. "Gummy fucker, is that right! Well, for your information lady, Jud loved my gums around his plums. He said I was the best lover he's had, just like his brother said too."

Dawn jumped on her and she was going for gold, she had no respect whatsoever for her now and she was pummelling her fists deep into her. Screaming filled the air. Maureen never stood a chance and she just curled her body up in a tiny ball. Dawn was yelling at the top of her voice. She swung her foot back and surged it deep into her mother's frail body. "He was mine mother. I loved him and you had to get your dirty claws into him. Where is your respect for me, ay? I'm your fucking daughter, not a stranger. What the hell is going on inside that warped mind of yours?"

Dawn stepped away from her and stood with her back to the wall. Reality was hitting home now and she'd realised what she'd just done. The front door opened and Sally ran inside. She took one look at Maureen and she was white. "Dawn what the fuck have you done to her, fuck me, you've half killed her."

Maureen was a tough old bird and it would have taken more than that to keep her mouth shut. With a swift flick of her wrist she wiped the blood trickling down from the side of her mouth and scrambled to her feet. "Oh, you no good bastard. Just you wait now. Sally, go and get my trainers from upstairs will you. And, get me a bobble for me to tie my hair back. I'm going to kick her bony arse. You just watch now. How dare you raise your hands to me?"

Sally stood in between them, there were punches flying and Sally had to duck to dodge one. "Fucking turn it in now the pair of you. Dawn just piss off in the front room will you and calm down. I can't believe you could do this to her. She's an old woman, a pensioner nearly."

Dawn growled at her. "Oh, don't you come that with me. Ask the tart what's she's done, go on ask her about Jud and her sleazy secret." Dawn bounced inside the other room and slammed the door behind her.

Sally was alert, what the hell was Dawn talking about, she needed to know. "Come on Mo, let's get you cleaned up, bleeding hell your mouth is cut too. She's really gone to town on you hasn't she. What the hell has gone on?"

Maureen started to walk up the stairs as Sally followed closely behind her. Dawn ran to the bottom of the stairs and shouted up after them. "She's been sleeping with Jud, sucking his cock, Sally. It's been going on for years. Let's see her talk her way out of this one. Sally keep her away from me, because, I'll put her six foot under if I get my hands on her." Sally turned her head behind her and her jaw dropped. She pushed Maureen into the bathroom and bolted the door behind them both.

Maureen walked to the sink and lifted her head up to the mirror. "Orr, look at my lip now. And my eye, it's bleeding swelling. How the hell can I go to bingo looking like this?"

Sally filled the sink up with warm water and Maureen

stood there with her hands resting on the bowl. Sally studied her from the corner of her eye. It wasn't true, surely Dawn was making it up. This woman was nearly a pensioner. There was no way she was having any of it. "Mo, what's Dawn going on about? She said you've been sleeping with Jud, is that true or what?"

Maureen was throwing water over her face and dabbing an old crusty towel on the side of her lip. She never looked at Sally as she spoke. "Yeah, it's true. I'm sorry, but it just happened. It was all him though, he came onto me, he did all the running."

Sally looked like she was going to collapse. She blew her breath out in front of her and sat on the toilet bowl. "Mo, come on, you're just saying that to hurt her. You've never slept with Jud have you? Stop pissing about. A joke's a joke and this has gone too far!"

Maureen snapped, her voice roared. "Yes, I bleeding well have Sally. I'm not ashamed of it either. Mrs fucking fancy pants downstairs was sleeping with Larry, she didn't want him. So why couldn't I have a bit of fun too."

Sally ran to the door and slid the bolt from the top of it. She was retching into her cupped hands. Standing outside the bathroom for a few minutes she tried to calm down. She needed more information, she needed to know he hadn't cheated on her whilst they'd been together. Popping her head inside the door she watched Maureen looking in the mirror, dragging at the baggy skin around her eyes. She edged back inside and let out a laboured breath. "Mo, when did this all happen. Are we talking years ago or recently, come on, when was it?"

Maureen rolled her eyes and licked the tip of her top

lip. "About two months ago was the last time I think. I was pissed, you know what I'm like when I'm steaming. Jud just comes to me when he's fed up. You know, when he needs to bend my ear, a shoulder to cry on." Maureen pressed her hands against the sink and gripped it with force. "Don't listen to Dawn either, he doesn't pay me for sex. I'm not a brass. We have sex together because we enjoy it. No other reason."

Sally paced the bathroom floor, this couldn't be true. Her insides were churning and the thought of the man she loved having sex with this old fossil was making her ill. "So, two months ago you slept with him. Are you sure?"

Maureen barged past her and went into her bedroom. Sally ran after her needing to know the answer. Maureen chuckled as she sucked on the blood still dribbling down her lip. "Men always have a bit on the side, Sally. I don't care what anyone says, they do. I keep marriages alive I do. If it wasn't for me, Jud would have probably dumped Dawn years ago. She's hard work. You know that more than me." Maureen turned to face Sally and snarled. "So, that cunt downstairs should count herself lucky. I did her a favour. What did she expect when she treats him like that?"

Sally was speechless, she stood biting her fingernails. Dawn was shouting from downstairs and Sally went to see her. "Mo, you just stay up here out of the way. I'll try and calm her down. For fucks sake I don't believe this mess. You've really gone and done it this time haven't you?"

Maureen sat on the bed snivelling. The truth was hitting home now. "I'm not a bad person am I Sally? You understand me don't you?" Sally closed the bedroom door behind her and headed downstairs. She never replied.

Sally opened the living room door and Dawn stood screaming at her. "She'd better keep well out of my way, Sally. I swear, let her come within an inch of me and I won't be held responsible for my actions. I'll kick her head right in."

Sally walked over to the window and stared outside. Her eyes clouded over and she shook her head slowly. Dawn was on her phone and she was sat eagerly waiting for the call to be answered. "I'm leaving Manchester, Sally. Once I get hold of Larry, that's it, I'm gone. I can't do this anymore." Sally never said a word. Dawn seemed genuinely sad for a change. "I've lost Jud now anyway so what's the point in staying around here? I may as well give it a go with Larry. I need out of this place. I need to make a new life for myself."

Sally sat down and dipped her head. "How have you lost Jud? I thought you two loved each other?"

"No, it's over. We finished last night. The guy is a complete tosser. He told me about her upstairs last night," she raised her eyes to the ceiling. "I'm fuming, fucking livid. I can't believe it, she's one dirty bitch." Sally was thinking but her mind wasn't on the job. Dawn was still on one. "She thinks she's smart, but let me tell you now, she's finished with me. I'll never speak to her again after this. She's dead as far as I'm concerned."

Sally sucked hard on her gums. "I've got to go Dawn. I've got too many of my own troubles to be listening to this."

Dawn stamped her feet and ragged her fingers through her hair. "What, you're just leaving me. Well, thanks for fuck all then. What kind of friend are you? I've just told you I'm leaving Manchester with Larry and you're not even arsed. Some kind of friend you turned out to be. Go on piss off. I don't need you. I never have." Sally took a deep breath and it was there on the tip of her tongue, she was ready to confess all but stopped at the last minute.

Spencer barged in and he just stood there gawping at them both. He'd been listening for sure, his ears were pinned back and his cheeks were bright red. "Fuck me, who's died. Dawn, what's up with your mush?" Sally wasn't waiting around, she nodded her head at Spencer and left. No banter, no conversation, nothing. "What's up with Sally? Have you two been arguing again?"

Dawn sat down on the sofa and folded her arms tightly around her chest. "Oh, just leave her Spencer. I'm sick to death of her blowing hot and cold with me lately. If truth be told I'm glad to see the back of her. She does my head in." Spencer could see Dawn had been crying, her eyes were red raw. He hunched his shoulders and raised his eyes at her. Dawn took a deep breath and sat back. "Spencer, you better sit down for this. Trust me, get a cig or something, you're going to need it."

Dawn watched as her brother sat down and he was urging her to talk. "Come on then, spill the beans, what's gone on?"

Dawn hung her head and even to tell Spencer what their mother had done was painful. "That slut of a mother has been sleeping with Jud. It's been going on for months, he's been paying her too."

Spencer burst out laughing, his shoulders were shaking up and down. "Orr, stop it Dawn you're killing me now. Stop fucking about and tell me what's up."

"Honest, on my life," she held her hands out in front of her. "Jud told me last night and she's even admitted it, the dirty bastard."

Spencer was still laughing, he looked like he had a feather up his arse. Looking at his sister in more detail his face dropped, she was actually telling the truth for once. He was still smirking though, this was unbelievable. "And, what has she said about it all?" He was thinking out loud. "Why didn't she just deny it? At least then she could have saved some face."

"Oh no, she's proud as punch Spencer. She said he loved it and the only reason Jud stayed with me was to see her. I feel sick, honest to God I just want to strangle her."

Spencer walked to the door and turned his head back slowly. This was shocking news. Okay, he thought it was funny at first but now he'd thought about it he realised how bad his mother really was. "I'm going upstairs to see her. You just stay down here and let me see what she's got to say for herself."

Dawn's mobile was ringing as he left the room. "Where the hell have you been Larry? I've been ringing you for ages. Listen, we're leaving Manchester. Pack your stuff and meet me at the pub." Dawn carried on speaking and you could see the door closing slowly in the front room, someone was listening.

★

Maureen was getting ready, she'd plastered herself in make-up and she was sat looking in the mirror in the bedroom. Spencer came inside the room and shook his head. "Well, you've done it this time haven't you? Just when I thought you couldn't surprise me anymore you go and do something like this."

Maureen turned her head slowly and he could see the state of her injuries for the first time. "Listen, don't you come in here lecturing me about my life when you're just as bad."

Spencer ran inside the room and slammed the door shut behind him. He walked over to the bed. "You're evil you are, pure fucking evil. What, are you trying to blackmail me now just because your life has gone tits up?"

Maureen dabbed a cotton bud on her lip and you could see she didn't have any shame about what she'd done. "We all have secrets, so those without sin cast the first stone." She snarled at her son and knew her point was made.

"You keep your big mouth shut, mother. I'm telling you now, you breathe one word to anyone and I'll do more than kill you."

They stared at each other. "As long as you know then," she whispered. Spencer rushed out of the room and left his mother to get ready. Whatever it was that she knew, he was scared to death of her telling anyone, he was petrified.

Larry sat waiting for Dawn in his car. She was late and he was beginning to get frustrated. Tapping his fingers on the steering wheel he hummed a tune that was on the radio.

The car door opened and in jumped Dawn. "I need to pick up my suitcase from my house. Then we're off. I can't stay here any longer." She shot her eyes around the car and looked puzzled. "Where's your stuff. I mean your clothes and that?"

Larry smirked. "I'm not going anywhere Dawn. I need to sort Jud out first. If he goes down then we don't have to go anywhere."

"No, we need to leave. I've just got to go somewhere later on and once I've done that I'm free to leave."

Larry touched her thigh with his fingers sliding softly over her skin. "You're not listening are you? I said, I'm not going anywhere until I've done what I have to do. Jud's at the pub tonight and I'm going to take him down."

Dawn dropped her head into her hands and lifted her head up slowly. "He's been shagging my mam, he told me last night." Larry wasn't listening and he was checking his phone constantly. "Larry, are you even listening" she shrieked.

"Sorry, what did you say again, I was miles away?"

"I said Jud has been sleeping with my mam."

Larry's jaw dropped, he wasn't sure if she was joking. "Nar, our Jud wouldn't touch her. Why would he have mincemeat when he's already got steak?"

Dawn let out a laboured breath and twiddled with her hair. "Exactly, what's fucking wrong with him?"

Larry could actually see the funny side of it and he was trying his best not to laugh. "Well, the kinky fucker. Who'd have thought he was into the old wrinklies, the fossils?"

Dawn didn't want to talk about it anymore. She was concentrating more on her own life and how to get that sorted. "Larry, tell me you love me and want me."

Dawn was sat waiting for him to answer, she needed him to tell her, she needed for him to want her. He was taking his time though, thinking longer than he should have. Finally he gave her an answer. "Dawn, I do want you, and yes I think I love you."

Dawn snapped, here she was putting her heart on the line and this wanker could only come up with that he thought he loved her. "You think you love me isn't good enough Larry. If we're going to start a new life together don't you think we should be on the same wavelength? I've given it all up for you Larry, everything."

Larry started the engine, he looked over his shoulder and edged into the traffic. "I'll phone you later. I've got enough on my plate at the moment without you adding to it. Just chill, and let's see where we are when everything's sorted out. At the moment I can't think straight."

Dawn checked the time and growled at him. "Just drop me off near the pub. I'll tell you something for nothing Larry Watson," she took a deep breath and looked him straight in the eye. "I'm not waiting about for any man. If you've not called me by ten o'clock tonight then I'm done with you. Do you hear me, I'm gone."

Larry turned the music up and tapped his fingers to the beat of the music. Her heart was low and she knew he was slipping away. The greed for his brother's empire was much stronger than any love he felt for her. All this time, all the words he'd ever said to her were lies. He never wanted her, he just wanted everything his brother had, including his woman. The car stopped and he took a few seconds to open the door. "So, let's see if it's real, Larry. If you ring me, then you ring and if you don't you don't."

Larry pulled her back by her arm. "Stop being such a drama queen, fucking hell, relax. Give me a kiss before you go."

Dawn pulled away from him and dipped her head back inside the car. "There's no more taster sessions from now on Larry, no try before you buy. Make the choices you need to, then ring me." She slammed the door and started to walk off in the opposite direction. Looking at her through the rear view mirror he smirked. He loved watching her arse swing but he knew he'd upset her. Larry edged back into the traffic, he had bigger fish to fry at this moment in time. Dawn would keep until he was ready, she was going nowhere.

★

Later that night, Dawn stood in the shadows, she was edgy and forever checking her phone. Her suitcase was near her feet and the way she was handling it, it didn't look like anything was inside. Dawn jumped out of her skin when she saw Michelle Buckley coming towards her. Just the look of this woman was enough to scare anyone. She had small beady eyes and a nose that looked like it had taken a few belts over the years. Michelle was sniffing hard as she neared her. Dawn swallowed hard and stood tall. It was time, it was all or nothing. Michelle looked Larry's other woman up and down and edged closer to her. Her warm breath tickled her cheeks as she spoke. "So, this is it then. You're leaving?"

Dawn had small balls of sweat forming on her brow and hot sweaty palms, her breathing struggled. "Yes, once you've given me the money I'm getting off from around here. I've got nothing left anymore." Michelle was pacing around her, thinking, not sure of her next move. She had her hand in her pocket and she was holding something. "Have you got the money then or what?" Dawn asked, eager to get away.

"Just hold your horses Dawn. I have to be sure about this before I give you any money." Dawn sighed, she was so impatient.

"Fucking hell, I've just told you I'm leaving. You can come and watch me get on the train if you want."

"I might just do that," Michelle hissed. Opening her jacket Michelle revealed her baby bump. "You see this Dawn, this is how much Larry loves me. This is our child, the baby that means everything to us both."

Dawn dropped her head, she was struggling to see properly. Michelle placed her hand on top of her stomach and closed her eyes slowly. "You nearly ruined my baby's chance of having a father and I don't know if I can let you get away with what you did."

Dawn picked her suitcase up from the floor and stood chewing on her bottom lip. "I'm glad you got your happy ending Michelle. Once you've given me the money we agreed then I might find mine too. We don't need to say anything else do we. Just give me the money and I'm gone. You won't see me around here again."

Michelle reached deep inside her pocket and pulled out an envelope. She held it in her hand and sneered. She was kicking the arse out of this situation and there was no way she was giving it up that easy. Walking closer to Dawn she held the money out to her. She had her hand in her other pocket and her eyes were dancing with madness as she neared her. Dawn reached over to take the money and before she knew it she was looking down the barrel of a gun, a silver pistol shoved deep into her mouth. Dawn tried to move but she didn't stand a chance. Michelle pushed her up against the wall and held one hand around her neck. "Did you really think I would give you the money, Dawn?" The gun was choking her, pressing deep into the back of her throat. "Do you think I bought your little story about Larry loving me either?" Dawn was trying desperately to suck some air inside her lungs but the gun was going deeper and deeper into her mouth. "The only way he will ever love me is when you're gone my dear, fucking dead" Dawn's eyes were wide open and as the bullet fired into her head. Her head exploded like a water melon being dropped to the floor. Michelle was off her head. She flicked the pieces of flesh off her jacket and inhaled deeply. This woman held no remorse for her actions and left her victim's side with a smile on her face. Dawn's body lay lifeless, her face was blown apart. The sound of Michelle's footsteps leaving the scene of the crime filled the air. She was chuckling to herself as she pushed the gun back into her pocket.

Larry received the call he'd been waiting for and he was on his way to the meeting place. It was time to face his fears. Both Danny Morgan and his brothers would be there today. This was getting sorted once and for all. Larry was alone and the sound of his heart beating like a speeding train in his chest was all he had to keep him company. Paul had arranged the meeting, this shit had to be sorted and it was show time. Larry was going to bring his men with him but they all told him straight that this was family business and they wanted no part of it. Heads were going to roll, everybody knew that. Danny Morgan had arranged to come with his brother Mike and Ged just to even things out, in case it kicked off. It was the Watsons against the Morgan's.

The warehouse in Ancoats was deserted. Larry drove into the car park and his head was twisting one way then the other, his arse was flapping. A chill passed over his body and his nerves were on edge, small beads of sweat formed on his forehead and he kept taking deep breaths. There were no guns here today, no tools, no machetes, or bats. This was the rule. If it came to blows each man would fight with their fists or so they said. Larry turned the engine off and stood outside his car. Popping a cigarette into his mouth he stood for a few minutes gathering his thoughts. This was it, time to meet his brother, his enemy. Paul popped his head from the side of the building and whistled over to Larry. "Oi, fucking slug, we're all here, move your arse. This needs sorting as soon as." Larry sucked hard on his fag and casually flicked it to the side of him. With a quick glance over his shoulder he headed inside.

Jud Watson looked as hard as nails. Chest expanded fully and nostrils flared, he was ready for action. He was pacing the floor cracking his knuckles, these cunts were getting wasted, who was he trying to kid. There was no way he was here to talk, heads were going to roll. Paul came back into the room and he was ragging his hands through his hair. "Larry's here now. Jud, remember, let's sort this out. Don't be flipping out. Just let's talk."

Danny Morgan and his brothers all sat together, whispering, ready to fight if needed. Mike could fight too and he was the one who'd be tackling Jud if it all went pear-shaped. There was an eerie silence as Larry walked inside the room. His footsteps could be heard marching along the concrete floor. Jud snarled at him and never took his eyes from him as he sat down. Larry positioned himself between each group, he couldn't sit with his brothers or the Morgan's. He had gripes with both groups and didn't trust any of them. Paul paced up and down and he was the one who began to talk first. He wanted an easy life, things to go back to normal. "Listen, there is enough graft for us all to work together on this. Danny, you deserved what you got because you broke the rules. You tried to have us over and you got caught. Simple as really."

Mike was a big mouth and there was no way he was having this prick talk to them like kids. "Paul, wind your neck in for a minute. Jud has done what we've done a hundred times before so don't come all this loyalty shit with us. It's a dog eat dog world and you lot have got greedy. We want a piece of the action too."

Jud spoke up, there was no way he was keeping quiet. He spoke directly to Mike. He had no fear whatsoever and if this dick-head wanted some, he was more than ready to rumble. "We take what we want, that's the way it works. If there is anything left then you're free to take it. That's how it is." Mike's back was up and you could see this situation was getting out of control. "We are the Watson's and we're allowed to do whatever we want."

Larry hissed as he clocked where his brother was stood. Jud held his head back and let out a menacing laugh. He was up for some beef and he was sick of talking. In his world people didn't talk, they fought. It was winner take it all. Jud slipped his jacket off and flexed his muscles. He looked bulkier than normal. Paul was running around like a headless chicken, he knew it was going off and there was nothing he could do to change it. Jud walked over to Mike and went nose to nose with him. "So, big boy, are you ready to sort things out the proper way. I'm not a talker and we both know that at the end of the day talking never solved anything." Jud was a snidey bastard, he jerked his head back and head-butted Mike. Blood gushed from his mouth and he was a sitting target. This was it, the shit hit the fan. Danny Morgan jumped on Larry and Paul was fighting with Ged. Punches were being flung and it was just a free for all.

Danny Morgan shoved his hands down the front of his pants and pulled out a blade. Larry was dodging it as he came closer to him wafting it about. With all the commotion nobody heard the door open. There were gun shots fired and each man fell to the ground like a sack of spuds. The attacker ran into the room and held the gun firmly in their hand as they approached each of the victims. Heavy breathing could be heard, struggled breaths. Jud was lifted up by his hair and thrown back to the ground. His skull crashed against the floor. Jud's eyes were staring into space. The attacker chuckled as they clipped Jud's Rolex watch from his wrist. "Not so smart now are you gobshite," the man sneered as he pushed the silver watch into his jacket pocket.

Larry Watson wasn't dead, his eyes were flickering rapidly. The murderer crept over to him and smirked. "Nighty night wanker." He held the gun to the side of Larry's head and squeezed the trigger slowly. This was a blood bath, a crime scene, six men lay dead on the floor. The attacker searched each of his victims and whatever he found he shoved into his coat pocket. With one last glance over his shoulder he fled the crime scene.

★

Maureen sat watching the clock. She was pissed and every time she heard a noise she was up to the window checking the area. Flicking through the TV stations she found something to keep her occupied. Her mind was working overtime and she didn't know if she was coming or going, she was stressed. The letterbox was flicking at speed and she knew this time it wasn't the wind blowing at her front door, there was somebody there. Fastening her housecoat up tightly she ran into the hallway. "Hold on, bleeding hell, give me a minute," she shrieked. Hands shaking, she fumbled to twist the catch. "Fucking hell, where the hell have you been? I thought you were never coming home?"

Spencer was sweating, he was white and he was constantly licking at his lips. Maureen walked back to the front room and poured herself a large glass of brandy, she was nervous and she was shaking from head to toe. "So, is it done?"

Spencer nodded. "It's done mother. I took the fucking lot of them down just like we planned. It's all ours now, we can have it all. Fuck the Watson's and the Morgan's, we rule the crime scene now. Yep, us the fucking Pritchard's. They underestimated us, did they think we were just some kind of pricks who they could walk over?"

Maureen rubbed her hands together, she was clapping like a seal, eyes wide open with greed written across her wrinkled face. "So, everything went to plan? Did they know it was you?"

Spencer dipped his head low and his breathing was rapid, he was a nervous wreck. "Larry knew it was me. You should have seen his face before I blasted the bullet into his skull. That shot was for our Dawn mam. It was for the way he'd treated her and fucked her life up. It had to be done. Larry Watson is a cunning twat who got what he deserved. The Watson's have ruled Manchester for too long now. Why shouldn't our family have our turn, ay? I've worked for them both for months running about doing this and doing that and for what mother, fuck all." Spencer sat down and dipped his head low. "Danny Morgan told me everything about his grafts, where the money was kept, fucking everything. What did he expect?"

Maureen tapped her finger against her teeth and she was edgy. "Are you sure they're dead? The last thing we need is this coming back to bite us on the arse."

Spencer rolled his eyes. "The lot of them were wiped out. Give me a bit of credit, mother, I'm no amateur." Maureen sat thinking as she watched her son pull wads of money out from his jacket. He placed it on the table and smirked as he held the watch in his hand. "This is worth a right few quid too. Mother for the first time in our lives we're going to be loaded. We never have to go without again. Look, I've got the keys to Danny's safe too."

Maureen reached over and touched the cash on the table. She took forty pound out of it and casually shoved it down the front of her bra. "I'll nip down to the shops love and get us some bread and milk. I'll get some electric cards too, there's only a couple of quid left on it so I'll top it up."

Maureen reached over to the table and tried to get some more money. Spencer was alert and slapped her wrist. "Just keep your hands off it you greedy fucker. You've got enough there for what we need. I don't need you flashing the cash about either. People will start talking if they see you going over the top."

Maureen patted the top of his shoulder. "I just thought I could get us something to eat, you know, like some fresh steak and that." She was a cunning cow and any chance she had she would have had her son over.

Spencer stood to his feet and peeped through the crack in the curtain. "Where the hell is Sally? She should have been here ages ago." Maureen was in a world of her own and the money she had was burning a hole in her pocket. She slipped her slippers on and grabbed her coat from the arm of the chair. She was still wearing her nightwear and didn't seem to bother that she was going to go to the shop in them, she had no shame. Spencer held his phone to his ear listening to the ringing tone. "Mam, she's not answering. I'm getting worried about her."

Maureen held her hand on her hip near the door and sighed. "Sally will be here when she's ready. She loves you for crying out loud. Stop flapping, just relax. I'm bobbing down to the shops and I'll be back soon. I'll get us some brandy to celebrate, fuck buying any steak it's too expensive anyway. I'll just make us some toast." Maureen left and the front door slammed behind her. Spencer clipped the Rolex watch onto his wrist and sniggered to himself. He held his hand to the side admiring his ill-gotten gains.

Sally stood at Maureen's front door and knocked rapidly on the letterbox. She was freezing and her teeth chattered together. It was cold outside and the wind was picking up. Stepping up to the letterbox she squashed her perished lips up against it. "Maureen, it's me Sally. Open the door." Rubbing her hands together she stood back looking at the house for any sign of life.

Spencer opened the door and she stood frozen looking at him. "For fucks sake where the hell have you been? I've been worried about you. Come on, get inside and get warm. My mam's just gone down to the shop to get us some brandy to celebrate." Sally didn't budge, she was glued to the spot. Her head twisted to the alleyway close to the door. Spencer reached out and grabbed her by the arm. "What's wrong, come on, get inside." There was a loud coughing noise and Spencer twisted his head to get a better look at who was in the garden. The colour drained from his face and he looked like he'd seen a ghost. "Sally, what's going on, how on earth is he here?"

Spencer didn't stand a chance, he was gripped by the throat and dragged inside the house. "Did you think you would get away with it? You daft bastard you know

I always wear a bullet proof vest when I go to meet anyone." Spencer was flung to the floor and Jud dragged him inside the living room. Sally was petrified, her heart was in her mouth and she knew Spencer was drawing his final breath before he met his maker.

Spencer held his hands out begging. "Why Sally, you've double-crossed me, you daft bitch. We had it all there for the taking. You said you loved me, why have you done this to us. We could have had it all but now you've ruined it!"

Jud surged his foot deep in Spencer's ribs. His body folded in two and he knew he wouldn't be walking out of this alive. Jud bent down and squeezed Spencer's cheeks together so his lips were touching at the sides. His hot breath sprayed into his face as he lifted his hand up and unclipped the watch. "I think this belongs to me doesn't it?" Sally was just stood with her back to the wall, she was in some kind of trance and nothing was making sense anymore, her head was in bits. Yes, she'd loved Spencer at the start but he'd changed. For crying out loud he'd slept with the same man that she had, in his quest to take over the crime scene. Nothing was safe with him about, she could never trust him. And, there was Jud, yes she'd loved him for as long as she could remember but he was just the same as all the rest of the men she'd met in her life. He'd been sleeping with Maureen behind her back for months! No. No man could ever be trusted.

The front door slammed shut and Maureen was singing her head off in the hallway. She opened the living room door and the dance she was doing just stopped. Her mouth was wide open and her jaw was swinging low. She clocked Spencer and knew the game was up. Lifting her head slowly she met the eyes of Jud. "Bleeding hell, what have you done this for Jud? Take your fucking hands from him before I ring the police." Jud made sure Spencer was going nowhere and stood on him. His foot pressed deep into his neck, his windpipe was squashed. Sally walked slowly to the chair and sat down.

Jud growled over at Dawn's mother. "Maureen this runt tried to kill me. He's shot my brothers and now he's going to pay. An eye for an eye and all that."

Sally watched the gun being pulled from Jud's jacket and she screamed at the top of her voice. "Jud, no. Please, for me, let him live."

Jud turned his head slowly and growled at her. The penny had dropped now and he realised that she had feelings for Spencer. "Is this who you want Sally? Do you really want to end up with a lying deadbeat like him? He doesn't love you, he loves money, the power, the control of making people feel worthless. And, he'd do anything to get it."

Maureen stepped in, this was her son's neck on the line and she had to think on her feet. "Jud, for me, walk away from this. I'll make sure he never comes near you again. I swear to you on my life if you spare him he'll leave Manchester," she sighed as her hand stroked the side of his cheek. "We go back a long way, please, he's my boy. You owe me."

What the hell was happening here? Was Jud going soft or what? This man had wiped his family out and nothing would ever be the same again. Spencer held Jud's ankle and tried to speak, he was spitting blood. "Please Jud, I'll do anything. I'm sorry. You're right, I just got caught up in my own jealousy and greed."

Jud backed off and ragged his fingers through his hair. He had nothing left and his body folded to the floor. All the money and all the power meant nothing anymore, his family, his world was crumbling around him. His eyes clouded over and he let out a roar like a caged lion. Sally walked over to him and placed her hand on his shoulder. "Jud, it's over. Come on, let's go. Just walk away." Maureen flicked her eyes over at Sally, was she missing something here or what, she thought Spencer and Sally were an item, in love, a couple. Spencer was struggling for breath as he scrambled to his mother's side.

Maureen stood tall and placed her hand on top of his head. Her eyes met Sally's. "So, it's you who Jud has been seeing all this time." She walked over to her and spat in her eye. Her fist curled at the side of her legs and she was ready to blow. "You know when our Dawn finds out about this she'll string you up, you dirty slapper. You're finished with me Sally. What a snake in the grass you turned out to be. I thought I knew you, I trusted you. It just goes to show how wrong I was. Go on, piss off with him you both deserve each other, fucking scum the pair of you. There's no honour amongst thieves and that includes you love."

Spencer dipped his head. He was in a bad way and lucky to be alive. He whispered Sally's name under his breath as he watched her leave. Once the front door slammed shut Maureen opened the bottle of brandy and swigged at it. "I thought you said that cunt was dead, how did I know you couldn't be trusted to do a proper job. I'll tell you what Spencer you're going to have to leave here now because he'll be back, mark my words he'll be back. Both you and Dawn can never live under my roof again. Jud Watson will always rule the streets of Manchester and nobody will ever knock him off his throne. Quick, get a bag together and fuck off." Spencer knew she was right, his plan had gone tits up. Maureen was right about her son though, he was an amateur and he'd never be a match for Jud Watson.

Sally sat in the car with Jud, she was quiet and her eyes never looked at him once. Jud was in pieces and now for the first time he broke down crying. Big fat salty tears streamed down his cheeks. He carried on driving and he was driving dangerously. Sally licked the edge of her mouth, her cheeks were bright red. Turning to face him she held a serious look. "Can you just take me to pick something up from the pub? My mate is there and I need to see her. Pull over Jud, I'll drive, you're in no fit state, look at you, you're a bag of nerves?" Jud nodded as he pulled over. Here he was breaking his heart and all she cared about was going to see her friend, selfish bitch she was.

The car pulled up at the back of the pub. Jud stayed in the car as she left. "Just give me two minutes, I won't be long," she said as she left the car. Jud never replied, he hung is head low and smashed his clenched fist against the dashboard. "Fuck, fuck,fuck."

Sally ran into the night pub and her eyes were everywhere, she was looking for somebody. Waving her hand above her head she got the attention she wanted from the woman she was meeting. "I'll wait in the car for you," she shouted as she started to walk back outside. Her heart was jumping about inside her chest and it seemed like it was going to leap out of her rib- cage and splatter onto the floor. Sally looked over her shoulder just to check the woman was following her, she was. Her feet stomped along the pavement as she headed back to the car.

Sally opened the driver's door slowly. Once inside she sat gripping the steering wheel tightly. Jud sat back in his seat, he was a mess, not just crying now he was sobbing his heart out. "I have nothing left Sally. My brothers are all gone, and for what," he ragged his fingers through his hair. "For fuck all, nothing, just me and my daft stupid pride." Sally was watching him but never once did she comfort him. No kiss, no soft touch, nothing. A flat palm banged on the window next to her and she swallowed hard. Michelle Buckley was stood there and she shot a look at Jud. Sally nodded for her to get into the back of the car. The car shook as the door slammed shut.

Michelle leaned forward and her hot breath tickled the side of Jud's cheek. "What's up with you?"

Sally shook her head as she flicked the engine over. "Leave it Michelle, his head's in bits. I'll tell you later."

Michelle sat back and looked at Sally through the rear-view mirror. Their eyes met and they held a cunning look. Sally starting driving and Jud just sat with his head resting on the window. Sally headed onto the motorway and Jud didn't flinch, he just sat frozen. His head was spinning and he was still in shock. Sally's breathing was rapid and she was constantly licking at her lips. The lights on the motorway faded as they left at the next exit. They were heading on the A roads now and each lane was harder to make out. Michelle Buckley was humming a tune as she patted her hand on her stomach slowly. She was definitely with child, her shape had changed and her baby bump was there for everyone to see. Jud wiped his nose with a swift movement and checked the area around him. He dipped his head through the windscreen and looked for any landmarks. Sally could see he was agitated and turned the radio up. "Where the hell are we?" Jud asked.

Michelle Buckley was fidgeting in the back of the car and you could hear rustling noises. "I've just got to pick something up Jud and Sally said she would give me a lift with it." Jud sat thinking and just as he was about to turn his head to face her, Michelle Buckley smashed him over the head with a claw hammer. The blow knocked him for six and he was out of it. Grabbing the rope from her bag she sat forward and hooked it around his neck. He was mumbling but no words were coming out. Michelle tied the rope around the seat and made sure this beast wasn't moving. Jud's head hung low and a small trickle of blood seeped down the side of his forehead. "Hurry up Sally, come on, before this cunt wakes up. We know what we're doing, so don't fuck it up." Sally accelerated and she was swerving in and out of the traffic. Their destination was near and they were living on borrowed time. Michelle leaned forward in her seat and squeezed the top of Sally's shoulder. "It's what this bastard deserves Sally. I can see you looking at him feeling sorry for him but don't. He's no good. He's a cunt, nothing else."

Sally drove down a country lane and parked at the

top of a cliff. She was tearful and not really sure she'd made the right choices. "I know Michelle but I trusted him and he let me down. I loved him too, loved him more than he will ever know." Michelle bolted out of the car. She was a strong as an ox as she dragged Jud from his seat. Sally headed to the top of the cliff and peeped over it. Would this drop be enough to finish him off or did they have to kill him where they were stood. Sally walked over to where Jud was lay. His eyes were open and he was aware she was there. Bending over slightly she touched the side of his cheek. "You fucked Maureen, Jud. I could understand Dawn, but old Mo, you dirty no good bastard. I could never love you after this. You betrayed me." Sally stood up and sucked a large mouthful of air. She tilted her head to the side and snarled over to Michelle. "Finish him, make sure the last of the Watson brothers never breathes again."

Michelle blew a laboured breath and shook her head. "Larry's gone too. His blood lives on though. This child is the last bloodline of the Watson brothers. I'll make sure my child has it all. It will want for nothing."

Sally grabbed Jud's legs and Michelle came to join her. It was time to end his life. The drop was high and no man nor beast could ever survive it. Michelle looked over at Sally. "It's our time now. We can take over the crime scene in Manchester. We have everything we need, fucking everything." The wind howled in the midnight air as Jud's body was hauled over the edge of the cliff. Michelle smirked as she watched him fall. They could hear his skull crashing against the rocks.

Once he hit the bottom Michelle Buckley gritted her

teeth together tightly. "Fuck you Jud Watson, Fuck the lot of you." Sally headed back to the car and once inside she turned the engine over. It was done, it was over.

The heavens opened and the sky was grey. Mary Watson stood tall as she laid her sons to rest. Stan Morgan was by her side and he knew exactly how she felt as he'd buried his sons a few days before. Michelle Buckley and Sally were there and they held their secrets close to their chest. They would never tell anyone about this. Michelle was the one calling the shots now in the area and her own family were making sure they were never had over again. Sally was paid off and after today she was going to leave the area for a new life. Dawn's dead body was discovered and Sally's relationship with Mo and Spencer was over. Of course she could have stayed with Michelle and do what they set out to do but that wasn't for her, she wanted a quiet life. The police didn't have one stitch of evidence who had masterminded the downfall of both the gangs and every day they were searching high and low for any scrap of evidence that would lead to an arrest, but up until now they were pissing in the wind. They had nothing to go on.

Michelle held her waist as Larry's coffin was lowered to the ground. She was tearful but something in her eye said this was all for show, crocodile tears some might say. Mary Watson walked to Michelle's side and placed her flat palm on her stomach. "You look after my grandchild, it's all I've got left of my boys. Don't be a stranger with me. I want to be part of this child's life." Michelle kissed the side of Mary's cheek and kept her eyes low. A Judas she was, a lying conniving bitch who would do anything she needed to do to get what she wanted. Sally shot her eyes around the graveside. All the main heads were there and each of them held a hard look in their eyes. Spencer Pritchard was hidden away watching the funeral. His face was battered and bruised and one of his eyes was still badly swollen. Sat smoking in the shadows he smirked as the last coffin was lowered to the ground. This wasn't over for him yet. He still craved the power, the respect.

Jud's body was never found and everyone said he'd been cut up into tiny pieces and fed to the pigs. It was a mystery what had happened to him and for years to come people would always tell the story about the mighty Jud Watson and his fallen empire.

Mary Watson sat around the dining table with Stan Morgan. Both of them were empty, nothing left to give, drained of any emotion. Mary stared into the bottom of her empty glass and ran her finger along it slowly. "It's up to us now Stan. We need to work together and make sure we take back what belongs to us. Our boys died for this and we're just sat here letting it all go. We both know who is running things now and I say we act quickly. I've got our Jud's money stashed and we both know money talks around these parts. We have enough cash to take it all back."

Stan sighed and blew his breath. He reached over and touched the end of Mary's fingers. "Let it go love, just let it go. We're too old for all this. Just let's move away and enjoy our twilight years together. Mary, you're all I've got left. Just walk away and let our sons rest in peace." Mary swallowed hard. She knew he was right but something inside her wanted revenge, she wanted her family's name to live on. She never answered him.

Sally stood in the train station toilets. Sat in the cubicle she slowly opened the box in her hand. Squatting down on the toilet bowl she held a plastic strip between her legs. The seconds that passed seemed like hours and as she peered at the pregnancy test her jaw dropped. The positive result was not what she was looking for. Her head dropped into her hands and she dragged at her hair. Tears fell and she covered her mouth with her hand so nobody could hear her sobbing. This was a nightmare, what the hell was she going to do? Slowly Sally left the cubicle and walked to the mirror. Dipping her head she looked deep into her eyes. The tears seemed to dry up quickly. The corners of her mouth started to rise and she smirked one last time at her reflection in the mirror. Sally left the toilets and stood at the platform waiting for her train to arrive. She was edgy and she kept lifting her suitcase up and dropping it back down again onto the floor. Slowly she made her way to the exit. Sally looked up at the sky as she left the train station and spoke in a low voice. "Jud, the journey begins again. I'll make sure your son's name will be on the map forever. Nobody will stop me. I owe you Jud. Our child will rule Manchester, just like you did."

Michelle Buckley looked down at the son in her arms. He was the spit of Larry Watson. Mary sobbed as she held him in her arms. He was innocent looking and his face was angelic. Michelle reached over and touched his fingers slowly. "He's my boy Mary and nobody will ever hurt him. Everything I own he can have. His name will be something nobody ever forgets. The Watson Empire is his. Nobody will ever take that from him ever." Mary nodded her head slowly, she had no words left to give. This child was all she needed now and she too would do everything she could to protect him. Lee Watson would soon be a name everyone knew in the Manchester area. Michelle Buckley would make sure of that. He was the heir to the throne and nobody would ever stand in his way, or would they?

THE END

Other books by this author

Broken Youth
Black Tears
Northern Girls Love Gravy
Bagheads
Teabags & Tears
The Visitors
Sleepless in Manchester
Covering Up
Riding Solo
The Pudding Club
Grow Wars
The Square